When I Remember You

A NOVEL

To Kathy

♡ Claire Springfield

Claire Cobb Springfield

Charleston, SC
www.PalmettoPublishing.com

When I Remember You
Copyright © 2022 by Claire Cobb Springfield

First Edition

Hardcover ISBN: 978-1-68515-808-8
Paperback ISBN: 978-1-68515-809-5
eBook ISBN: 978-1-68515-810-1

Registration Number: TXu 2-292-976
Effective Date of Registration: December 07, 2021
Registration Decision Date: January 04, 2022

For all the friends I've made through music
and the rock stars we adore

"....It's funny to think you can be lonesome so long for something you really didn't want. It's really funny, I mean. First you get hurt and then you get lonesome and then you get used to it and then you get busy. And it really doesn't cross your mind after that, that it could start all over again and everything be the same. Only maybe it won't..."

—*Excerpt from* The Pride of the Peacock,
Ruth Chatterton, 1954

Chapter 1

EVERY ONCE IN A WHILE I GO ONLINE AND search for some little artifact of his, an old '45 record or a magazine with his picture on the cover. He had such an expansive career, so there are plenty of things available. But I'm looking for something different, something to remind me of how I felt when I was with him.

It's a challenge though because the way he made me feel was like nothing I can find. That's what I want to tell you about, how it all happened and what it meant to me.

What *he* meant to me.

I'm going to put it together for you, but it floats through my mind in fragments. Soundless nights. The lilt of water. Comforting solitude. Pie. And music and joy and no-plans days and how he helped me see I was real and full of potential after I'd been stuck and uncertain for so long. He made me feel so many things. He made me see myself.

His name was Cliff Wood, and while he'd been a favorite of many on the radio when I was growing up, I wasn't paying attention to that. Not because his songs weren't catchy or because he wasn't sexy and handsome or had the right moves. He was all those things and more. But I was a contemplative girl, one who'd rather spend an evening with Edith Wharton or Toni Morrison than listen to records or go to a party. That introversion carried into my adulthood.

When I met Sydney, who would help me out of my reclusive tendencies and become my best friend, I was thirty-five years old, yet I often felt like an uncertain girl in many ways. Womanhood, maturity, however you might look at it, seemed something bizarre and elusive to me. I still had the vulnerability and timidity that accompanies being young, not quite knowing if I belonged and where I was headed. Maybe that feeling was because I had not ventured far enough into the world's offerings and was still figuring out my way.

Sydney would ensure I marched past my own realm of experience without knowing she was taking me there. It was a late afternoon at the bookstore I frequented in St. Mark's Place when she first showed up, unknowingly about to change things for me.

Sydney. Beautiful in an effortlessly cool way with flecked hazel eyes and a vivacious attitude.

Beautiful in both looks and spirit. She had the most petite stature of anyone I'd known, just reaching five feet tall with a small-boned frame, made to be tiny and so perfect as I saw it. The day we met, she'd recently had her fortieth birthday, a fact that surprised me when I'd learn it later.

At first I would often think about our age difference, her being a little older and having a leg up on life's experiences, but I would come to feel our ages to be reversed as time went on and we got to know each other. Her nonstop energy would defy my thoughts on what it was to hit forty. I knew I didn't want to grow older, fearing the passage of time because I felt so unsettled. But here was *tiny Sydney*—as I thought of her back then—showing me that youth came in all ages and never had to stop or be labeled.

I had been dwelling in a self-imposed world of *should haves* and *must haves* and rules for things I was supposed to achieve by certain dates. I felt I was failing at them all.

Sydney was nothing like that. She imposed no set of guidelines on herself, living life by the day, loving each second of it, making it count—in her own way. Even at forty, she was a spitfire with a sharp but playful and inquiring mind. Sydney gave herself must haves and should haves too, but they were fun ones. Getting to know her changed my fixed ideas on age as well as plenty of other things.

St. Mark's Place is the section between Third Avenue and Avenue A in New York's East Village. It has always been my favorite part of the city. Back then, I had this need to roam and get away, from myself mostly, though I didn't see it that way at the time. The area made for just the right nest to escape with its offbeat vibe, vintage shopping, and relaxing cafés. I loved taking walks and could easily get to the area from my apartment. A mile or thereabouts, a perfect distance for a stroll unless winter had its foothold in which case I'd either pile on another layer of warmth or take a taxi.

On my drifting about, I'd often find my way to this one hole-in-the-wall bookstore with a shotgun layout, nose to nose with stacks of previously loved literature. I felt a sense of lost happiness in the cramped but cozy space, just me and heaps of literary works for days tucked away in a miniscule part of the enormous city. In my frequency there, I'd gotten to know the owner of the store, a soft-spoken man named Marlon.

Marlon had shaky hands and sported an involved white beard, and on occasion let me cover the store for him, usually at the end of the day when he didn't expect much to happen. I reveled in being there and enjoyed imagining what it would be like if I'd read all the books. Of course, I had not read many of them. They were stacked in every corner of the tight space, but I knew them well having perused them endlessly. On the days when I was there, Marlon could leave early to be with his wife or take her to dinner. I envied the closeness of their decades-long relationship and the way Marlon talked modestly about her and set aside mysteries he knew she'd like.

The informal arrangement with him was a great partnership, and though I didn't want or need the money for the few hours I put in there, it was a matter of pride for him to compensate me. But I just liked to be with the books.

I was tending things for him on a Thursday when Sydney made her entrance in a fluster.

There hadn't been any customers since Marlon had left, and after doing my usual meandering about the place, I had settled myself on the floor behind the cash register with a pile of records that had been mixed in with a delivery of books from an estate sale. It was understood I could go through any albums that came in and keep the ones I liked before Marlon dropped them by a thrift store. Rarely did I take any home, but I liked the idea of rummaging through them just the same.

The door's latch clicked, and I heard a woman's voice. "Anyone here?"

Within seconds, I was bolt upright with a dusty Stonewall Jackson album in hand, my face probably looking both bewildered and annoyed. *Who was interrupting my tranquil atmosphere?* I preferred customers who wanted to quietly browse the same way I did.

"I need some help, please." The voice came again, loud yet out of breath.

Then a small hand pushed a heavy stack of biographies to one side of the counter and peered around them. "Oh, hi! I hope you can help me. I left something important here."

There stood Sydney. Tiny Sydney. My eyes took in her dark hair, cut short and nearly shaved on one side, the rest of it landing wherever it wanted. My mother would have described the style as severe. But my mother found many things severe. On Sydney it had an adorable effect.

I could never have gotten away with that.

For most of my life, I had light brown hair with a flicker of curl at the end hitting my shoulder blades as I still did. My face was overall pleasant, but my best feature was my eyes which someone had once described as sail blue.

All in all, I wasn't that memorable. Not in the manner Sydney was anyway. I felt intrigued by her severe hairstyle alone—even if she had interrupted me. As she awaited my reply, she swept a row of jagged bangs to the side by sliding her fingers across her forehead.

"What did you lose?" I set down the record.

Moving from behind the cash register, I continued to study her. Tattered jeans. Converse sneakers. A perfectly fitted white t-shirt draped with an assortment of necklaces, one of them a large turquoise cross. She was one of those women with an unrestricted sense of fashion who could pull off pairing random pieces of clothing and somehow still manage to look universally appealing. I was around people like that all day where I worked.

It was a common event each morning for me to teeter on the side of being late to the office as I tried to commandeer a suitable outfit for a job at a fashion magazine. Whatever combination I tried to put together never felt as though it quite worked, at least not like it did for someone like Sydney. She could look well put together no matter what.

"I lost some concert tickets. I think I dropped them when I was here earlier. Did anyone turn them in?" Her eyes pleaded with mine for a positive response.

I had no idea about her tickets. I'd scarcely even been in the shop but so wished I could have said yes to her and sent her on her way.

I paused to make her feel I was considering her situation. "I don't think so, but I haven't been here long."

"If it helps, there was an old man here earlier helping me look for a book by Cliff Wood. So it would have to be near that section." She made off further into the store.

"Cliff Wood?" I followed, having to move double time to keep up. Her candy scented perfume left a pleasant trail behind her.

"Yes, I know—you had a crush on him in high school, listened to his music backward and forward, and likely made out with posters of him on your bedroom wall, kissing him every night before bed. Same as me and every other girl—probably some guys as well." She laughed, and I did, too, in the polite way one does in an awkward social situation.

Next she moved to scan a different shelf, gently stroking the spines of the books as if engrossed in some deep love affair with each of them. I stood behind her as she continued her one-woman search party for the case of the missing tickets. Her sardonic comments seconds ago hadn't been lost on me, but I was trying to place Cliff Wood in my mind.

"He's a musician. A singer." I felt pleased with myself for recalling this fact and demonstrating I wasn't completely ignorant to his fame.

"And an awesome guitar player. And an author." She shuffled the books before her. "I know he's not someone people take seriously as a writer, but have you read him?" She was only half-talking to me. The way she phrased her question with the words *read him* made me smile inside.

I hadn't made out with his posters, but Amelia, my sister, she was the Cliff Wood fan, the kind of girl Sydney seemed to be describing. Amelia had collected all his records and any magazine featuring him back in the day. I knew exactly who he was. He was a rock star mostly known for being good-looking.

"Cliff Wood. I know who you mean. My older sister was into him. She *did* have a poster of him." *Several in fact*. I was glad to share this, feeling it added further credibility to my understanding of who Cliff was which was obviously important to this girl.

Sydney wasn't listening to me though, and I didn't care. I wanted her to find the tickets and leave. My alone time in my comforting hideout was rapidly dwindling.

"Maybe over here." She motioned with ring-clad fingers, a silver one on all but her thumbs. In the new section, she was dwarfed by the ceiling-high rows of books.

"I was definitely in this area here." She separated a few hardbacks, shoving them side to side more impatiently than she had in the beginning of her quest. Putting a finger to her lips, she smudged her nude lipstick as she turned to me. "You don't think that old man would have taken them, do you? Is he here? Can I check with him?" Her eyes were filled with optimism.

"Marlon? No. He's the owner. And he's not here."

I knew Marlon looked a bit weathered, but I didn't like her referring to him as an old man or that he had potentially stolen her tickets. While I considered if I should say something more in his defense, she turned back to continue the search, again softly fingering the spines. "If he were helping me find Cliff's books, they would be here it seems."

"This section is fiction. But if it's an autobiography—"

"Novels," she said as if I should have known. "They're novels. That's what he writes."

Her tone said I'd made an unforgivable error and disconcerted me.

I tried to further summon in my mind what I could of this musician—this rock star—picturing Amelia glued to her teen magazines as his music blared in the background. All I could see was him in a pair of faux leather pants with his shirt unbuttoned revealing a few sprigs of chest hair, the way he looked back when he'd been at his career peak. I knew he had probably continued with his music along the way, but I had a regular subscription to more than one literary website that sent monthly updates. I had no idea of him being a published author. I felt surprised and intrigued by the idea.

"What time is it?" Sydney looked at her wrist overpowered by a silver watch. "Almost six. Show is at eight, and there's an opener."

She was not so much talking to me as reviewing these details with herself.

I stood a full head taller than she did and scanned the book section directly above her. There they were: two novels by Cliff Wood. Westerns.

Oddly, I hadn't noticed them in all my leisurely musings about the store. Extracting one from its slot, I flipped through it, and a pair of concert tickets fluttered to the ground.

"Oh my gosh. Thank God!" Sydney stooped to retrieve the prized paper rectangles from the worn hardwood. "Thank you so much!" Her mouth dropped open with a breath of relief. "Sorry about my question over the possible intentions of the store owner. I was—"

"Really, don't worry about it." I cut her off, not meaning to be rude but wanting the exchange over and done with. "It's all fine."

I took a few steps beyond her, ready to lead her toward the exit. Looking back at her, I saw she was put off by my behavior, her face a hurt frustration. She had tried to offer some parting words of appreciation, and I had denied her that moment with my hasty send-off.

I stopped and peered at the Cliff Wood novel still in my hand. "Are they any good?" I hoped my interest provided a pseudo-apology for my rush to get her out the door.

"I'm not that big of a reader, but I guess so if you like that kind of thing."

I assumed she meant westerns. The one in my hand was titled *Lucky Jack* with a field of horses on the cover.

"He has another one coming out soon, too." She headed back to the front of the store taking the helm of her departure.

At the counter she stopped where she had left her purse, a black square that looked as though it might hold her identification and a few credit cards. I hadn't even noticed when she'd set it there. It seemed she moved around depositing things in random places, unseen. No wonder she'd misplaced the tickets.

I was more than ready to resume my position behind the cash register with the records when she said loudly, "Oh no. No. I can't believe this. Geezus."

"Is everything okay?"

"Well, so much for finding the tickets." Her tone was one of both irritation and defeat. "My friend can't come to the show tonight. She didn't even give me a reason. I think she's just bailing on me." She looked at her cell phone as though it were an important document.

I didn't know what to say. Finally, she began to make a path to the door, her hand swaying by her side with the tickets. I watched her, wanting to be sure she didn't lose them again. As she reached for the doorknob, she turned around and brushed her bangs to the side once more. "Do *you* want to go?"

"I'm sorry?" I wasn't sure I'd heard her correctly.

"I said, do *you* want to go?" She held up the tickets, waving them in the air. "To the concert. To see Cliff."

"Cliff Wood?" I don't know why I felt the need to clarify.

"It's too late for me to sell it. You should come."
She set the ticket on top of the closest book stack.
"It's right here on *The Wonderful Private World of
Liberace.*" She grimaced. "I'll leave the ticket here
for you. Your sister will be so jealous. I'm Sydney,
by the way."

"I'm Claudine."

She was already out the door, the latch sounding
behind her.

In seconds, I moved across the room to view the
ticket. Cliff Wood's printed name stared up at me
magnified and out of proportion as in a strange
dream. The concert was uptown at the Beacon
Theatre. I couldn't remember the last time I'd been
to the landmark venue.

I tried to visualize myself there, how I'd react to the show, the possibility of enjoying it or
wishing I hadn't come. I pictured this diminutive
Sydney person and what it might be like to be
around her.

But she hadn't invited me along as her guest.
Had she? She'd only left the ticket for me to use, no
suggestion we would be seeing the concert together.
It was a little strange, but I always thought about
things way too hard.

"Claudine, go. Just go," I heard myself say.

Then it all started.

This man, this guitar-playing author, wasn't
the slightest bit on my radar at the time, but his

concerts, his whereabouts, every facet of his life, was about to consume a major portion of mine. And so much more.

Chapter 2

THE SECTION OF MY LIFE WHEN I MET Sydney followed a few years of doubt about my career path, where I was headed, dating—everything—and left me unclear about what I was doing. Or rather, what I wanted to do and wasn't making happen.

After having several jobs at media outlets around Manhattan I thought would lead to meaningful employment as a writer, I bounced around with my negligible savings to a few other cities attending writers' workshops hoping the experiences would give me a jumpstart into the literary world. Yet I ended up taking a job at a magazine where my days were mainly comprised of assisting Nina, a stylish fifty-something woman who was the editor of the publication. Following up on commissioned articles, arranging schedules for modeling shoots, or even running out for a fresh tube of mascara were all things I might do on a given day.

Not so much writing.

As for Nina, I was sure she truly wanted me to succeed in my endeavors at the keyboard. She was that type of driven woman who had made it and wanted to see other females reach their potential, too. But with Nina, there was no corner-cutting, never a way to get there faster. She felt you had to put in your time, go through the hard slog of climbing the ladder and slowly come to understand all the nuts and bolts of whatever it was you wanted to pursue.

I think she also knew I wasn't interested in the fashion industry and thought my contribution on the page would be lackluster. Still, I lived in hope she'd throw a writing assignment to me eventually so I could prove her wrong. That was enough to make me stay. I figured it allowed me to reserve my creative energies for my ultimate goal of writing books.

I locked the door to Marlon's bookstore, leaving the stack of records where I'd found them and set off walking the three blocks to the 8th Street NYU station at Astor Place. During a ride on the subway's R train heading to 42nd Street, I sat next to a woman who looked to be going to a funeral, black dress with matching hat, stately purse resting in her lap, hands clasped on its elegant handle.

It made me think about my own attire, still in my work clothes.

I'd been lazy that morning, pulling on khaki pants with a navy sweater and adding a basic gold chain I erroneously believed gave the ensemble some life. It was understated dressing to say the least.

She's sensible, my mother often described me.

She was right about that. Sensible. And maybe even dull. I liked to spend my time on other things.

The thing was, I had a stylish wardrobe—one of the best benefits of having a job at a fashion magazine where I had insights into the latest trends and occasionally received an apparel sample. But I had no flair for putting pieces together. The only thing I had going for me in that arena was that clothes fit me well, and I remained the same size through the years.

When I switched to the one train heading toward 72nd, I landed within walking distance of the venue with time to spare. It had rained that morning leaving the air moist and my hair flatter than it already would have been on its own.

After returning from my first outing of the day for Nina, I had planned to correct the situation, maybe sneak away to a salon and get a blowout. We were supposed to have a department meeting after lunch, and I wanted to look good being around the rest of the team where personal presentation was often scrutinized. But when the meeting was canceled, and I knew I'd be alone at my desk, I abandoned worrying about any salon outing for the day.

Now as I stood outside of the Beacon Theatre, I was in full regret on that decision. My usually soft hair had an overall look of flyaway strands, and a piece kept falling into one eye. I managed to locate an elastic band in my purse and rope the mess into a low ponytail, thinking it might make me look more put together. But it really didn't matter. I wasn't going to know anyone other than this Sydney—though I had a sense I wanted her to like me, to feel I was worth giving me her extra ticket to see Cliff Wood whom she liked so much.

I felt out of place beneath the marquee announcing his performance. A girl on my right wearing a sweatshirt featuring a photo of a young Cliff Wood gestured at the sign, and more women clustered around her for a picture underneath his name.

It was cold, the kind of wet cold that creeps into every bone, and I shivered, watching as the women removed their jackets to make their concert tees visible. It was a good time for me to go inside.

The opening band had just finished. As people flowed from the theater for their requisite bathroom breaks and beverage runs, I looked around for the only way I knew to spot Sydney—her dark, edgy hair. I wanted to let her know I had decided to use the ticket.

In minutes I spotted her standing at the front of a long line for the bar in the lobby.

I felt myself smile. Gone were her jeans and Converse. Now she wore a black short skirt, though not an attention-seeking length, with thick tights, knee-high boots, and a ribbed top under a long black sweater. Her only jewelry was a single bangle bracelet. I was jealous she could look both sporty and girlish at the same time.

I wished I'd had enough time to go to my apartment and change into something more suitable for the evening, something concert-ish. Even a basic little black dress would have been better than my plain work outfit.

If Sydney cared about my attire, she didn't show it. "You made it!" She grabbed me by the bicep, her clasp remarkably strong, and pulled me into the line with her. I was surprised by how happy she was to see me. "I didn't get your name earlier."

"It's Claudine."

The room was heavy with body heat, so many people crammed in the area between those at the bar and others buying concert t-shirts in between acts. At least the closeness of everyone mitigated my chill from being outside.

I glanced over at the table to see an assortment of merchandise emblazoned with Cliff Wood's likeness of yesteryear, stacks of CDs, and keychains bearing what I'd come to recognize later as his logo.

"Claudine. That's pretty. I'm sorry. I was so stressed over those tickets. Do you want a beer or something?" She flaunted a twenty-dollar bill as if this would help me decide.

"Whatever you're getting is fine with me."

She was next in line and asked for two Michelobs. She handed the twenty to the bartender. "Are you ready?" She had an exaggerated glimmer in her eyes. "For Cliff Wood?"

What was to be ready for exactly? Other than the fondness Amelia had for him, I hadn't given much thought about it on the ride over. My plan was to see most of the show and leave early to get some dinner. There were several restaurants I liked in the area. It was also near my aunt's apartment though I wasn't planning to stop by.

Before I could say anything, she added, "I'm super excited. I haven't seen him in a while." She paused to accept the beers, handing one to me and tilting hers to her mouth. "He's been finishing his next book so there hasn't been much happening with him lately." She licked her lips. "I think it's been about six weeks. Six whole weeks. Too long."

At the time, her comment blew right by me. I thought she meant Cliff had been doing things related to his book for the last six weeks, but she meant that was how long it had been since she'd been to a Cliff Wood concert. To Sydney, that was an eternity. So many things would make sense later, things that would become important to me. I had no idea I was right on the precipice of my life's new trajectory.

Next we were trekking into the theater, winding our way between people to get there and trying to stay together among everyone else headed in the same direction. She would walk ahead a little, then turn to see if I was still with her, never letting me go astray. Then finally, we lingered at the back of the theater behind the last rows of burgundy velvet seats as Sydney took several swallows of her beer.

"I need to finish most of this." She pressed the bottle to her lips again. "I'll barely set it down, and someone will end up kicking it over. Then I'd have to get physical." She took another large gulp. "I hope you know I'm not serious. But some of these girls can get pushy, especially where we're sitting." She gazed around as if fascinated by the seating arrangement and the room's opulent decor.

Columns and arched doorways. A mammoth, glittering chandelier suspended from the ornate recessed ceiling. It felt too posh of a place for a rock concert, but many famous acts had performed at the venerable theater through the years.

I looked at my ticket, noticing the section information for the first time. "Is this really a front-row seat?"

Sydney had a look of self-congratulations as she reached into her purse for her ticket as well. "Yep."

"Now I know why you were so worked up about finding them."

"Exactly. It's much more fun when you get to be really close. I'd almost rather not even go if I can't be right up front where you can see him in full detail."

She took me by the arm and led the way to our seats. I moved along not sure I was ready for the front row experience. But it was a change of scenery in my world, and I had committed to it.

On the way, I had tried to visualize what kind of audience might come to see Cliff Wood in concert. I imagined the attendees to be a subdued bunch of women who had been interested in him back in the day, ones who had kissed posters of him in their bedrooms the way Sydney had described and who now wanted to relive those memories from their teen years.

Maybe some were women now missing their spent youth, feeling the years pass them by, unhappily left behind. Maybe some were just lonely and hankered for the kind of camaraderie shared fandom brings, longing for someone to talk to, even if only polite chitchat about the concert.

The place turned out to be filled with people of all ages, even some men, all talking in groups or sipping pre-show drinks. No one looked lonely. Nothing seemed out of the ordinary.

As we neared the front, I heard someone say, "There she is," and a handful of women rushed over surrounding Sydney for a photo. Then another wanted a picture with her alone. Sydney complied as she pressed her cheek against the girl who looked overjoyed and grateful.

For a moment, I asked myself, *is she famous?*

She possessed the look, the confidence, the attitude. Clearly, money was also not a problem for her. The cost of tonight's ticket alone plus all the others—under six weeks in between each concert— was her usual schedule based on what she'd said.

"What was all that?" I asked.

We had reached the front row now after inching our way past a few more who also greeted her.

"All what?"

"You seemed like quite a celebrity back there."

She shook her head. "I just go to a lot of these. That's all."

When we got to our seats, to my right was a woman with a homemade sign featuring a young photo of Cliff Wood and the words Come Home With Me, a reference to a song about which I would later learn more. Her face was beset with a nervous happiness as she cocked her head toward us both. "Can you believe we're front row?"

I looked to Sydney who leaned over, all vivid white teeth and animated eyes as she responded to the woman. "I know! Fantastic, isn't it?"

I was impressed by how easily she spoke to the stranger. There was something so vibrant and excitable about her. She exuded a feeling of goodness while also wanting to walk on the wild side and enjoyed others who displayed the same potential for abandon.

This other girl was nothing like that. She appeared the opposite of my new friend Sydney. She fit more of the stereotype I had pictured about the audience, a little on the frumpy side, wearing an outfit worse than mine, glasses, and with a nervous enthusiasm that suggested she didn't get out much and was relishing the evening.

"It should be pretty amazing," I heard myself say, but as my words came out, I knew I was only trying to support their excitement. I couldn't say I shared it.

To me, Cliff Wood was a has-been, probably lucky people were interested in seeing him at all. He'd had a string of hits years ago but wasn't someone you'd see on the cover of a current magazine or otherwise hear about. At least that was my idea of him.

I had acted on Sydney's invitation partly because I thought she was someone who could be my friend. After watching the reactions to her among the other fans, however, I wondered if she could even fit me in. Moreover, did she want to? She was someone important and interesting, at least in the

Cliff Wood world, and with her, even at that early juncture, I felt like someone, too.

A bathroom run was calling to me before the show started, but then the room fell dark.

I knew I'd missed my chance when Sydney turned to me, her face a picture of pure joy. "It's about to happen! Your first Cliff Wood concert!"

My first? Oh God—will there be more?

Next came an elevation of sighs from the audience fusing together into one passionate roar, a unified signal that everyone was excited about Cliff Wood's impending presence and ready to dive into the music. I took a last sip of my beer, set the bottle on the floor, and glanced behind me. The room was now at capacity. All those who previously had looked so reserved were now on their feet, hollering, whistling, and making noise in whatever way they could. You could even smell the energy pulsating.

At my side, the frumpy woman put her hand to her forehead as though it were all too much for her, the thrumming of Cliff's entrance music, the hyped crowd, and the idea Cliff Wood was mere seconds away from being within feet of us. The atmosphere gave me an unexpected swell of nauseous anticipation.

Snowy lights illuminated the dark platform area as band members darted from backstage to their positions. A crew member rushed into view setting out water bottles, a last-minute forgotten task.

But Cliff was so covert, so practiced at his entrance, I didn't even notice him until he was right before us with a shimmering blue guitar hanging dangerously at his hip. He paraded to each side of the stage playfully gauging the audience's level of excitement, an exercise immediately heightening the already noisy anticipation in the room.

When he was satisfied with his evaluation, he swaggered back to the microphone, slid his guitar into place, and forcefully dragged a pick across the strings to play the first chord to his opening song. This time, after investigating the spectators from his center vantage point, the playful smirk he'd arrived with gave way to a sincere and warmhearted smile. It was clear he was just as glad to be performing for us as we were to be watching him. The response from the audience was a sharp if not delighted thunder of voices reverberating throughout the theater.

The moment was not lost on me.

Cliff Wood was no has-been.

At least not to anyone there. They were one hundred percent elated, ready for him to take over their night.

As the cheering continued, I was caught off guard when the occupants of the first several rows flooded toward the stage edge. Now with Cliff ripping away at his guitar in full rock star mode, it was as though any rules about staying in place didn't apply. What felt like chaos to me was a routine jockeying into position to fill the gap between the stage and the front row before security could interfere. I looked at Sydney for something, help maybe, but she was too caught up in the moment, spellbound by Cliff's presence as if this were *her* first Cliff Wood concert, too.

These kinds of standard concert mechanics I'd learn over time, but for now, I was literally going with the flow. There was no choice anyway. It was a good thing I didn't know all that was going to happen. In the moment, it was terrifying and confusing but also exhilarating.

When the migration was done, we had shifted down and forward, and now maybe two feet of space was all that separated us from the disarming rock star. Sydney and I had ended up directly beneath the microphone stand, the frumpy woman with the sign right there beside us. She was so overcome by our new location she threw her arms around me in celebration.

I had never experienced someone famous up close like that. Not like Cliff Wood. My eyes worked their way up him. His lace-up boots carried the scuffs and creases from many a concert gone by. Form-fitting jeans were exquisitely cut against him, hugging the muscles and firm tone of his frame. While time had played its inevitable role as it did with everyone, it had not interfered with his conventionally handsome features. His black hair was giving way to silver, yet it still wasn't going any-where. He'd idly run his hand through it leaving it charmingly tousled. All that and the world's most adorable dimpled smile.

I couldn't take my eyes off him.

I leaned close to Sydney's ear. "How old is he?" The music was so loud I was sure she'd ask me to repeat myself.

"Sixty-three," she yelled with a note of pride, not losing her focus on Cliff.

I had to let that number sit. It was hard to think this man was in his sixties. My lusty fascination now turned into wonder.

I didn't recognize the opening song while Sydney and what felt like everyone else in the place sang along to not only the chorus but also the rapid lyr-ics in the verses. If Cliff looked in our direction, I pretended to concentrate on taking a photo, not wanting to stand out as someone unacquainted with his music. It felt like sacrilege to be in such a prime viewing spot and ignorant to what everyone else knew so well.

"That one was from the new album." Sydney had worked off her initial Cliff Wood adrenaline and could talk like a normal person to me now as we waited on a tech who situated Cliff with a different guitar. He'd broken a string.

"He has a new album?" I hated I sounded so astonished.

"It came out about a few months ago." Sydney's eyes stayed on Cliff, following his every move. "It's pretty good. Not his best, but there are a couple of good ones."

As the show progressed, it turned out I did know some of his music, his hits. They came back to me as I recalled muffled versions from our bedroom when Amelia had played records with her friends, their chatty teen conversation mingled with the music.

I felt like Sydney forgot I was standing right by her at some moments during the show. When things began, she'd been extra-attentive, clueing me in to nuances about the songs, and the band, and the overall scene. But anytime Cliff played an intricate guitar solo, she was entranced. Now, I could see why.

There was an authenticity to the care he gave each note, squeezing his fingers against the strings, making sure the melody came out right. And there was something special in the way Sydney observed him. Joining in her fascination, I followed Cliff's hands crawl up and down the guitar's neck. He had an engaging presence, something that breathed right into you, making you want more—crave, really.

We were halfway through the concert when Cliff pitched his guitar to someone in the wings who quickly tossed back a tambourine. Cliff caught it casually in one hand.

With his new instrument, he patrolled the rim of the stage, once again taking in the audience. Fans waved their hands wildly for his attention, some pushing their way closer to the front. Cliff slapped hands with a few of them pacifying their exuberance and then returned to center stage looking across the crowd, clearly enjoying the anticipation he had spurred.

Then it happened. Cliff Wood hovered over me with his microphone in one hand and the tambourine in the other, a devilishly handsome smirk on his face.

"Can you sing?" He looked right into my eyes.

I froze.

Sydney had not warned me about this part of the agenda, just like she hadn't mentioned what would happen with our positioning after Cliff took the stage.

When I didn't respond, Cliff Wood bent forward to reach for me, his fingers clasping mine, and began pulling me toward him. Fans eagerly assisted. I felt a multitude of hands pressing across my back as they helped elevate me. As all this was in motion, I tried to reach back and yank the ponytail holder loose, but it only ended up sliding down and twisting the end of my hair into a funky knot. *So attractive, Claudine.*

It was too late to do anything about it. Cliff and his super-supportive fans had finished propelling me to him, and the deed was done.

I winced as Cliff's solid grip had activated an old wrist injury sending a shock of pain up my arm. By the look on his face I could tell he was concerned he'd hurt me. I massaged the bones at the edge of my palm and then let my arm fall by my hip so he'd know I was okay.

There I was. Side by side, on stage, with Cliff Wood. As I looked at his twinkling eyes, I imagined how envious Amelia would be. All that time she'd spent poring over pictures of him in magazines made sense now. I wished she could trade places with me, even if I were now starstruck myself.

"Can you sing?" Cliff was still waiting for my answer, but I first had to take in this new angle and what it felt like to be inches from his beautifully designed face. He was like a cozy blanket of masculinity, a place you could curl into, soothing yet seductive. *Sigh*.

"Not really," I said finally. I thought my answer might get me out of whatever was at play. No such luck.

"Oh, that's perfect!" Cliff beamed at the crowd with a deep laugh. He knew what he was doing, knew I wasn't a familiar fan he had seen at his concerts in the past. I sensed he could tell I was nervous and wanted to make the moment fun for me.

"We're gonna do a little something here together, okay?" His eyes met mine, warm yet playful.

Before I could agree or disagree, the band amped up the pace of notes they had been playing in a loop since the whole bit had begun and then rolled right into the opening of a song I recognized but couldn't name. Cliff raised his tambourine in the air and began singing, and when he reached the line, "Her eyes were brown, her hair was long, and her smile was right," the audience joined in with, "And she was coming home with me tonight!"

The line from the frumpy lady's poster, *Come home with me,* now registered. I guess she was hoping to be the one invited on stage for this moment with him.

My mind was all over the place. I was amazed by how much I was enjoying being in that desired spot with Cliff Wood—a man who had meant nothing to me a few hours ago.

I surveyed the mass of people in the room, all those eyes on me in my khaki pants and sweater. I wondered if his concerts were always sold out. How could they not be?

Cliff's voice brought me back to the situation at hand. "You ready to do this with me?" He danced a little shaking his hips, a move meant more to amuse everyone than a suggestion of his skills. I later realized he had wanted me to join him, but I didn't recognize it fast enough.

Then he put his arm around me as the notes started again, singing as he had the first time and when he finished with, "and her smile was right," he put the microphone to my lips, and somehow, I knew to sing "And I'm coming home with him tonight."

It was obvious I didn't hit the right tempo of the lyric, but no one cared, Cliff Wood especially. Cheers erupted across the theater as if I'd won an Olympic competition, and he pulled me against him in a sideways hug. "That was gorgeous, completely gorgeous." He winked at me as his eyes danced with mine.

I wanted to linger in that space with him for a few seconds longer, even though it was time for me to go back to my spot next to Sydney. I had never liked being picked out and put into the spotlight, but Cliff had succeeded at making it fun. As I started to walk away, I had an urge to reach up and touch his hair to commemorate the experience but even in my euphoric if not distorted state, I knew that would be too much.

Sydney and fans helped me off the stage. When Cliff started the next song, I pretended to join in, but I was still thinking about this unusual setting I'd stumbled into, meeting Sydney, and being such a prominent part of the night's show. I felt proud of myself for going with it so wholeheartedly. Yet this was only the beginning of where things were headed.

Chapter 3

CLIFF WOOD'S ENCORE HAD EVERYONE ON their feet if they weren't already as he played an updated version of his biggest hit with the audience at full throttle the whole the way through. Hearing the song live was often the thrill of the night for most in attendance while Sydney used the time as a kind of cooldown. She'd heard the song enough.

Now she had her phone clutched in her hand, rapidly typing texts to someone, her original concert buddy I supposed. From my accidental view over her shoulder, I'd seen her comments about everything from what Cliff Wood had worn to how he introduced certain songs. The last reply I saw inquired whether Cliff had invited anyone on stage. I hoped she had mentioned me.

When he finished the song, Cliff let his guitar gently fall by his side and then headed over with an outstretched arm, touching hands with half a dozen people before exiting to the right. A crew member met him in the wings with a fresh bottle of water and a towel and then he was out of sight. That was when our section of the audience began the search for used guitar picks haphazardly discarded in between songs.

Not us though. Sydney didn't have time for that kind of nonsense. That was how she saw it. Used picks were not for people at her fan level. She already had a jar full.

Instead she took my hand and guided me out of the theater, dodging people who were lingering in the aisles, until we arrived in the lobby. Once there, she read and sent more text messages while I waited by the Cliff Wood merchandise table watching the t-shirt selection dwindle as post-concert impulse purchases were made in the afterglow of Cliff's explosive performance. I considered buying one, but when I moved into the line, Sydney motioned for us to leave and waited impatiently as I scrambled into my coat.

"There's a better selection on his website." I felt she'd said so as an apology for hindering my purchase.

On my way to meet her at the venue, I had thought about nearby restaurants I could go to after the concert, imagining myself somewhere lowkey and casual, a place offering a cup of coffee with a sandwich, then a rich dessert. Afterward, I'd catch the express train home and read until my eyes got heavy, like always.

But Sydney had more in store for the night and wanted me along for that, too. She was both mesmerizing and captivating, and already I was falling prey to her unique brand of fun. Instead of thanking her for the concert and being on my way, I was willing to go along for the ride with her not knowing what was going to happen, the same as I had done on stage with Cliff.

I was still trying to zip the front of my jacket as we walked up Broadway and past the hotel adjoining the theater. The air was sharp and damp and even though I hated feeling cold, I was curious enough about where we were headed not to complain. The cuff of my sweater was caught in the elastic of my puffy coat, and as I stopped to untangle the material, I glanced through the window of the hotel lobby bar.

Sydney reached for my arm. "Let's not waste time. We need to keep moving and see what he does first."

In the moment, I didn't even know what she meant about *what he does*. I was just enjoying being on the outside, looking in. I liked peering into the windows of illuminated places as I passed by in the dark, wondering what kind of a life the people inside were leading. I thought I might find inspiration for better orchestrating my own life or perhaps something I could tuck away for my writing someday.

That wasn't on Sydney's agenda. It was then I started to learn her favorite part of a concert night:

the quest for a post-show Cliff Wood sighting, or better yet, an opportunity to talk to him.

The pursuit usually started at the venue. It depended on the situation. There were rules and protocol around such things, how to properly go about locating him and then approaching him. I'd learn more about all of that down the road. For now, I was an innocent bystander. Sydney was the one in the driver's seat with her hands firmly on the wheel.

At the next corner, we walked past the Viand Restaurant and in steps discovered a group of fans assembled in a jagged clump within view of the backstage door on West 75th Street. It was clear Sydney was surprised by the cluster the way she came to a hard stop at the sight of it.

A security guard worked to arrange a protective gate as he dragged a section of a metal barrier into place to keep the crowd at bay. He looked annoyed he had to do so. These intense fan types made his life more difficult, that was for certain. The thoughts were written all over his face.

I had a knit hat in my pocket and arranged it on my head. I sensed we might be a while. "What's everyone waiting for? Autographs from the band or something?"

"Cliff. To see Cliff." Her tone said, *I can't believe you're even asking. It's obvious.*

Though Sydney answered me, she also sounded like her mind was miles away. Her jaw tensed as though she were fighting a profane outburst.

Then, reaching out and swiftly taking me by the hand, she steered me further in search of a better viewing spot as the guard hollered orders about staying put on the group's deaf ears. Defying his directive, we continued moving until we landed beyond the other side of the barrier with a sideways view of the backstage door but still part of the fan swarm waiting in the cold.

Sydney folded her arms across her chest and evaluated the scene. "I wonder what he's going to do. Sometimes he waits a while and lets the band trickle out first." She looked strangely solemn now, much different than the girl who had just danced through a two-hour concert with the energy of a twelve-year-old.

I felt like I was in some strange dream. One minute, I was sifting through records at Marlon's store in solitude, then I was onstage with a 1980s rock star, and now we were waiting in the freezing cold for him. It was fun in an odd sort of way. I would never have thought to hang out after a concert for a simple glimpse of an artist, but for Sydney, not doing so would have diminished the night's experience.

"Anyway, did you like the concert?" she asked. I could tell she was making small talk, possibly worried I might lose interest in what we were doing.

Before I could answer, we heard excited screams as a black sedan slid into place. The guard yelled again to make room, and only a small part of the crowd responded.

"Well this is different." Sydney folded her arms. "Normally with the band it's a passenger van, but this definitely means he's not staying here."

"Staying here?" I was confused, too.

"He doesn't live in New York. But I mean, he's not staying in the hotel attached to the theater where you were looking for him a few minutes ago."

I was about to explain that I hadn't been looking for Cliff and didn't even know doing so was on the agenda at that point. Then someone yelled, "I love you!" It made us both laugh because the voice sounded like a man's, and no one had come out of the door yet. I lost my train of thought and let it go. I knew Sydney wasn't listening to me. She was busy concentrating on the scene.

I tried to anticipate what might happen next so I could figure out what I should do and not disappoint her with my lack of understanding. I thought Cliff might make his appearance and stop to sign autographs and then shake a few hands as he headed to the car. Before I could finish my mental sketch, Sydney started to run. I felt her fingertips graze mine as she attempted to grab my hand but didn't catch it.

Her body became a silhouette behind the mob as she moved closer to it while I stayed in place trying to decipher things. Then I got it—Cliff Wood was making his exit.

A white cloud of breath twirled in the air before him as he appeared from behind the metal service entrance doors into the brisk night. His height made him easy to see, especially with that black and silver gift of hair. The fitted button-up he'd worn at the concert had been replaced by a leather jacket and loose t-shirt. A security guard accompanied him as he began a slow stride toward the waiting sedan.

"Great show," came one voice.

"I've been a fan since forever!"

"Awesome guitar playing, man!"

Cliff didn't react to any of it except to give a brief wave.

As I listened to the chorus of shouts and compliments, I admonished and even laughed at myself for having thought of him as a has-been.

Then another man joined him, and they both climbed inside the car. Brake lights flickered, and soon they made their departure easing onto 75th carefully navigating the pedestrian blockade.

Sydney drifted back to me. She looked dejected but no way was her disappointment going to stop her quest. She wasn't done yet—not by far.

"We have to go." She led the way back down 75th to Broadway taking us along the sidewalk once more past the theater.

I looked back at Cliff's car now making a turn onto Broadway itself and passing us. I felt a nudge of hunger and knew my after-show relaxed dining wasn't going to happen. Too bad we couldn't have stayed and eaten at the Viand. I loved that place. But I didn't mind really. I was enjoying the unconventional turn the evening had taken.

We were nearing a subway station, and I saw Sydney produce her Metro card from her purse.

I did the same. "Where are we going?"

"To look for Cliff. I have some ideas where he might be headed." She adjusted her sweater folding the flaps across her stomach as we trailed though the damp night.

I decided it was best not to ask further questions. None of the answers mattered as I was game to see what this was all about.

We waited on the subway platform with a handful of others and minutes later boarded the express line to Times Square. An elderly woman wearing a battered red scarf sat across from us clinging to an umbrella and a bag of pretzels. I was so hungry I thought about asking her for one.

"What did you see?" Sydney asked as the train started moving. I hadn't thought about how her view of Cliff's departure from the venue had been obstructed by her taller counterparts.

"He got into the car with some guy." I wished I'd had something more useful to offer her.

"His manager, probably."

I told her Cliff was wearing sunglasses and about him wearing a t-shirt.

"Was it the one that says *Parkdale* on the front?"

I tried to remember. "I couldn't see it completely under his jacket."

"Hmm. It's so worn out. He wears it all the time." Her eyes darted about in thought. "I wonder where the band was. We would have had more time to get in place to see him if they'd come out first."

"Maybe they were breaking down their instruments or something?"

"They have people who do that for them." Again, her tone was slightly clipped suggesting that any fan would know such a thing.

I was not a fan, but she seemed to forget that. My mind, too, started to forget it.

The train rattled to our stop. We scaled the grubby concrete stairs emerging from below the city into the electric view of Times Square and immediately had no choice but to mix with scads of tourists. Lights glowed high above as massive billboards heralded the latest Broadway shows with the featured actors' likenesses hovering over us like interlopers to our excursion.

A heavy scent of nuts and sugar filled the air from a street vendor's cart offering an assortment of heated candied cashews, pecans, and walnuts. I could practically feel their glorious taste inside my mouth and was about to suggest we get a bag when Sydney pointed upward. "This is where he hung out after the show last time when he played in Manhattan."

We stood across the street from a chain hotel. The sign over the electric doors fought to compete with the rest of the area's luster.

"Really?" I was surprised. It was hardly befitting of a celebrity in my estimation.

She knew what I was thinking. "Yeah, that was after a concert at the Best Buy Theatre. He probably wanted to be close by, but a lot of times he likes to stay in Soho or the Village."

I was surprised again. "Wow, that's where I live."

She edged toward the hotel's entrance, and I followed her inside. The lobby was largely empty except for a woman with a baby and group of men in suits gathered around and engrossed in conversation. Nothing to see, no Cliff Wood. I thought our exploration was done, but I didn't understand the complete search process for a rock star.

Sydney turned to me. "I don't think this is the right place. No one else is here. Usually there's at least one other fan lurking which would mean others have insider details on his whereabouts. Maybe he hasn't had time to get here."

"The car he got into passed us when we were walking to the subway."

"That doesn't really mean anything. We need to find the bar." She continued to look around, seemingly for another such fan or sign of Cliff.

I wasn't sure how to weigh in on her evaluation of the scene. "I wonder what Cliff Wood drinks?" I mused aloud. In doing so, I had instigated getting my first Cliff-spotting lesson.

Sydney spun around on the heels of her tiny boots. She grabbed my wrists, momentarily wrenching the bad one, and pulled me a few steps to the side as if this minute change in our location would afford us some privacy. "Don't do that. Don't say his name."

She had a forceful whisper, and I felt like a wayward child being disciplined. That was when I realized the gravitas of the whole Cliff Wood scene for her. Her familiarity with his standard t-shirt choice should have been a clear enough signal on its own.

"We need a code. I know this is a new situation for you." She thought about it for a moment as I tried to decide whether I felt offended. "How about rock star?"

"You think that would cause less attention than Cliff W—"

"Don't say it!" Her voice was terse. She released my arms to consult her phone. "What's your phone number?"

I said the numbers aloud for her as she dialed me. I felt the vibration in my hand of the call coming through.

"You've got me now. I'll go search for the bar and any activity—a band member or fan regular—just to be sure. You stay here. If you see him arrive, send me a text." She took a few steps and turned back. "Don't try to talk to him. Be inconspicuous."

Taking a seat on a nearby couch, I accepted my post to monitor the entrance. It was an average hotel, nothing notable. From the overhead speakers came staid classical music. Sydney had nothing to worry about. I would have been at a loss if Cliff Wood were to appear. *Don't talk to him* she had said. As if I even could. Apprehension aside, I couldn't imagine what I might say that would interest him.

Sydney returned. "Two bars. Nothing." She held up her middle and forefinger for emphasis and looked at me for a report.

"Nothing here either."

More handfuls of people strode into the lobby, gloves and jackets coming off in the welcome warmth of the space. Cliff Wood wasn't among them.

Sydney studied her phone. I assumed she was awaiting more information relevant to our rock star pursuit but must not have received any. She shook her head in apparent frustration, her face drawn in disappointment.

At first it seemed a little irrational and borderline stalking behavior to go to a celebrity's potential hotel in hopes of finding him, but I'd had such a memorable moment being on stage at the concert. I wanted Sydney to have something special from the evening, too. And I had never had an adventure like this. I wasn't the adventurous sort. But

Sydney's scope of interest in Cliff Wood, which I didn't know the half of at that point, had grown on me in the short window of time I'd been with her. I wanted the adventure to keep going.

I was about to suggest we try the Marriott Marquis or another hotel to locate him, when Sydney asked, "Want to get something to eat?"

We slid into a booth in a back corner of a bar blocks away and ordered martinis and appetizers. Sydney gave me her life story in between our reflections on the concert and nibbles of broccoli bites and potato skins. It felt good to have conversation. We asked for more martinis along with desserts and drank and talked some more.

She told me she worked out of her apartment on the Upper West Side running a marketing business mostly designing web pages for corporate clients of varying sizes. She'd done similar work as an employee for a couple of companies but liked having the freedom to determine her own schedule and be selective about the projects she accepted. Dating wasn't on her current radar. She had been in two long-term relationships and was married for most of her twenties. While she explained this history, I could see in her personality how she functioned better being single. She had very specific ideas about how she liked to do things. I had already experienced this with her over the course of the night.

As for Cliff Wood, she had seen him in concert too many times to count and attended any meet-and-greet or autograph signing opportunity. It was a hobby of sorts—an expensive one—she confessed. She had been a fan since she was a teenager and had followed his career through the years, buying his albums, seeing his concerts. Only in recent years had she become involved with his fan community.

"It's like a sisterhood. Kind of like a sorority—comes with some drama, too." She rolled her eyes and shook her head simultaneously. "You see a lot of the same fans at the concerts. Cliff hasn't ever slowed down except he doesn't go all over the globe as much as he used to. He lives in Jamestown."

"Where's that?" I followed the question with a broccoli bite.

"In Rhode Island. It's not that far, a few hours I think. It makes it easy for him to come here. Sometimes, there are long periods where he falls off the map. I figure that's when he's writing."

"Like how long?"

"A couple of months." She pushed her chocolate cake toward me, offering to share it, and took a sip of her martini. "Then suddenly, a show will get announced or a fan retreat."

"What does that mean, fan retreat?"

"It's like this mini-weekend of concerts. Only about a hundred fans can go. One time, it was tied to an album coming out, and he played some of the unreleased songs. The last one was about two years ago. It was at a lake place near Nashville. I didn't go. Someone had said it was mostly going to be about his books and discussions on writing, some readings, but he ended up doing some different sets, too. I was sorry I missed it."

"I wonder why Tennessee?"

"He has family there I think. He's super private, doesn't talk a lot about his personal life. He's not into social media at all."

"You seem to know a lot about him," I countered. I was astounded by her array of Cliff Wood knowledge. I felt like I could ask her anything about him, and she'd have an answer.

She started to lift her martini glass but then set it down. "It's not that hard to figure things out. I read everything there is about him. I pay attention anytime he's interviewed. When you do that enough, you pick up on things, subtle stuff he doesn't even realize he's putting out there. But I'd love to sit and talk to him. Just have some one-on-one time, really find out what is going on in his mind. You can tell from his songs he's a deep thinker." She pulled the plate of cake back toward her and scraped a heap of icing off with her fork and shuttled it to her mouth. "I wonder if he's as fascinating as I think he'd be."

I wanted to contribute more to the conversation, but I had never felt that passionate about anyone or anything really. I had heard about people who were obsessed with bands or celebrities, but I didn't know anyone like that. I loved how she made no attempt to hide how submerged she was in it all, the world of Cliff Wood.

"Okay, no more." She set the cake aside. There was hardly a square inch left.

We sat there for a few moments, not talking.

Then Sydney said, "I'm really glad you came. I hope you enjoyed the concert." She spoke as though we'd come to the end of a first date. "You did enjoy it, right?"

"I did. His whole band is talented."

What I didn't say was how I wouldn't forget my experience being on stage, but the best part overall had been being with Sydney. I hadn't enjoyed an evening of such fun banter in a long time. It was nice, being with someone it was easy to talk to.

"They really are talented!" Excitement ignited in her voice. "The keyboard player is extra cute. Did you notice?"

I'd only glanced at the band now and then during the performance. Cliff's stage presence had been too distracting.

Before I responded she said, "His name is Brent. Married. British. He's the member of the group who seems to have his act together. Has twin girls. His wife is twenty years younger than he is, but they've been together for a long time."

Again, I was surprised by the esoteric insight she had not only for Cliff Wood but also for his bandmates as well. That was some true dedication and enthusiasm.

I thought back to my times at writers' workshops, stumbling around, hoping the right idea for a book would surface. The whole point of being there was to immerse myself in the writing process and be with others who sought the same and act as a sounding board for one another's ideas. I'd scribbled in notebooks, mostly words I liked, sometimes a paragraph that felt well-constructed. A few poems had come out of it. Other attendees left with the bones of a book in place. I didn't and wondered why.

Now I knew. I had never become one with my supposed dream— never ate, slept, and breathed my stated passion the way Sydney did for hers. She had a tenacity and a drive I lacked. Not for anything in my life. It didn't matter Cliff Wood was some fangirl obsession she had. She was committed to it. Listening to her deep dive about all things Cliff Wood and how hard she worked to cultivate such a whimsical hobby, I thought I must not have a sincere enough thirst for a career in writing. If I did, I wouldn't be working as an assistant at a magazine at this point in my career. *Career?*

"Too bad we don't live closer. We could share a cab." Sydney counted some twenty-dollar-bills from her purse. "It's on me." She set them on the table. "It's the least I can do, what with dragging you through the cold to unsuccessfully hunt down a rock star you aren't even into."

"I'm sorry we didn't find him." And I really was. I stood up to get back into my coat.

She wiped her bangs to the side. "It's okay. There are always other opportunities."

On the sidewalk outside the restaurant, she gave me a hug as if she didn't expect to see me again. Her small frame pressing against my longer, taller one felt like a missing puzzle piece.

"Thank you for coming, Claudine. Be safe going home." It made me feel good she cared enough to say such.

Walking through New York City at night can either make you feel wonderfully alive as if you're holding hands with a sea of people enjoying life's potential or like you're at a party where you don't know anyone.

I'd felt the latter for a long time, tuning out any possibilities that may have helped me pick up the pieces of my damaged soul, an endeavor I felt too challenging to attempt. But spending that evening with Sydney had awakened my spirit. She made me a part of something important to her when she didn't even know me, an outstretched hand in that sea.

As I started my short trek to the subway station at 50th Street, I felt the temptation to turn around and run back to her and offer to canvas a few more places to find Cliff Wood, anything to hold onto the moment and to her welcome and warm hand. Even if I backtracked, her pint-sized frame was long gone in the crowded landscape of people. Sending a text to ask if she wanted to hang out a while more seemed desperate.

The city felt larger than usual, foreboding and avaricious, the lights brighter, the dark sky more ominous as though every cloud and every shadow reached out to grab me. I worked my way along the crowded sidewalks of mostly tourists until I reached the subway and descended into the stark under-ground of the mass transit system I knew so well.

As I swiped my metro card to get through the turnstile, I heard the train. Its approach sounded like distant thunder as it rumbled along the tracks. I felt decidedly alone as the doors swished open, and I got on. At least below the city the air was warm.

After the twenty-minute ride with a handful of people who looked ready to call it a day, I was in Greenwich Village at my apartment and walk-ing through the ridged front door, happy to see I had a book I had been enjoying waiting for me on the couch. I was down to the last couple of chapters and had forgotten all about it while I was with Sydney.

I let her know I was home with a text message, *Hey, made it. Had a great time!* Her reply was a thumbs up and a smiley face emoji. I had hoped she'd say something about getting together again.

After changing clothes, I fell into bed. I couldn't help thinking about her more. I wished I had found something to share about myself to connect us on a deeper level. I never felt good at small talk with women.

As I lay there, the gears in my head continued to rotate thinking about the whole evening, being on stage, waiting after the concert with the fans, and Sydney's explanations about everything. I knew I wasn't going to be able to fall asleep for a while. Kicking away the covers, I rolled over to reach my laptop and downloaded Cliff Wood's latest album.

Chapter 4

MY MOTHER DECORATED HER APARTMENT the same way she had all my young days: lots of little collections on surfaces and in display cabinets, from tiny teapots to an assortment of thimbles she'd been accumulating for years. She didn't have room for all her treasures, and as such, the space felt cluttered but gave the feel of a life of history.

I liked to keep my own apartment devoid of any collections other than books, but even those were carefully chosen and tastefully organized. My love of the printed word had been inherited from my mother. She kept heaps of paperbacks behind the wingback chair where she did her reading. All my life, books had been stored by that chair, some from the library, some she'd received from friends, Marlon's, lots of places. And she read all of them, every single word.

Outside of her literary decor, the rest of the place held simple but sturdy furniture. She would never have entertained the idea of replacing any of it unless it became unusable. I liked being around the comfort of my childhood home that had remained the same year after year, and I tried to visit at least once a week, easy to do with it being a ten-minute walk from my own apartment.

That Friday, I left work early, having finished the things Nina had asked me to do before she herself left earlier than usual. It had been a long week. Each day when I wasn't focused on the myriad of details I had to juggle between two photoshoots, I thought—hoped—I might hear from Sydney. I had enjoyed being with her, learning about this Cliff Wood world she inhabited. I'd experienced her energy and fun and wanted to know more about other facets of her life. I thought being around her could help me get back to the creative side of my mind, and a new friendship would be good for me.

My mother and her sister, Trudy, were having one of their evenings of jewelry making, a hobby they'd shared for as long as I could remember. I didn't usually participate other than to be in their company and enjoy their chatting. They discussed anything and everything and liked to reminisce about relatives who'd passed on before my time. The rhythm of their voices made me feel comforted, even discussion on mundane topics.

Their relationship sometimes made me jealous. They had an effortless connection to one another and never a strained silence between them. Amelia and I didn't have that type of relationship, though I would've liked it if we had. We had such different personalities. Still, I admired her and saw her as someone who could give me advice, and as we got older, we both started to appreciate the value of having a sister.

At a card table in the middle of the living room, my mother, Aunt Trudy, and I sat before an assortment of containers filled with beads, wire, and tiny charms. I rummaged through the components while they talked about some late cousins I'd never known and then went to the kitchen for some water. That was when my mother intercepted the long-awaited message.

"Someone wants you to come to the Bowery." My mother squinted at my phone next to her. She didn't see something like announcing the content of a text message as intrusive, but helpful, a tendency I was used to. "Isn't it a little late for something like that? Trudy, what time is it?"

I abandoned the water. "Can I see the text?"

My aunt nudged her glasses back into place and consulted her watch. "It's only nine, Joyce, still early for someone Claudey's age, especially on a Friday night." She glanced up to wink at me as if letting me know she was in support of whatever mischief I might be considering.

I tapped my phone to see the full message. As I viewed the screen, another text arrived from the same number. *What are you doing? You awake?*

Maybe it was Sydney. I hadn't filled in her contact information when we were looking for Cliff at the hotel.

I stepped away from my mother and aunt and typed, *yes awake.*

Great. Hurry. Get here. It was definitely Sydney. Always commanding and in a rush.

I didn't get into the specifics with my mother and Aunt Trudy about what I was doing because I didn't know. I just knew I wanted to see Sydney again. And I wasn't ready to tell them about my initial experience with her either. It would only spur multiple questions from my mother who had the propensity to be a well-intentioned busybody as demonstrated by her announcing the text message.

I ducked into the bedroom to see if there was something I could wear that would lend itself to whatever unique outing might be on tap. Would we be going on the hunt for another rock star? I didn't want to end up on stage again in a pair of khaki pants. Sydney represented spontaneity to me even though I'd only spent one evening with her.

In my old bedroom closet, I found a pair of jeans and an apricot colored tee I remembered I'd left there a few weeks ago. The black coat I'd worn to work would have to do.

Aunt Trudy removed the chandelier earrings she was wearing, oversized but elegant in their own way with an oval-shaped blue topaz in the middle.

"These will dress you up, wherever you're off to."

"I'm just meeting a friend for a drink." I hooked the earrings into my ears.

Aunt Trudy suppressed a smile. I knew she assumed it was a man.

Outside my mother's building, the street was quiet as I waited for the rideshare I'd ordered. It wasn't the time of night to get a taxi. I'd have to walk up to the main drag at Houston and hope for one to come along, and Sydney had directed me to *hurry*. Avoiding the staggering cold of early February was also top of mind.

When the driver arrived, I was happy to climb into the heated cabin of his Nissan Maxima. He'd taken care to create a welcoming atmosphere for his occupants providing a phone charger and a cupholder of mints. Several bottles of water lined a compartment on the door. He even told me he had individual bags of chips should I want one.

But I didn't need any of those things. My phone was fully charged, and my mother had swiftly put together a bag of snacks to send with me. It was her way to prepare for the unlikely. "Just in case you get hungry or stranded," she had said cheerfully if not ominously.

I had accepted her offering knowing I'd hurt her feelings if I turned her down. And really, who knew what kind of emergency snack occasion might occur? If things turned out like last time with Sydney, the possibility for a snack might very likely happen.

As I rode along, I wondered if her invitation was related to Cliff Wood again. I hoped so. The fun of it all aside, I wanted a run-in with him to happen for her. But when I walked into the Bowery Hotel's lobby, and she was nowhere in sight, I thought her plans for us might be something entirely different.

I sat down on a long, modular couch to wait for her. Knowing Sydney, she was off in a corner, texting someone. It could be a while. I now wished I had the plastic bag stuffed full of my mother's homemade popcorn to keep me company. It was too bad I'd handed the snacks to a homeless woman after I departed the car having decided arriving with a food bag wasn't exactly a great look.

Another text from Sydney showed up. *How far away are you?*

I'm in the hotel lobby now.

Hotel? She wrote further saying she was at the Bowery Electric, a nightspot, not the hotel. And Cliff was about to play.

I shook my head, annoyed at myself. I should have asked for more specific details before heading out, but I had been so excited to hear from her. Thankfully the venue was only a short walk, and I was ready to hit the pavement. My spirits were boosted that our outing again involved Cliff Wood.

A bachelorette party arrived, weaving their way through the lobby and wearing pink boas and t-shirts reading, *Team Mrs. Greg Gates.* As I gathered my purse and sidestepped them on my way out, a security guard and two men emerged from the elevator.

After all my years in New York, official-looking activity like this still made me extra alert, thinking there could be a disturbance I'd prefer to avoid. Looking over my shoulder as I moved toward the exit, I saw a fourth man join the group. He had greyish black hair, sunglasses, and a searing casualness about him. He studied his phone as the other men led the way. I slowed.

I would not have so easily recognized Cliff Wood had I not seen him only a week ago when I'd been with him on stage, plus had almost two hours of a front row view—more than enough time to burn the way he looked now into my memory. I had a passing thought that no one else who happened by right then would be able to place him, the young bachelorettes especially.

While I waited only feet away, he and the three men headed outside. I felt a jolt of excitement, the way most do in the presence of celebrity. Had I been thinking clearly, I would have followed them to the venue. Instead, I consulted my phone's map to be sure I went to the right place this time.

Sydney was at the entrance waiting for me. As always, her outfit was sporty and smart with an elegant flair. White jeans with an electric blue off-the-shoulder blouse with the words *Mascara and Rock and Roll*. She didn't look as if she were trying for attention or to look young. It was just her fun style. Meanwhile, here I was at another event looking as if I had no taste in clothing much less worked at a fashion magazine.

It had been my plan to tell her about seeing Cliff in the hotel lobby as soon as I got there. I felt bad I'd had such an effortless brush with him after we tried so hard to find him after the show the week before. But things were happening too fast. Sydney practically threw the ticket she had for me at the doorman and rushed me inside toward the bar. I was fine with it, glad to be out of the cold. And with her again.

The place had a relaxed industrial feel to it. Strings of lights draped across the rafters added a tone of charm and intimacy. It was more casual than I'd anticipated. My uninspired ensemble was fine for the night.

"Sorry this is so last minute." Sydney pushed her way into the congested area getting us closer to the bar. Even amid the packed room, her candy scented perfume prevailed. "This is kind of a pop-up show. Let's grab a drink."

"Pop-up show?"

She either didn't hear me or ignored my question.

"Two screwdrivers," she yelled as she leaned between others already with their cocktails in hand. Then turning back to me, "Are you good with that?"

When I nodded, she signaled the bartender to proceed and then fully faced me, looking up to meet my eyes as she always had to, given her tiny stature. "My friend who was supposed to be here is the same one who bailed on me last time. She literally told me she wasn't coming as I was walking inside. That's why you got a late text." She had to shout in the noise-filled room.

"I'm glad I was able to come." Even if the invitation had been the result of her being stood up, I was glad she'd reached out to me. I hoped there would be a time when joining her would be planned, not because someone had stood her up. Those times would be many and soon.

When our drinks were in hand, we clinked glasses, each taking a sip. Then Sydney grabbed my arm and hustled us to our seats. It felt like déjà vu from our first Cliff Wood show together.

Second row this time, seats on the aisle.

I didn't ask her how she secured such prime spots. I had a feeling she enjoyed some of the cloaks around the Cliff Wood concert scene, and I would learn about them myself if she continued to include me.

We had just taken our spots when she asked me to hold her drink and abandoned me to join a group in conversation in the aisle. There were hugs, a photo, and a couple of others coming into the scene. Sydney gave me a sidelong glance and motioned me over.

I set our drinks under my chair and headed their way. I still needed to tell her about seeing Cliff at the hotel. I'd wait until we were done with the interlude at hand.

"Claudine, these are some friends of mine— Doreen, Paige, Evelyn, Lorie, and Jerry," who said, "Yes, I'm a fan, but I also happen to be Lorie's boyfriend."

Everyone laughed as he shook my hand. It was true, the women more than outnumbered the men in the crowd.

"Oh, come on, Jerry," Doreen said. "You have the hots for him just like we do."

Jerry made a face as if to playfully agree. "I get the attraction to him. He's a great-looking guy and all, but it's his guitars I have the hots for." He gestured toward the stage where a combination of both electric and acoustic guitars formed a semi-circle around a stool.

"What about you, Claudine?" It was Evelyn, a striking woman my height with a perfect blanket of dark hair, cranberry lipstick, and professionally applied eyelashes. "How long have you been a fan? And I go by Evvi. No one calls me Evelyn."

I was ready to say I had known about Cliff Wood since his heyday and mention Amelia's interest, but Sydney jumped ahead of me. "Wait, where are our drinks? Did we leave them somewhere? We'll catch up later. Good seeing you all."

She squeezed Paige's forearm before we turned away. It felt like a too-abrupt departure.

I waited until we were out of earshot to comment. "What was that about? They seemed nice."

Sydney nodded her head agreeing. "Most of us are. We've known each other a long time. Many people here are friends *because of* Cliff and his music. And the friendships go way beyond his concerts." She looked behind her. "But there's another side to it, and some think they're better at being a fan than someone else is. If they think you're new in this Cliff Wood world, they'll be less accepting of you. It's all very immature."

I didn't know what to make of such information and didn't feel it applied to me. I was there to hang out with Sydney. I had listened to Cliff's latest album off and on during the week, wanting to be more in the know on him should I see her again.

One of the album's online reviews I'd found said the lyrics were "a myriad of poignancy" and would "grab your soul." I had planned to listen again to see if I agreed, but Nina had me neck-deep in tasks, and the one evening I'd left the office on time, I helped Marlon at the bookstore with inventory.

"You said something about this being a pop-up show," I reminded Sydney.

"Oh yeah. It's essentially a solo show, just Cliff, no band. And he improvises a lot."

"What does that mean though? Pop-up?" I took a swallow of my drink. The ice had melted leaving the mixture too weak to enjoy. I set it below my chair again.

"It's a show that doesn't get formally announced. And there isn't much notice. You have to be on watch. They pop up here and there, so we call them that." She sipped her drink. "He likes to grab his guitar and be in a room of people in a small venue. It's like therapy for him."

"Therapy for what?"

The lights dimmed before she could answer. One of the men I'd seen in the hotel lobby crept from stage left and tweaked the height of the microphone while people hurried to their seats with last-minute drink purchases in hand.

Cliff Wood's entrance soon after was much less dramatic than the last week's concert at the Beacon. Though much applause and whistling still greeted his arrival, there was no cascading of lights as he collected a guitar and trailed over to the stool.

He took a seat and plucked a few strings. "Hope everyone's evening is going well so far."

I had forgotten how good his voice sounded.

More whistles and cheers exploded from the room along with cries of *I love you*. These declarations seemed to tickle him though he didn't respond.

Black suit jacket, faded Stones tee, indigo jeans. Same scuffed boots. His mussed was hair in need of a trim, but that would have interfered with his charming rock star look. I thought in the hotel he had worn a different style of jacket, something more casual. That was the kind of thing Sydney would have easily remembered. I flinched inside thinking how I'd forgotten to tell her about seeing him.

The show started. It would have to wait.

Cliff anchored one of his boots against the stool's frame and hoisted the guitar further onto his thigh. As he started to play, he shared one of his electric smiles, and the rush of excitement in the room increased and then leveled. Sydney, who had been furiously texting, now tucked away her phone saying to me, "I think you're going to love this."

I am not one who exaggerates. In my first college writing class, I was told by the instructor I needed to work on my descriptions, to learn to embellish. It was this directive that had almost pushed me away from the idea of being a writer. I wanted my words to come from a place of authenticity, not feel forced to magnify them or alter them for the sake of effect.

So when I say from the moment the concert began I was completely transfixed—from how Cliff cradled the guitar, to the way his lyrics airbrushed the room, to his accompanying facial expressions conveying a full spectrum of emotion—then you can know my memory of the evening isn't overstated.

Transfixed. Fascinated. Rivetted. Pick one. They all fit. Sydney was right. It was a different show, full of spontaneity and intimacy. Only Cliff and his guitar, his voice, his thoughts. I could have watched him all night.

He started with a few variations on his hits. Even a novice of his music like me could tell he was deviating from the original tempos, putting the brakes on some melodies while accelerating others. It felt like watching an artist mixing colors and creating a painting on impulse.

He'd gaze into the rafters, working out a new section until he found the right rhythm, and then ease back into the song, sometimes inserting a change in the lyrics meant to amuse us. He looked comfortable as if hanging out with friends in his living room.

Whether Cliff sang fast or slow, a known song or not, Sydney was having her own spiritual experience. A soft smile rested on her face as she slowly rocked her head to the beat and sometimes closed her eyes. I wondered what she was thinking.

In my early twenties, I'd gone to some concerts but never gotten that into it. It was just something to do. This show though had such a different feeling to it, Cliff's gracious presence, the way he responded to the crowd. It was something special.

"Are you enjoying this?" Sydney momentarily came out of her blissful trance.

Cliff had stopped to drink some water before getting a different guitar.

"I'm blown away by his artistry."

"Yes! I'm so happy you were the one who ended up coming. He's really putting it out there tonight."

Back on the stool, Cliff positioned his guitar once again. "Thanks for coming." He cast a half-smile and then winked at someone to our right.

Sydney's head whipped around like lightning to see if she could pinpoint the recipient. At the same time, Cliff introduced the next song.

"This one's called 'Out of Tune.' It's about, well," he chuckled, "a lot of things. Relationships, the pursuit of dreams. And a girl, of course." Laughter flickered across the room. "I wrote it when I was thirty." He clamped his fingers on the strings. "Thought I knew everything back then."

A silence fell over the room as the song began, first with a reference to the aforementioned girl, then giving way to lyrics describing how inner demons can triumph when you think you've made the wrong decision.

"I think this one is my favorite," Sydney said at the end, "of his older stuff."

I added it to my mental list of songs to look up, picturing myself with my laptop, locating the original recordings, with the privacy to concentrate as much as I wanted on them. The writer in me wanted to know about his musical history, but I also thought having more knowledge of his song catalog might endear me to Sydney.

Becoming her friend, a real friend, not one who'd be invited after another dropped out, was important to me now. I had acknowledged her impact on me. It would be much later before I'd know Cliff's full influence as well as the effect of everything else in the Cliff Wood world which had started to bud in those first experiences with Sydney.

But the next song would speak to me immediately. It crept in like a shadow and embraced every despairing thought I had, every wound I'd felt, all the brokenness I kept to myself and fought daily to ignore. I'd turn to it over and over down the road.

"Oh gosh, he hardly ever does this one, hardly ever." Sydney's tone was breathy and earnest as she gripped my thigh with absent-minded enthusiasm.

"What is this?" The first notes were just hitting the air, but I could already tell something was different about this song by the look in Cliff's soft yet concentrated eyes.

Sydney whispered the title. "'When I Remember You.'"

For most of the performance, Cliff had introduced each song by sharing a story illustrating what had sparked its theme. But not for this one. The story was in the words, in his tone, and his troubled eyes as he sang it. His delivery carried an anguish he made no attempt to hide. He had lost someone, and the grief was still with him, the haunting song bringing it all back.

"You will always be, always be…. a light for me," he sang wistfully.

I sat there with my hands loose in my lap as the melody fell over me like welcome rain with lyrics addressing things hidden in my mind that now rolled into the forefront of my thoughts.

Halfway through the song, Sydney added, "It's about his sister."

Now I understood what she had meant by the show being like therapy. But it wasn't just therapy for Cliff. It was for us as well. When he came to the end of the song, he took a moment to compose himself, his head tilted downward, getting his bearings. When he looked up at the crowd, his eyes were wet with sorrow, the same as mine.

Chapter 5

I WISH I HAD MORE CURRENT, MEANINGFUL memories of Amelia.

When she died, we had just started getting to know each other as adults. With us having shared a bedroom most of our younger lives, it would seem we would have bonded in multiple ways, but we were five years apart in age and very different. I was always knee-deep reading while she talked on the phone, usually buried under the covers so I couldn't hear her silly teenage fascinations. As we got older, we continued moving in opposite directions as our personalities developed.

She was more interested in things like setting off on a hiking trip with friends or going on a snow skiing weekend while I wanted to wander around libraries and study authors' writing techniques in magazines like *The New Yorker*. Even thinking about it now, I can't come up with much we had in common, other than we both had a sweet tooth.

Once a month, our parents would take us to Economy Candy on the Lower East Side. Amelia and I would plot ahead of time agreeing how to get the most from the outing. Our typical plan included each getting a different candy bar to split and then one of us would get a package of gum and the other a roll of something we could also share. When our dad produced his wallet, we'd talk him into a few extra things we couldn't live without. As Amelia got older, she lost interest in that kind of thing. She wanted to be with her friends. My friends were books and words. Our worlds didn't have much overlap.

After I got out of my teens, she started inviting me to her apartment to watch obscure movies or help her organize something, usually her closet. She had a roommate who did prop work at an off-Broadway theater and was often gone at night leaving Amelia and me the privacy to dish about family issues or whatever we wanted to discuss. We were finally revealing some of our secrets to one another, nothing heavy, but the conversations were often laced with, "But Mom doesn't know, so don't say anything."

There was also some shopping and some passing down of clothes she either no longer wanted or that wouldn't fit in the one shared closet in her sublet. Sometimes we'd hop the Hudson line train to Tarrytown and wander around the vintage town. Other days we rented bikes and rode around Central Park. We started finding our way as sisters. After she was gone, the idea I couldn't bring her back was a constant weight, and I worked to put her absence out of my head. It was brutal and sad and probably not the way to handle it.

The subject of her was especially difficult with my mother. I always knew she liked Amelia more than me, and I was okay with that. They had an innate understanding of one another. But my mother needed to make sense of things and couldn't find a way to do that with her death.

That was what my therapist thought about it anyway. I went to a few sessions trying to get a handle on things for myself, but it wasn't working. Truth is, I didn't know what I needed and couldn't adequately describe my feelings. I decided to let things sit and find their own resting spot.

But I didn't need a therapist's input to know another effect of losing her was being fearful about my future and what it would be like someday when I'd be alone in the world, facing life's inevitable challenges with no parent or sibling to help me through. I thought I needed to get myself nailed down in an existence that made me feel safer and more optimistic as time marched.

I moved in with a guy I'd dated only a few months. I stowed some clothes at his apartment, along with some hair products, and a few books. Never truly moved in. He lived in Brooklyn which gave me the sensation of being away from home. But in the end, it was just another part of the city and did nothing to change my outlook.

After that, I found an eight-week writers' workshop in Oxford, Mississippi. I decided to commit beyond the course—not just move a few clothes. I thought being so far from all I'd known would be what I needed to disconnect me from Amelia's loss. I would learn about writing while I also filled my mind with new things to see and have fun setting up my life there. Instead, it only made all the sadness I felt more pronounced. I wanted to be able to tell Amelia about what was happening and make plans for her to visit.

I dated some there, mostly a guy named Rob, thinking a relationship would help seal my new life. But that also inflamed my mind. Again, I wanted to tell Amelia about him and the nuances that accompany the beginnings of relationships. It was easy to see a change in geography wasn't the answer.

That's when I went back to New York, resigned to it all, to my uncertainty and fears, knowing I'd have to find a way to face life no matter where I lived. Rob asked if he could come visit. I'd said maybe, but I knew I meant no.

Thank goodness Aunt Trudy had a friend who retired to Florida and needed someone to live in her apartment since she wasn't ready to sell it. I had given up my loft where I'd lived for years with a landlord who liked me and had yet to raise my rent.

———

At the end of Cliff's performance, I finally bought a t-shirt while Sydney did her usual involved post-concert texting. I knew that meant we were likely going on the search for Cliff Wood again. While I was excited I already had knowledge on where to find him, I hated I would have to admit I'd held the information all through the show.

A combination of events changed that and led us to Cliff without my ever saying anything. I decided bringing it up late wouldn't matter. It wasn't as though I'd had an actual encounter with him. That would be the kind of thing I'd need to share with Sydney, but my minor run-in could be swept aside.

As Sydney studied her string of messages, it gave me time to recover from the emotions brought on by Cliff's last song. It was not a time to give in and be sentimental. I wanted to be present for this experience with Sydney and focus on the sacred business of the rock star hunt. I hoped this time she would get her moment with him.

It was Paige from the group I'd met earlier who gave us the lowdown on his real whereabouts. Cliff was not going to be hanging out at the Bowery Hotel. According to her, he would be at a nearby restaurant and bar. How fans like she and Sydney got such information was a mystery to me, but it was so important to them. Seeing Cliff even for a fleeting moment outside of the venue made for a more complete experience. They wanted something extra, a quick smile or two seconds of eye contact from him would suffice.

There were factions, divisions, and a fair amount of weirdness among the fans. Sydney explained it to me saying, "Paige is one of the good ones." Like Sydney, she had recently turned forty and had followed Cliff for years which meant she was seasoned in the after-show rock star drill. Sydney seemed to regard her as more of a concert associate than a friend.

When I came out of the bathroom after the show, Paige was in the hallway ending a call to someone, her husband, I figured out when she hung up.

"Men, men." She shook her head. "I just want a few hours away. He knows this is *my time*. And then I have to talk him through some minor thing I know he could handle."

I followed her back out to the merchandise table where Sydney waited. Paige shared her details on Cliff.

"Oh, perfect." Sydney looked relieved.

"I think my people have disappeared." Paige's head bobbed around like a magpie. She looked forlorn, though only briefly. "Yep, I've been abandoned. Can I walk with you?"

Sydney started toward the door. "We need to get moving."

"Yes, we're already behind." Paige ran a comb through her short, white-blond hair and then tossed it into an oversized purse.

Dashing off with them as if I had long been part of their intimate fan adventures felt good. I didn't care if we found Cliff or not.

I liked Paige right away. She had a bold spirit about her, nothing to hide, and seemed to be fine if the world knew her every facet. She linked arms with me as we walked along and told me her Cliff Wood history. All of Sydney's fan acquaintances had backstories on growing up with his music and were eager to share their fan credentials. Paige, too, described the experience as being part of a sisterhood and said she never got tired of seeing Cliff perform.

As she unapologetically puffed on a cigarette and wafted the smoke away from my direction, she told me she had grown up in Detroit and had a daughter and son aged fourteen and eleven. She loved Cliff's 1982 album best, and could, if asked, name the songs in order on each side of the record. She still had her original copy. Cliff had signed it *Adoringly Yours* at a record store event. Most notably, she had been on stage with him three times in the same way I had, a fact I could tell Sydney did not enjoy hearing given the way she refrained from making a comment.

A five-minute walk brought us to a corner restaurant I'd never heard of called The Block. It was a dimly lit place with high round tables. A bar stretched the length of the room on one side, fully stocked with every imaginable brand and type of spirit.

At first glance, there was nothing to suggest Cliff Wood was anywhere to be found.

Sydney told the young hostess we were looking for a friend, and she allowed us to go beyond the entryway to survey the room. The noise level made the music playing overhead unintelligible, and I was surprised to see how packed it was for a weeknight.

"Is that Alternative Kyle at the bar?" Sydney raised onto her toes for a better view.

I knew she was talking to Paige and not me. Their Cliff homing devices were in the extreme *on* position. The analysis of the scene had begun. I still didn't know the full scope of the process, but I knew it was a mission to be taken seriously and had its own set of guidelines. I'd had but a glimpse of all that could be involved on my prior excursion with Sydney.

"That's him. I see Bruce, too." Paige flung her giant purse over her shoulder as though she needed to be ready to move quickly.

"Where?" Sydney sounded anxious.

As Paige discreetly pointed toward the bar, I turned to her. "Who is Alternative Kyle?"

They both ignored me, at least momentarily as they continued their FBI-like surveillance of the place. Then Sydney said, "He's this guy who's at a lot of the concerts, but he doesn't fit in. He looks more like he's dressed for some underground club show. He's super low-key, doesn't talk to anyone."

"He always knows where Cliff's going to be hanging out," Paige chimed in. "And Bruce—he's Cliff's manager. In the red shirt. Bushy hair, see him? He's always easy to spot."

I thought for sure we would rush over to them, but we stood there, eyeing Bruce's wild hair and ordinary behavior. So far, we had watched him pay for drinks and put his wallet in his back pocket, neither of which elicited any useful information.

I felt shards of cold air hit my back each time someone entered or left and was ready to move more into the room. I wished we could at least mill about and get away from the draft, but I knew better than to make a suggestion at this critical stage of the search.

That was when Evvi appeared, gliding into view through a doorway off the bar, her blown-out hair swaying as she moved. She said something to Bruce making him laugh out loud, and within seconds, he vanished through the same doorway followed by Alternative Kyle.

"Well now things are getting interesting," said Sydney.

"Yeah. Wonder where they went?" Paige's eyes stayed gripped on the area Evvi had just exited.

We both looked at Sydney who fiddled with the wisps of hair at the base of her neck. I could see an idea brewing. "Claudine can check it out."

"Check what out?" I looked at her, curious.

"You just need to confirm Cliff is really here and see what's going on back there." Sydney said this as if it were no big deal—me wandering into what was clearly a private section of the restaurant.

I bit my lip, unsure about it. "Isn't there someone you could text and ask?" After all, Sydney had spoken earlier about the tight friendship between fans.

Paige explained, "It's not like that. Everyone gets really possessive about Cliff. No one's going to share that information."

They both looked worried I wouldn't agree to the plan, but as unnerved as I was, I still felt pleased they trusted me for the task. After giving it only a second of thought, I weaved my way across the dining area, passing through the mysterious doorway to find a nondescript room probably used for the occasional private party like the one at hand.

If I'd known the full extent of the territorial element to the Cliff Wood fan world, what Sydney had described earlier, and that some would view my outsider presence as discussion worthy, I would have felt more intimidated waltzing into their midst as though it were nothing. But it was all so new to

me. The people I was getting to know were adding a positive and missing piece to my life, and I
was game for anything to keep it going. Especially
if it might bring me a step closer to attaining a firm
friendship with Sydney.

Strolling into the darkened room, I pretended to
be looking for someone. There were people everywhere, some standing and others at tables, but the
majority were part of a dense group huddled next
to a long rectangular table. I waded deeper into the
scene to find out why.

His back was to me, but his lush, greying black
hair gave him away. I had confirmed the Cliff Wood
hideaway of the evening as Sydney and Paige had
hoped. I moved closer and edged around the table
and into the huddle near enough to see him take a
sip of white wine. He licked his lips and set down
the glass.

A slim blonde stood to his left, looking amused
by whatever was said by those nearby. I couldn't
distinguish the identity of anyone at the table except for Bruce, the manager, who I'd only learned
about at the bar moments ago.

I knew this scene was what Sydney had wanted
to find the last time we'd gone looking for Cliff after
the concert. I anxiously sent a text to her, *He's here.
At a table.* Then I drifted back to the doorway to
wait. In seconds, she and Paige joined me, both still
in surveillance mode scanning the room.

"Who are all these people?" I moved so Sydney could be in the front of our trio.

She didn't waste any time. Knowing exactly what the gathering by the table meant, she immediately led us toward it. She stopped at intervals ostensibly suggesting our migration wasn't calculated. Eventually, she answered me saying, "Fans."

"Really, all of them?"

"Most of them. *Those* two guys," she said with a forward nod, "longtime friends of his, but the rest, fans."

It was all so curious to me. "Did he invite them?"

Paige waved her hand as though brushing off the idea. "They like to act like they were invited."

I could see what she meant. Most of those surrounding the table weren't even part of the conversation among those seated. And Cliff was paying little attention to anyone. He played with a silver bracelet on his left wrist.

Sydney continued inching further until the three of us blended with the cluster by Cliff's table. I could see the girl who had been standing behind him now occupied the seat to his right. She looked to be about twenty-five, out of place among those of the Cliff Wood era. She maintained an expressive interest in all that was being said but wasn't contributing anything herself other than to smile and toss her hair from time to time.

"Okay, I'll be back." Sydney was ready to make her rounds.

Paige fished in her purse for some cash. "We need drinks."

"Get a waitress." Sydney turned back to us, stern. "Don't lose this spot."

As soon as Sydney moved away to mingle, Paige ignored her directive and left for the bar. Until then, I had been fine having Paige and Sydney to call the shots. Now, I felt uncomfortable standing on the sidelines alone.

"Hey sweets, can you take over my seat for a moment?" It was a man's voice close to my ear.

I looked behind me to find Bruce. Up close, I now saw he had a worn face, dark eyes, and a set of wild eyebrows to match his wayward hair. As he awaited my response, he lightly took hold of my shoulder, seeking to maintain my attention as he looked back at his chair, guarding it with his eyes.

"I'm sorry. What?" I knew I sounded bewildered.

"Would you sit there and save my seat for me? I'm getting drinks. Takes too long for the waitress. I'll get you something, too. What do you like?"

I was so caught off guard I couldn't think of a specific drink name and heard myself say, "Something with citrus." I didn't have a clue what I meant by that.

"You got it." He gave me a thumbs up and then pointed toward his chair—his chair right next to Cliff Wood.

I couldn't believe my luck, and not in a good way either. There I was, having another accidental Cliff Wood encounter.

I tried to appear nonchalant, but I could feel my heart begin to pound inside my chest, understanding the term heartthrob firsthand now. I closed my eyes and took in a breath, then crept the two steps putting me right at the table.

It wasn't even logical, how worked up I felt. Being around the celebrity of Cliff was exciting, but it wasn't the same for me as it was for fans like Sydney and Paige. Maybe it was because all eyes would be on me for a second time because of him. And now that I knew about the territorial fan aspect Sydney had described, there was a bigger issue at hand—my desire to be accepted.

Floating into the chair, I saw Evvi standing on the opposite side. She was pinned in between two similar-looking girls with their professional eyelashes and spiced-up hair. She looked bored with one arm folded and a margarita in the other hand.

When she saw me, her expression turned to one of sheer disdain. I watched her whisper to her friends who then eyed me as if I'd committed an unforgivable crime. Sydney had been right. Their reaction was immature as though we were in the high school lunchroom, and I'd sat next to the quarterback, uninvited.

I started to text Sydney about what was going on when Cliff turned to me. "How are things going tonight?" His voice was deep and cozy.

I shuddered inside. I hadn't expected he'd talk to me. It would have been so much better if I could have sat quietly and been done with the task before Sydney returned.

I looked behind me hoping to see Bruce coming back, but not enough time had passed.

Say something, Claudine. "I enjoyed your concert tonight." Hardly a profound statement. How many times had he heard that? He was probably used to such compliments and maybe even tired of them.

I tried to look right at him, but it was unnerving being so close. His knee was touching mine. I could feel the warmth through his jeans. He smelled something of a somber day, a lost kiss, ineffable but magnetic all the same. His only response was a simple but kind smile. Then he reached for his wine and finished the small amount in the glass before looking at his watch.

That was when I noticed Sydney had arrived, balancing a cosmopolitan in the tight space where she landed on the opposite side of the table near Evvi and company. Did the look on her face say she was thrilled or devastated by my new location? I couldn't read her. When she gave me a thumbs up, I was relieved. She furtively pressed her hand toward me, her palm out as if to say *stay there, and play it cool.*

Her tacit guidance made me even more nervous. I was afraid I'd foul something up. I already knew my response to Cliff moments before had been the wrong thing to say. It was just the kind of idiotic comment Sydney would likely advise against, sounding too much like a fan. Cliff had given me a conversation opener, and I had closed it down with a banal answer that led nowhere. I hoped there'd be no reason for me to tell her about it later.

Someone nudged my shoulder. Bruce was back. "Hi again, and thanks. Appreciate it." He had not brought me *something with citrus* after all. I looked at his hands bearing a glass of white wine and two beers which he held outward and away from his body attempting not to spill them. I would have laughed except I felt way too nervous, trying to fathom which of these drinks was supposed to be for me.

He handed me one of the beers and our fingers touched for the briefest moment. "Sorry, I couldn't remember what you wanted. Hope this is okay." We skimmed past each other for the switchover.

I tried to step back, but so many people had crowded behind me that my location didn't change much. I looked to Sydney, and she signaled me to check my phone by pointing at hers.

Stay and listen, she'd written in a text message.

I tried. There wasn't much to hear, only some chatter by the two men, something about a football game.

Then Cliff took a large swallow of the wine Bruce had provided. "Let's get rolling."

"Now? Really? Jesus, I just got us these drinks." Bruce sounded aggravated. "Remember you owe me for these."

I wondered if they really kept tabs on who paid for what.

It surprised me no security personnel were on hand to escort Cliff out of the place. He acknowledged a few fans with eye contact and simple nods as he stood up, and then Bruce, taking a final sip of the beer he had to forsake, carved a path toward the exit, a familiar process to him judging by the way he easily began to pilot the mob.

If the volume of fans there knew Cliff well enough to have determined his whereabouts after a concert, then they also knew to give him room to get by without trying to engage or delay him. Still, a few reached out to pat his shoulder or his back as he moved but in general gave him the space and courtesy to depart.

Courtesy aside, no one was giving up on the potential for further interaction with him. Neither were we, apparently. Out of nowhere, Sydney and Paige were next to me, and we all joined hands. Sydney led the way, clinging to Paige's hand and

Paige's to mine. We proceeded in single file as we followed Cliff and Bruce along with everyone else, one big entourage.

This seemed so crazy to me with Cliff trying to leave, everyone tailing him as though we couldn't find our way out of the room on our own. Sydney would explain later it was all part of the process, how if Cliff Wood happened to be in sight and you could also go where he was headed, that's what you did. This wasn't the first time she and Paige had participated in such. Sydney would say Cliff was used to the unorthodox attention, possibly even secretly liked it.

"Keep up! We have to stay with him." Sydney gave the orders. Her pint-sized physique was lost in the herd of people, but her voice was loud and clear.

I didn't know what she was worried about. Everyone involved was more than keeping up with him, but I knew to defer to Sydney's direction. Maybe Cliff was known to bolt when he reached a certain point? He hadn't done that when he'd exited the Beacon Theatre. I didn't have enough experience yet with any of it to evaluate the situation. I complied with whatever Sydney said we should do.

We took a left down a short hallway to exit through a backdoor we wouldn't have known existed. Outside, a black SUV waited with its taillights aglow like flames in the darkness. In the distance a siren screeched, a customary sound against the city's backdrop. A pile of the day's garbage lay stacked against a wall. I had forgotten how cold it was.

Everyone stood alongside the SUV causing the driver to get out and motion us away. We moved enough to appear as if we were complying with his direction.

I dug my hands into my pockets as wind gusted my hair. The last time we'd been outside by his waiting car, Cliff had only waved, hardly worth the effort of our time and discomfort. Perhaps now he was in a different mood and would offer a few words. Or maybe he *didn't* secretly like that we'd followed him.

I considered Bruce would remember I'd been the one to hold his seat, and I could go over and joke with him about getting my drink wrong. Then Sydney would have an avenue to talk to Cliff. Having thoughts around such mechanics, I wondered if this was how Sydney's mind operated. It was kind of overwhelming. It was also kind of nice, having something else circulating in my head other than uncertainty and sadness.

A short, dark-haired man with a stack of records under one arm approached Cliff who had already taken a seat in the SUV. The man displayed the array of albums and said something in a voice too low to hear. Cliff swiveled in his seat and anchored one scuffed boot on the ledge of the doorway. Out of nowhere, Bruce appeared producing a felt marker, and the man steadied the records as Cliff scribbled across a couple of the covers. The man thanked Cliff multiple times and moved away as Cliff said, "Appreciate the support, man."

I was impressed by his gracious attitude.

Somewhere in there, Sydney had moved away from Paige and me. I hadn't noticed. But I should have known she'd seize the moment with Cliff in such close range. As he started to shut the door, Sydney lunged from the SUV's rear blocking the door's closure. I would have expected Cliff to be startled by her surprise appearance, but it didn't faze him. He let go of the door's handle and lightly caressed her shoulder as she grasped his forearm. After she backed away I could see his look of re-served appreciation at her boldness.

She joined Paige and me full of breathless joy. "Did you see me? I was able to give him a little hug!"

The rest of the group dispersed, and some headed back through the exit door. Sydney watched the SUV drive away as though a long-lost friend were departing. No matter her skewed perception of what had hap-pened in those seconds with Cliff, I was in full support of her moment with him. She looked so happy.

Paige exhaled her cigarette. "Another successful quest in the life of Sydney Watts. Except it wasn't really a hug." She teased her friend whose eyes re-mained starry.

"Hey, watch it." Sydney's reply was lighthearted. "It *was* a real one. It counts as one. So, what do you think, Claudine? Do you want to do this again sometime, swim around in the Cliff Wood underworld? Are you up for it?"

That made me laugh because an *underworld* was exactly what it felt like. Here we were in the dark having just seen this rock star off while so many others had left the show with no concern about his whereabouts.

As I opened my lips to speak, Sydney added, "I think you're a good luck charm, Claudine. You should come to all of Cliff Wood's concerts with me."

I didn't want to sound overly excited, but I felt like I'd hit the jackpot. Was her remark a joke or was I now more than a stand-in for her usual concert buddy? To me, it meant we were friends. I would never stand her up like the other girl had.

We moved down the alley behind the restaurant, heading toward the opening at the street. After Paige climbed into a taxi, Sydney and I continued along the sidewalk in the brisk air. I felt in my jacket pocket for a tube of lip balm and smeared it on my lips.

I had never been called a good luck charm.

Chapter 6

THE NEXT MORNING, I TOOK A THREE-MIN-ute shower, tamed my hair into a ponytail, and headed to Aunt Trudy's. I'd almost forgotten we had made plans to go thrift-store shopping together. I had also agreed to help Marlon re-organize the back section of the bookstore. I hated my Saturday was mostly spoken for. Sunday would have to be my day for hibernating under a comfy blanket, reading.

I'd had trouble falling asleep after the adventurous night with Sydney and Paige. My brain had stayed wide awake, thinking how we'd infiltrated Cliff's post-concert location and been part of the abstruse fan world. It was hard to believe I'd met Sydney only a week ago. I was elated for her getting to have a moment with Cliff outside the restaurant. It might have killed her if she didn't achieve some encounter of her own after I'd so easily ended up sitting next to him albeit only for a few minutes.

As we walked around after Paige left, she'd talked about hugging him as though he'd swept her into his arms. I understood it made her feel good to think about it that way, and I validated it by saying he had a pleasant look on his face when it happened.

It was a quick trip to Aunt Trudy's apartment on the Upper West Side from my location in the Village by taking a twenty minute ride on the subway straight up to 79th and Broadway. I was happy to do so. She was the one person around whom I felt I could be myself. She always made me feel good.

Wearing a heavy, hooded jacket over the concert tee I'd bought the night before, I jogged the short distance to the Christopher Street subway station near my apartment as my breath billowed into small clouds before me. I was tired of it being cold.

While I waited for the train, Sydney sent me a text asking for details on how I'd ended up sitting with Cliff, plus she wanted to know if anything interesting had been said at the table. I was surprised she hadn't asked about all of that right after Paige left. I had already started learning how the post-mortem banter on the outcome of the Cliff Wood hunt was equally as important as the hunt itself.

When I reached my train stop, I headed through the turnstile and stepped aside to stay out of the chilly air, tapping out a text explaining my role as

Bruce's seat-filler. I deliberately didn't mention Cliff had spoken to me.

At the time, I thought withholding that part was because doing so meant I'd have to share my uninspired comment to him about enjoying his concert, possibly having her criticize me over it. Looking back, it seemed more that I wanted to keep it for myself as a private memento.

Aunt Trudy lived in a pre-war apartment building on the Upper West Side at 78th and Amsterdam. She had been living in the same one-bedroom residence since the late 1960s, though it didn't seem like it as she had consistently changed its décor through the years.

She loved to stay on trend and spent much time and investment in keeping it up to date. The current theme gave the aura of bohemian chic with funky accents and mismatched furniture pieces. A set of beads hung from the ceiling setting off her kitchen from the main living area.

I liked that section of Manhattan and would have enjoyed living there, too, but the Village really was the place for me, keeping me close to the bookstore and within a walk to my mother's apartment where I grew up.

Our trip had us spending two hours in one thrift store alone, a large warehouse of a place with rows and rows of every kind of clothing organized according to color, plus a large section of odds and ends.

We visited for a few minutes before heading there as we sat on her oblong couch while a 70s sitcom played in the background. I knew she was expecting I'd share some tidbits about where I had been off to the night before wearing her earrings. I downplayed the outing, saying it was some girls from work and that we'd listened to a local band one of them liked. It was almost a true statement, I thought as I told her, save the part about the girls being from my office.

Normally, I wouldn't hold back from my aunt, but I didn't feel ready to talk about Sydney and the experience of Cliff's performance, the touching song about his sister, plus the antics after the show both then and the previous time. I was still understanding for myself this Cliff Wood world I'd gotten into.

I also knew it would invite a mountain of questions on whether this new interest could potentially lead to a boyfriend for me. Aunt Trudy was big on boyfriends and typically had one, even if it was only a companion she met for dinner now and then. The latest beau was into foreign films. Each time they saw a new flick, Aunt Trudy sent me her review.

Roaming the thrift store aisles, we searched the array of cast-offs for unexpected treasures as we caught up on other things. Usually, I had some gossip I could share about working at the magazine, nothing harmful, just entertaining.

Aunt Trudy saw my job to be an avenue for a splashy event she could attend and be my plus-one. She often talked about it in a fantasy way, describing the dress she would wear.

"This is interesting." Across a clothing rack, Aunt Trudy held up a long-sleeved orange shirt with the words *No Limits* across it in stark white lettering. Well-worn and slightly faded, it reminded me of Amelia's style. I could see her wearing the top, sleeves pushed up with the backpack she often carried suspended from her shoulder. It reminded me of Sydney, too. I wondered if the similar vibe between the two of them was part of what attracted me to her.

I kept remembering how she'd said I was like a good luck charm. Even though I knew she hadn't meant it as a profound declaration of our friendship, it meant something to me—that my company was worth having. I hadn't been sure about that for a while. I'd kept to myself in recent years, uncertain of things, uninterested in relationships, believing I didn't have much to offer given I felt so troubled.

She said she wanted me to come to all her future Cliff Wood events. Had she meant it? I wondered when the next one would be. I had been filling my shopping cart with tank tops and other essentials for my much-anticipated arrival of warm weather.

I should have been looking for concert attire.

Aunt Trudy came away with giraffe-shaped bookends and a gold Buddha lamp, perfect accents for her eclectic apartment. Her plump girth made finding clothing more of a challenge, but she landed an orange blouse and a flowy leopard print dress, both of which suited her bold personality.

We'd determined our haul was too cumbersome for the subway and returned to her apartment via taxi. She wanted me to stay for a late lunch.

"I can make you the best tomato sandwich, and I've got a new brand of chips to try." She held up the bag for me to view in further persuasion.

Her exuberance was enticing but not enough to ignore I was still full following the donut binge we'd had from my detour into a bakery before arriving. More than that, the day was going by so fast. I needed to get over to Marlon's.

Aunt Trudy followed me to the door and handed me a bag of things she'd apparently snuck in with her purchases. "You can have some fun looking through this later." She was always doing things like that for me. She gave me a robust hug. Her flower-scented perfume swirled between us as I turned to head out for my trek back to my apartment.

At home, I tossed my thrift store loot on my bed and grabbed a cab to save time. Marlon usually didn't give much direction on what he wanted me to help him with. I'd just look around and figure out what part of the store needed attention.

Today he had a project for me. He waved his hand at the paperbacks in haphazard stacks around us. "It needs a new look, some kind of system. Customers can't see what we have back here."

I wouldn't get it done in one evening but had an idea for what to do. I liked that Marlon gave me such latitude. I treated the place as if it were my own, he knew. As much as I enjoyed being there, it also reminded me I wasn't writing and that I had no mechanism in place to address that need. Moreover, it said that I had put a hold on finding one. My work at the magazine gave me the illusion I hadn't *completely* abandoned my writing ambitions. Still, on a deeper level, I felt discouraged with my lack of determination in finding a way to something I knew was important to me.

All of this skipped around in my mind while I evaluated how to best rearrange the cramped far end of the store's narrow layout. I sat down on the floor with a pile of paperbacks, and one of Cliff's stared up at me. The cover featured a man looking lost next to a horse as a hawk soared in the distance. In some way, I felt the illustration could be me.

Chapter 7

WE DIDN'T GO TO ANOTHER CONCERT FOR two weeks which felt like a long time given the initial momentum of things.

Sydney and I met at a hidden Chinese restaurant in the heart of Times Square after work one evening to go over Cliff's concert schedule. I wouldn't have found the place had she not met me outside. It was one of those secret New York gems. All that time I'd spent roaming around in the area, and I'd never noticed it. I'd end up coming back to it often on my own.

After we were seated and put in our order, she revealed a document-sized envelope housing printouts of venue information, seating charts, and copies of emails she'd exchanged through the years with other fans about prior show experiences at the upcoming locations. It was like she'd prepared to give an oral term paper on concert attendance although when she started reviewing the information with me, it was more like she was confirming the details of a crucial world summit.

There were so many pieces to think through, all essential, to be ready for what to her were not just concerts but a mission as well. Mission: hang out with Cliff Wood.

Over vegetable lo mein and moo shu shrimp, we talked about which of Cliff's concerts I should see with her. She said she wasn't sure how *deep into it all* I wanted to be.

I had assumed I'd go to all of them not knowing some required a flight or a few hours' drive. I had heard about dedicated fans like that who followed artists from city to city, but I'd always thought they must be people much younger than us. I had never envisioned them to be full-grown women who were out in the world with jobs and the weight of other time-consuming adult responsibilities.

"It's the people who have jobs and are financially self-sufficient who can afford to do it," Sydney offered when I'd said as much. "We've worked for this. We owe ourselves this kind of indulgence. Plus, it's Cliff Wood! Who doesn't want to see such a good-looking man like him sing as often as they can? He could stand there at the microphone and smile seductively and no one would complain, right?" She winked at me and then twirled another forkful of lo mein, ferrying it to her mouth. It was as if she were trying to sell me on it, but she didn't need to. I was fully on board for any adventure with her, Cliff Wood or otherwise.

That same week, Nina gave me the assignment of writing an article for an upcoming issue. It was the first time she'd invited me to do something like that, to write a featured piece for the magazine, and it felt good. I was finally making some headway.

She wanted something written about pink being the year's color for summer, tying it into a contrast of both classic and current celebrity fashion. She said she'd leave it up to me to find the best way to connect the subject to our readership. I didn't know how to go about doing that, but I knew one place to start was by studying a stack of past issues. Even if an article about pastel clothing wasn't exactly going to ignite my creativity, I wanted to give it my full effort. A good word from Nina could go a long way in my writing career if I could ever get it going. Maybe this was the start.

Sydney and I landed in Las Vegas just after eight on a Friday night and took a shuttle to the resort casino attached to the venue where Cliff was scheduled to play the following evening. I'd never visited the glitzy city but wouldn't have any time to explore it now either. We'd be on Cliff Wood patrol from pretty much the moment we arrived. Sydney had already set that expectation. I didn't mind.

Sydney had made me promise to be at LaGuardia airport an extra hour early to be sure everything went smoothly time-wise and so I wouldn't get caught in traffic on the way or experience some other glitch that could cause me to miss our flight.

She had so much invested emotionally in her Cliff Wood experiences that once she was in motion to see him, it would have felt like a catastrophic letdown were her plans to be derailed. Since it wasn't the same for me and I was still learning the ropes, I think she saw me as a calming force as well as a place to re-direct her energy, showing me the ins and outs of it all.

Things started happening as soon as we arrived. We'd checked in at the Delano and were rolling our bags toward the elevator with our complimentary bottles of water in hand when Sydney let go of her suitcase handle to cover her mouth.

"Look! There's Brian!" Her voice was sotto voce but clear.

I was several feet behind her, meandering along as I marveled at the hotel's swank ambiance full of glass figurines, oversized chandeliers, and the like.

"Who's Brian?" I landed beside her and took the cap off my water. The flight had left me dehydrated. I took a few gulps.

She turned to me, her eyes wide as though I had forgotten something vital. "The lead guitarist. I told you the band's names on the plane."

I was amused by her censure. "Oh, that's right. Brian." I took another sip, remembering her mentioning him in her vocal dossier that started right after we'd become airborne, but it wasn't as though it were that memorable of a name, not like Suede, the drummer. That one I did remember.

Plus, there was also the fact that while she talked about the band's names, she had also mixed in roundabout stories about previous events, each one meant to illustrate the many ways the band could play a part in a successful Cliff Wood interaction. It was all a bit overwhelming—so many intricate moving parts to it all—who was there fanwise, what their presence meant, and what kind of mood Cliff seemed to be in. I knew she'd be guiding me through the mechanics of everything, so I hadn't paid much attention.

As we flew, I wondered what our nearby seatmates must have been thinking of our conversation. I had laughed inside knowing it probably sounded as if we were planning a kidnapping or assassination. It certainly had a similar level of gravitas the way Sydney described it all.

"Here," she said suddenly. She reached across and took my water from me and tilted her suitcase handle so I'd take hold of it with mine. "You go to the room and drop our bags off. I'll mosey around and see who else is here."

I was a little put off. It felt like she was treating me as her personal assistant. I wanted to remind her I was the good luck charm as she'd said. When I made it to our room though, I was glad for a moment alone.

I'd fallen into a bit of a funk earlier in the day and had been trying to ignore it, deciding maybe it was related to my lack of enthusiasm for the subject of my magazine assignment. The time I'd spent sifting through old issues hadn't yielded any ideas. But as I put our suitcases to one side and removed my coat and boots, I realized the feeling was about Amelia. Here I was about to have another experience I'd want to tell her about, this time getting on a plane to travel for the express purpose of a Cliff Wood concert. This was big for me, adventurous. I could imagine the enthusiasm with which Amelia would respond. I felt my eyes dampen.

The room smelled like expensive soap and was dressed in shades of beiges and creams with an abstract architectural photo hanging above each bed. Heavy curtains held aside by thick ropes framed the glowing, classic view of Las Vegas at night. Every hotel and business lining the street below had some manner of neon sign promising the best of whatever they were offering.

I sank into the nearest mattress and wrapped myself around a pillow. It would make sense my dormant grief for Amelia would surface on a weekend like this. Usually, I was good at pushing it away, but it always idled beneath the surface.

My phone rang. I released the pillow and sat up.

"Did you get my text? He's here!" Sydney half-yelled. "Get down here. Come to the main bar, the one surrounded by all the slot machines past the fountain near where we were. Hurry!"

Her fervor had a way of being the best thing for me and also abated any lingering resentment from how I'd felt back in the lobby. I slid off the bed and back into my boots, abandoning my coat for a long, black cardigan. After tucking my ID and cash into my back pocket, I scrambled out the door, riding the elevator with an elderly lady holding a miniature poodle with a tiny pink bow in its hair.

Soon, I was in the bar Sydney had commanded me to while the glowing money machines dinged and flashed around us. The aroma of cigarette smoke dominated the air. Sydney had a huge smile as she greeted me with a glass of Champagne. I didn't see Cliff Wood anywhere.

She sipped the bubbly drink. "I got some intel. Come on."

Hand in hand, we slithered along the rim of the room to a new location. Trying not to spill my

Champagne as we moved, I stayed close as she shared the details.

"I overheard Evvi. It's Suede's birthday and they're having a party in a private room. Some fans are in there, too. We'll just walk in as though we were meant to be there."

"Evvi's here? What about Paige?"

She didn't answer me. Next thing, we were strolling past an official-looking casino person wearing a maroon jacket and black bowtie.

Our entry was a lot easier than I'd thought it would be. Sydney had already checked it out and was worried the room would fill up before we could secure a good spot. But she didn't want to risk me not getting in if something had changed by the time I got there. That made me feel even better as I realized her earlier dismissal of me had been about making the best use of our resources, the two of us. I was glad I hadn't said anything terse to her. As her friend now and official concert buddy, I wanted to help her succeed in her plans.

The scene was like it had been at our last Cliff Wood infiltration. He was stationed at a table with Bruce at his side along with a few others, except this time the band was there. I had to think for a moment why they had been absent the last time and remembered that one had been a solo performance, a pop-up.

Once inside, we inched our way about the room but couldn't see much of what was happening.

CHAPTER 7

Sydney said we needed a gimmick to get ourselves closer to Cliff.

I held my hand to my chin in thought. "We should send a cocktail over to Suede for his birthday." I'd meant it as a joke.

"He doesn't drink. He's the only one who doesn't."

"A piece of birthday cake then." I was still joking, but I saw her mulling it over.

She took a swallow of her Champagne while she thought about it further. "Oh Claudine, yes!" Her eyes brimmed with delight. "You're so good at this! Then he'll want to know who sent it and wave us over. You're brilliant!" She wrapped her tiny body around my waist hugging me in her elation.

Before I could weigh in on the idea or even put my arms out to reciprocate the hug, Sydney had vanished in search of a way to find a birthday-worthy slice of cake. I knew to hold her place. Our *Cliff procedures* were gradually becoming ingrained in me.

As I stood there feeling certain our little stunt would backfire, I glanced at the crowd by Cliff's table unable to imagine us ending up in the middle of it. There were too many people already with a steady flow coming and going. And if they were celebrating Suede's birthday, wouldn't they have a cake of their own? I didn't see one.

Cliff and his guests were eating now, so it seemed as if our idea, *my idea*, might only turn out to be an unwelcome intrusion. It could also come across as stalker-like if we didn't do it right. Sydney was usually big on evaluating things like that, but she was especially giddy right now having had such an easy time locating him. Now there was no stopping her.

She couldn't get birthday cake. Instead, we ended up with something that turned out to be far better. The waiter she'd found to assist us arrived carrying a piece of chocolate pie topped by a decorative swirl of whipped cream complete with a single candle at its center. He seemed pleased with his effort as was Sydney. Admittedly, I was also just as thrilled despite my worry about having been the one who had instigated the charade.

We were about to point out who to deliver it to when the waiter handed the dessert to Sydney along with a book of matches. He motioned us to follow him as he led the way to the table. We weren't sure if he thought we were friends with Cliff and the band or was just happy to help some enthusiastic fans.

We'd never find out, but after exchanging quick looks of amazement, Sydney and I maneuvered our way along with the helpful server and soon found ourselves standing right behind Suede, and more important, directly across from Cliff. It looked as though he'd had a seafood entrée given the leftover scales on his plate. The fact I remember such a detail shows I was truly embracing Sydney's ways of being extra focused on Cliff, but I didn't think about it like that at the time.

"Zeez ladies have a surprise for you." The waiter's accent made our arrival feel more official. He then left us to take things from there.

"Here goes," I heard Sydney say to herself before leaning in to set down the pie.

At the same time, Suede looked over his shoulder to see us—the ladies in question. "Hey! Great timing." His face launched into an appreciative smile. Luckily for us, he didn't appear angry or at all irritated, rather bemused and pleased. Much younger than Cliff, he was a slightly strange-looking guy with his unkempt, fuzzy beard and longish hair with a receding hairline.

I wasn't sure if it was nerves or excitement, but we didn't even say happy birthday, and Sydney had forgotten all about using the matches to light the thing. She stood there for an awkward few seconds before remembering and then thrust the matchbook to me to take over. I was taken aback; she was so confident compared to me, sassy even. But right now she was a jittery, pretty little mess.

Everyone both at the table and nearby watched as I struck the match and carefully guided it past Suede's head, cupping the flame to keep from setting him on fire. I smiled faintly, imagining the headlines if I managed to set alight the hair on one of Cliff's band members. It would give a whole new meaning to one of Cliff's songs called 'Light Up the Party.'

I thought we could start singing happy birthday at this point, having missed the first opportunity, but Suede blew out the candle immediately and then slid the plate toward Cliff.

"Hey, I can see your mouth watering over there. You want some? You're the pie guy."

Cliff had started tapping on his phone and didn't answer but reached for a fork and speared a chunk out of the dessert. After chewing for a moment, he took a sip of wine and pushed the plate back to Suede. "That's good stuff, man; but it's your birthday. You should finish it."

Next, Cliff looked at us with a thumbs up, and I could feel the electricity radiating from Sydney at this minor gesture, exactly the kind of thing she hoped for—an acknowledgement from the rock star himself and with so many onlookers. Such a moment went a long way in the fan world.

More than that, it made Sydney feel good, just like the pseudo hug the night by the car. She collected these moments with Cliff as though they were rare gemstones. She wanted him to see her as a special fan, maybe more, I didn't know. I was happy for her.

That was as far as we got though, but it was enough. Thanks to our ruse, we were able to stay right by Cliff's table for the rest of the evening, talking and drinking until he left. We didn't follow him although I felt Sydney was considering it. She said later it would have been too much given he was likely heading to his room. I was glad to learn she did have some boundaries with him. I had wondered what she considered to be going too far when it came to the tactics we used to find him.

The rest of the trip was smooth and brought much less tension from Sydney since we'd already had an encounter with Cliff. Of course, it didn't stop her from trying for another.

We spent a good part of the next day loitering in the lobby and again later in one of the nicer restaurants hoping he'd happen by, but no luck. We didn't find him at all after the concert either.

"He's probably having a catered dinner in his room. He likes to do that." That was Sydney's presumption when we came across Bruce having a drink on his own after we'd canvased all the likely Cliff locations. Bruce's solo status also gave her some comfort that Cliff truly wasn't to be found. She was always thinking he could be elsewhere, possibly with other fans, and she was missing out.

We closed out the night in the hotel room of one of her fan friends, chatting with a group there for a while, comparing notes on the concert. It was fun to hear more Cliff Wood backstories and their takes on the set list, and all the nuances they felt were important. Sydney liked relaying our experience with the birthday pie adding embellishments to how things had really happened.

Now we were flying back to New York in the comfy black sweat suits we'd gotten in the casino gift shop, the word *Vegas* bedazzled down the left leg. I hated we were leaving so soon. It had felt good to be somewhere else, but I needed to get going on my article and find some enthusiasm for pink clothing. Nina had given me a long lead time, and I needed it.

I took the window seat. Normally as the taller person I preferred the aisle, but I was looking forward to seeing some of the desert scenery as we departed. Sydney had coffee before we left the hotel and another cup as soon as we made it through security. She wanted to be able to get up easily when the need arose.

In Sydney's usual generous way, she offered to spring for an upgrade to the comfort seats. And that they were, too comfortable. I didn't even remember the plane taking off, missing the scenery altogether. I dozed the first leg, only awakening when a flight attendant asked the people in front of us what they wanted to drink.

"Welcome back." Sydney laughed. She had her photo stream open on her phone, scrolling through, entertaining herself. There were ones of us we'd taken before the concert after we got dressed and then dozens of Cliff playing his guitar throughout the performance. It occurred to me she probably had thousands of such pictures from God knew how many shows she'd seen by then.

She widened one of the shots with her fingers and studied it. "I still can't believe we pulled off the thing with Suede's birthday. I wish someone had videoed it."

I felt she would never stop talking about that.

"Cliff even had a bite of it! And he knew we were the ones who brought it!" She looked at me for confirmation on how exciting that part of things had been. "Did you hear Suede call him the *pie guy.*" She snickered. "What was *that?* Do you think that's some inside joke?"

"Maybe so," was all I could muster. I had run out of validating comments.

At times, I felt she enjoyed the subsequent analysis of such an experience more than the actual moment when it happened, seeming to place a lot of meaning on insignificant things. Such as how she thought Cliff might have given us more attention after tasting the pie but didn't, not wanting to take the spotlight away from Suede.

To me it seemed unlikely Cliff would think that hard about such a trivial moment. Also, at the concert Cliff had asked the audience to sing to Suede for his birthday introducing it by saying how Suede had already been doing some celebrating. Sydney thought this might be a reference to us coming over to the table with the pie, something even she said was a bit of a stretch but contended was possible. Wishful thinking appeared to figure significantly in her musings.

If these beliefs made Sydney happy who was I to put out the flames of her enthusiasm? None of it hurt anyone. And in the end, dissecting Cliff's behaviors was fun in an odd sort of way.

The flight attendant handed us our complimentary drinks. We'd both chosen ginger ale to dial things back from our weekend indulgence.

"Have you ever met him?" I opened the miniature package of airline nuts. We didn't have time to get any breakfast. They would have to do until I got home.

Sydney sipped her drink and then set it on the foldout tray in front of her. "Oh, of course! At meet and greets and book signings, those kinds of events. Fan stuff."

"So how do you get into a meet and greet?"

"For some shows, you can buy a ticket that comes with it as part of the price." She finished chewing her own mouthful of the meager snack. "Or if you know someone, they can put you on the after-show guest list. I don't have a connection like that. Occasionally I've talked my way back there. Not so easy to do."

She took another sip of her drink and picked up her phone opening her photo folder once more. She slid the pictures up until she'd found some of her with Cliff. Most of them were posed shots while a few were candid of her standing near him. As she scrolled past them, I could see the passage of time, his hair darker, only beginning to grey in a few of them.

"Wow. You've met him a lot." I leaned toward her so I could see better.

She vacillated between several of the posed ones. At six foot one, Cliff was taller than most, and next to Sydney he looked like a giant. He wore a serious expression in some of the photos, and in others a casual smile. Sydney, however, was beaming in every one.

"This one's my favorite." She held her phone before me. In the shot, she wore a red knit dress and a biker jacket as she gazed up at him, her face lit with laughter. His eyes were focused elsewhere, like he was reacting to something off to the side. She seemed not to notice it, or she wasn't dwelling on it anyway.

I took the phone out of her hand to view the shot more closely. "It's a great picture. He looks like he was having a good time. What were you talking about with him beforehand?"

As soon as I asked the question, I felt the mood change. Sydney took the phone back abruptly.

"I don't remember." She repositioned herself in her seat. "But it was fun."

It seemed I'd upset her in some way. Her words had come out cold, aloof. I should have rehashed the whole birthday thing more instead of asking about the photos. I tried to redirect the conversation by thanking her for bringing me along. Eventually, we both went back to dozing.

Back in my apartment later, I unpacked and then called my mother and Aunt Trudy to give them each a quick update about the weekend. By then I'd told them about meeting Sydney and what I'd been up to with her, part of it anyway.

As I carried a cup of hot chocolate to my couch, Sydney sent me a text saying she hoped I had gotten home safely, and I told her the same. Thankfully, things seemed to have returned to normal between us. I had tried not to think about the strange discord.

I took a sip from the mug and picked up my laptop, ready to do some research on the world of pink fashion when my phone dinged again, another text from Sydney.

She had sent a picture of me on stage with Cliff that first night at the Beacon Theatre, one of his arms was wrapped around me, his smile authentic and warm.

Sydney had written, *You were so cute with him. Lucky girl.*

Chapter 8

THE BEST PART OF MY JOB AT THE MAGAZINE, other than access to the wardrobe sample closet which didn't interest me much, and thus wasn't truly one of the best parts for me, was being able to fudge on the time I spent outside of the office when doing Nina's business errands.

The self-given perk came in handy on days when I couldn't get my mind to cooperate for the full eight hours. Fortunately, Nina was too busy herself to watch the clock and generally only cared I made sure the things she needed were handled. Her lowkey managerial style was a great gift to me during that time. So often I was ruminating over the dissatisfaction I felt about my life, and a lengthy walk through Bryant Park or along 57th Street was the best accompaniment to those reflections. Except when it was cold, in which case a subway ride out to Pier 53 could hit the spot or tucking myself away in a coffee shop with a latte in my grip.

March was nearing closure, its famous winds finally starting to take their bows with the promise on the horizon of me getting to wear my recent thrift store finds and other warm weather apparel. I couldn't wait to dive into my two-dollar tanks tops. Until then, another Monday was here, requiring the warmth of my favorite cable-knit sweater. I tried to liven it up with a strand of beads connected to a turquoise tassel. I know, so dull Claudine.

Arriving at work, it was the usual series of emails from Nina detailing her requests for the day. I was relieved not to find one asking if I had a first draft for her to review yet. I had already decided while getting dressed for the day and debating what necklace to wear I was going to maneuver the day's tasks so I could stop by Aunt Trudy's.

Having spent all my spare time of late at the bookstore, I hadn't seen her since our last jaunt, and I knew she was anxious to hear more about my trip to Vegas and the more involved details about all that was happening with this new friend, Sydney.

The whole thing was kind of strange. I felt as though I were living some secret underground life in the world of rock star prowling and wanted to reveal it to someone. Plus, I knew she'd enjoy a granular depiction of it all.

The first of Nina's emails contained instructions for me to return a set of eye shadow palettes we'd photographed for review in our cosmetics section.

The brand was new on the market and the palettes so exclusive the company had insisted we return them afterward but said they'd provide some samples for our staff.

I was planning to farm out the simple errand to an intern when I realized the boutique was near Aunt Trudy's. That worked out.

I called and told her I'd be near her place around lunchtime, and we picked a place to meet. Within a few hours, I was heading out of the magazine's office on 6th Avenue inside the Grace Building, carrying a shiny black bag packed with a full array of the latest eye-popping makeup.

Just a one-block walk to catch the one train at 42nd Street, and I was soon traveling to my stop at 79th. I loved the ease of the city's public transportation.

"Hi, can I help you?" A twenty-something cashier wearing a polka dot blouse underneath a plaid jumper greeted me inside the contemporary store.

"I'm Claudine Davis. I'm returning some palettes."

The girl traded bags with me, hers holding a collection of not just eye shadow samples but also the tiniest bottles of nail polish and a handful of mascara tubes as well. Toting the bag by my side, I left to meet Aunt Trudy at a restaurant a few blocks away on Amsterdam. She'd picked the place both for its location and its assortment of pastries. We both had a sweet tooth.

Each table in the minimalist space was adorned with a clear vase housing a mini carnation. Paper menus doubled as placemats. Aunt Trudy stood out, dressed in her usual creative genius donning a heavy purple sweater with an abstract brooch pinned to it. Her snow-white curls peeked from under a crocheted tam festooned with a mustard sunflower. If we hadn't been in New York City, she would have seemed eccentric or a little too creative.

She was already working her way through a plate of chickpea fries when I arrived.

"There you are," she proclaimed, spotting me with a giant smile. She pushed the fries toward me as I settled across from her. "Where have you been today? Doing something interesting?"

I half-rolled my eyes as I removed my scarf and gloves. "An errand involving eye shadow, if you can believe that. Very vivid eye shadow. Very exclusive. By that I mean stupid expensive."

Aunt Trudy didn't say anything. I knew she was thinking exactly what I was—how ridiculous it was for me to be doing this kind of thing, that I should be in a job involving writing. But she never went down that path. She was a good aunt. Always supportive. It would be great when I could tell her about the *pink* article, but I wanted to wait until I'd completed it.

I rummaged through the bag of samples and gave her a few. The boutique had more than made up for having us return their kits used for the shoot. If anyone could pull off wearing them, it was she.

"Oh nice. Look at that! Thank you. I've got a date tonight. I'll try them." She held a shimmery shade of rust next to her highly mascaraed eyes. "Paul. He's a retired plumber. That could come in handy, you know." Her eyes twinkled as she laughed and dropped the samples into her purse.

"Paul the plumber. Handy in more ways than one." I joined in with her laughter.

We studied the menus and put our order in, deciding to share a roasted potato pizza.

I had just taken a bite of a chickpea fry when Aunt Trudy rubbed her hands together conspiratorially. "Okay, don't make me wait. Tell me more about what's happening with you and your new friend. Shelby, is it?"

"Sydney."

"That's right. How was Las Vegas? Did you meet him? Mr. Wood?"

I shrugged. "Sort of. I mean, just brief things. Not really *meeting,* more like eyeing him. Poor guy. Fans are always looking for him, waiting on him. We certainly did. I wonder how he feels about it."

"It probably comes with the territory," Aunt Trudy ventured.

A waiter brought us each a miniscule glass of water. I took two swallows, and mine was gone. Aunt

Trudy offered hers to me as she tried to get the waiter's attention for more.

A small movie played in my head of my experiences so far at the hands of Sydney, being on stage with Cliff, the night at the table next to him before we'd been to Vegas, and the heartbreaking sight of him singing about his deceased sister. I wondered if Aunt Trudy remembered Cliff Wood being Amelia's teen idol. I decided probably not. Amelia hadn't shared the same closeness with Aunt Trudy. I didn't bring it up.

I told her about the stunt we'd pulled using Suede's birthday to get us to the band's table and more about Sydney and her involvement with the Cliff Wood scene. As I picked up my phone to show her the picture of me on stage with him, I noticed Sydney had sent me several text messages.

Two new ones! was the first.

I didn't know what she meant, but my mind should have automatically registered she was referring to Cliff's concert schedule.

Next, she'd written, *One is in Jamestown. That's where he lives! We HAVE to go. Other one's with Ramsey. Tix for that one go sale in an hour. Can you help?*

The pizza arrived, but the edge had been taken off my appetite. I suddenly felt under pressure. I wanted to enjoy my time with Aunt Trudy, but this news from Sydney was important for our concert-going exploits, and more than that, for my growing friendship with her. Plus, I didn't want to miss out on the unique concerts either. A shift was happening in me. Now I was beginning to see why Cliff's fans obsessed the way they did.

Though I'd only seen him perform a few times, I already knew the ones where he was on stage alone were my favorites, the intimacy of them and the way he revealed himself. At those solo performances, we were treated to songs outside of what he played with his band. The shows Sydney had just mentioned sounded like they'd be coming from a similar place.

As Aunt Trudy lifted a slice of pizza onto her plate, I replied to the messages.

I'm uptown away from my office. Don't know if I'll make it back in time.

I took a slice for myself and had a bite as I glanced at my phone again, trying not to look anxious. I knew Sydney was probably disappointed right now. In truth, so was I.

My eyes met Aunt Trudy's. "Sorry, it's something at work."

I don't know why I didn't just tell her what was going on. I guess I didn't want her to know exactly how involved I was becoming with Sydney and the Cliff Wood fan subculture.

Besides which, it was rude to allow myself to become so diverted when I barely saw my aunt. She deserved my full attention, not for me to behave like some teenager always checking her phone every two minutes. It was hardly considerate behavior, and I was ashamed of myself.

Still, I felt the urge to do it—my mind wouldn't let go of what Sydney had just told me.

Another text arrived from her. *Where are you? Come to my place. I'm between Riverside and West End.*

I knew she lived uptown but didn't know where until then. She wasn't that far away from the restaurant. Now I felt even worse than I had a few minutes ago as I started planning my escape. But it was what it was. I couldn't help it and wanted to go to Sydney. If I stayed long enough for one more slice of pizza and hopped over to the 72nd Street station, I could grab the one train again and be only a few blocks from her place.

I dabbed the napkin to my lips. "Aunt Trudy, I have to go soon. There's an impromptu meeting." That was technically true.

I wondered if she could tell I was lying. I hoped not as I didn't want to hurt her feelings with my made-up excuse to depart. She knew Nina gave me a lot of freedom but wouldn't want me to jeopardize it.

"You do what you need to do, Claudey, don't worry about me, but you're going to miss dessert."

I feigned a laugh but still felt bad about what I was doing.

Soon, I kissed my aunt goodbye with a heartfelt apology. She fingered the brooch on her sweater as she looked into my eyes. I felt she could read my soul right then, but it was probably the guilt gnawing.

———

Sydney opened the door wearing a floppy New York sweatshirt and denim leggings along with a pair of thick tube socks scrunched down by her ankles.

I hadn't seen her since our return flight from Las Vegas where I felt our closeness had blossomed. I'd been encouraged by the various dialogues we'd had since then as we'd watched for a sign of a pop-up concert.

I wanted to give her a hello hug, but she rushed me inside.

Her apartment was nothing like I'd imagined. It had a light and airy feel with lots of white and candles of all sizes in decorative holders. Only one of them was lit and filled the air with the scent of roses. Tall glass panes framed a view of the city's skyline on one side of the room. On the other, built-in bookshelves canvased the wall displaying a collection of zebra figurines, pieces of natural cut amethyst, and thick books about exotic countries.

With her hip vibe, I had expected her décor to be something more on the trendy side. I had also imagined there would be multiple pictures of Cliff Wood around. But not one.

A fluffy black cat rested on the couch in a ball. I walked over and stroked his head. "Who's this?"

"That's my boy, Lyric. You can pet him later." She motioned me over to her dining room table where a laptop awaited. "Oh my God, I'm so nervous."

I took a seat in front of the laptop, and she leaned over me to open a browser.

"Why nervous?" It seemed she'd have done this so many times that a ticket sale had to be routine for her.

"Look at it." She pointed to a seat map of the venue on the screen. "It's a tiny place. Everyone's going to be trying for tickets."

I studied the page. The venue was called The Bitter End. It wasn't far from my apartment, but it had been years since I'd attended anything there, didn't have much cause or interest to go. Until Sydney, I'd been a hermit after I'd come back to New York, mainly spending time with my mother and aunt or at Marlon's.

As I thought about that, I felt a rush of gratitude toward her for inviting me into her world. I wanted to do all I could to help with the impending ticket purchase.

"So tell me what to do." I pulled the laptop close.

"Get anything, any location, two seats. Even apart if necessary. It's not a time to be selective."

She loaded her credit card into the venue's ticket homepage. "I'll be right in there." She got up and moved to a computer in her bedroom nearby.

A green box with the words *On Sale Here* glowed at the top of the screen before me. Sydney's nerves were contagious. Even though I'd just eaten, I felt hollow, worried about coming through for her—for myself, too.

If someone had been listening to our conversation, they would have thought we were trying to buy something our life depended on. That was how it felt. To my psyche anyway. I'd already started relying on these outings with Sydney to keep my spirits elevated and my mind occupied from the negative lines of thinking I was prone to.

From her bedroom, she did a countdown beginning at the fifteen-second mark of the sale. When she got to the number one, she yelled, "Hit the refresh icon now!"

"Oh, dear Jesus," I heard her say immediately. "It already says there aren't any seats. That's impossible! Dammit! Claudine, are you pulling anything?"

Her tone reminded me of the Sydney who appeared during our Cliff-hunting, when stress overrides excitement.

My cursor was spinning, frozen. I hated to tell her I wasn't even in the sale and had no chance to try for a pair of tickets yet. "Nothing."

"Keep trying! Hit refresh."

I had already done that—a few times. Now I was on a completely different page that didn't even have a glowing sales box. More expletives were muttered by Sydney, and then, "This a nightmare. I have to re-login. Are you finding any seats *at all*?"

I almost wanted to say I'd had some and lost them, but I thought that might be worse, suggesting a foul-up on my part. I found the ticket box again. When I clicked on it, nothing happened.

"I'm back in." Her voice sounded more relaxed, but her optimism was short-lived. "Dammit! It says my ticket request exceeds the limit." She ran back into the room. "*Please* tell me you have something." She leaned in and saw my cursor spinning. "How long has it been like that?"

"Maybe a minute. Two."

She abruptly moved the laptop to the side and took over, first by clicking the refresh button and then moving the cursor all over the place as if the exercise would yield something different. Now the page wouldn't reload. She shook her head from side to side. "We're screwed."

She lowered herself into the seat beside me and held her head in frustration as her hair poked between her fingers like little spikes.

I tried to console her. "Maybe we can find some on an aftermarket site."

She sighed. "Unlikely. It's a super-small venue, not a lot of seats to begin with."

"What about the other show? The one where he lives?"

"Jamestown, in Rhode Island. Paige is working on those. It's a bigger place, so it shouldn't be an issue." She let go of her head and refreshed the page once more.

The original sales box on the page had been replaced with the words Sold Out. I thought Sydney might start crying or stab someone—me. She closed the lid of the laptop and pushed it away. "We're so screwed."

I didn't know what else I could do or say to help. I was disappointed, too, but I knew it wasn't the same. Her world revolved around Cliff Wood, and a special performance like this outside of his regular schedule was an epic event not to be missed.

In the kitchen steps away, she picked up Lyric and smoothed his head, holding him as she opened the refrigerator door to extract a beer. "You want something?"

I shook my head no. I still wished I had something helpful to say.

She stooped to let Lyric down and then returned to sit next to me. "It's just that—with Ramsey it will be such a different show. They've never performed together."

"Who's Ramsey?" I had meant to ask about that as soon as I arrived.

Sydney turned to the side in her chair, looking at me like I was crazy. "His daughter. She's in the indie music scene. She has a few songs of her own. They're on her YouTube channel. She's talented."

I hadn't thought about whether Cliff Wood had children. It made sense though. He probably had slept with dozens of women through the years what with so many eager for a night with a rock star. Maybe there were others besides Ramsey. I suddenly wondered if he'd ever been married.

I wanted to hear more about the personal details Sydney knew so well about him. And I knew she would have loved nothing more than to share them, but I couldn't blow off an entire afternoon from work.

I reached for my purse along with the bag of sample makeup I'd haphazardly dropped on the floor in my frenzied arrival. "I have to get back to the office. I have a mile-long to-do list."

Sydney trailed to the door with me. "Don't worry, I'll figure something out." She said this as if I were the one most upset by the ticket outcome.

I did like the idea of seeing Cliff sing with his daughter though and hearing some different songs.

Sydney held the brass handle of the door leading into the outer hallway. "Please stay. We could watch a movie or go shopping or something." Her hazel eyes looked downtrodden yet hopeful.

It made me feel good she wanted to spend time with me doing something unrelated to Cliff. So far those had been the only times we'd gotten together, but I'd have to hope for a future invitation. Right now, I needed to get back and find some ideas for my article.

"I wish I could, but I'm writing my first fashion piece and have zero inspiration. I need a good spark to get it going."

"Well this is the perfect place for stimulation. If we sit outside, you'll see all kinds of people wandering along. Mick Jagger even used to live in this area back in the 80s."

I knew that. Aunt Trudy had seen him a few times and said it always nearly stopped her heart to see someone so famous on the street. She'd once followed him for a few blocks. I hadn't fallen far from the same tree, it seemed.

Sydney's phone dinged. She headed back to the table to get it and then reviewed a text. "Here's some good news at least. We're set for the Jamestown show." *I hope they're decent seats*, she added to herself, and then louder to me, "It's only a few weeks away. I bet he wanted that to be more of a pop-up, but someone probably told him it wouldn't work given the location. Only thing is, he won't be somewhere afterward where we can find him." She frowned. "He'll go back to his house."

"How do you know that?" I hadn't meant to say it aloud. It was more of an inner curiosity.

"Because he's not going out to a bar when he has his house to go back to where he can be comfortable." She cracked open the beer.

I opened the door. "It's okay if we don't find him. We can still have fun. I've never been to Jamestown." And then I did hug her. The beer on her breath filled the air between us when we let go.

"I really appreciate you coming to help, Claudine."

I headed east on 81st taking a right on Broadway. Two more blocks and I was at the 79th Street subway station going downtown to 50th Street, close to the Grace Building.

The mixture of riding and walking gave me time to get my mind switched over from Cliff Wood concert matters to ruminating about what I would need to research for my article. Did Mick Jagger ever do his classic rooster move in pink? If he had, it might help as a starting point at least to satisfy the classic side of what Nina wanted. I was willing to try any morsel to kickstart things.

When I made it back to the office, a birthday party was in full swing in the breakroom for the front desk receptionist. I picked up a cake square covered in edible glitter and ate most of it en route to my desk. At my keyboard, I brainstormed about designers using pink, pink as a statement, celebrities in pink and pink in a dozen other variations. Nothing brilliant surfaced.

CHAPTER 8

I wished I'd stayed at Sydney's. No doubt she would've come up with a string of ideas in less time than it would take me to produce only one.

Chapter 9

A WEEK AND A HALF LATER, WE WERE IN Philadelphia on a Thursday night for more Cliff Wood, a regular full band concert, Sydney's favorite.

Paige had offered to drive, but she was giving Evvi a ride plus another girl we didn't know. Sydney was always skeptical about new people coming into the fold, a fact I found strange considering how much she had introduced to me the night she and I met. With us though, she hadn't expected things to go further than me using her extra ticket for that one show. Otherwise, anyone new in her Cliff Wood world felt like competition and an invasion of her jurisdiction in the fan community. She'd worked hard over time to figure out the nuances about him and his band and didn't want to freely distribute that coveted information. Other fans like Paige were less concerned about keeping it under lock and key.

I was disappointed we weren't going with Paige. Her candid personality made things interesting and fun, and I wanted to get to know her more. I also liked she had a family and the kind of life I used to imagine for myself. I'd given up on that lifestyle a while back and had gotten used to being on my own. Still, being around people like her and hearing about aspects of raising children and thinking about their needs made me feel good, similar to the way a book could take you away from reality and give you the sense and comfort of someone else's world.

Sydney and I met at Penn Station at four in the afternoon and took the train on an hour's ride to the 30th Street station in Philadelphia. Since she wouldn't tell me the price of the concert ticket so I could reimburse her, I arrived early enough to buy both of our seats on the train. I also picked up the tab for the sandwiches we ate when we got there.

I sensed she felt I was doing her a favor by coming along for these outings, thus wanting to ease the financial burden of it for me. But I wanted to be there.

It was special, the way she'd brought me into all of it, offering me not only her friendship, but also her secret Cliff Wood insights. I didn't want her to bear the expense of our fun all the time, though it felt good to be spoiled by someone.

By the time we finished eating and window shopping on South Street, Sydney said we might catch Cliff arriving at the venue if we could find the artists' entrance.

The concert was at the Theater of Living Arts which seemed like it would be more appropriate for his solo show than one with the band. Sydney had seen him play there a few years back when he'd also done a book signing event nearby.

While we headed to the venue, she tried to find a photo in her phone of her with him at the book-store that day as she recounted her memory of it, what Cliff had worn—always of importance—and the comments he'd made before the autograph ses-sion. She loved reminiscing about her Cliff Wood experiences, and I was a willing audience.

I only wished I had something as interesting to reciprocate with though I was sure it didn't mat-ter to her. We were now building our own bank of Cliff-related memories.

"Here it is." Sydney adjusted her knit hat.

We had come to an alleyway behind the theater. A group of fans we didn't know along with Evvi, Paige, and the new girl were already there, talking to the bass player, Matt Birch.

"You just missed him." Paige pointed to the back-stage door. This surprised me given how Sydney was so careful with her timing in Cliff Wood matters.

Evvi and Paige took a selfie with Matt and continued their conversation with him. Sydney whispered to me that Matt had recently done a solo album, and the girls were probably expressing

artificial interest in it in hopes he'd offer some details on Cliff's after-show plans.

We were about twenty feet from them, but
Sydney turned away to be sure only I could hear
her. "Cliff isn't going to tell anyone ahead of time
what he wants to do. He's not even thinking about
it himself."

There she was again with the confidence in his
routine. She didn't appear worried about finding
him later. There would be an inside tip of some
kind, that much I knew.

True to form, after a concert with an atypical
two encores—he probably wanted to impress someone, Sydney proposed—it was Alternative Kyle we
overheard, not so much saying the name of the Cliff
Wood rendezvous location as describing the atmosphere of it to someone else.

All we knew was it featured dollar bills stapled
to the ceiling and nautical memorabilia on the walls.
We asked a hostess in a restaurant two doors down
if she knew of any place with such decor.

"Oh yeah, sounds like you're looking for The
Lowdown. Lots of anchors on the wall there, old
portholes. The tables look like they're made of driftwood. If you take a right out the door you'll run
right into it."

Within minutes, we found the place. Sydney had
missed her calling as a detective. I wondered if any

of the skills she'd acquired in her Cliff Wood endeavors ever helped in her marketing business.

Nothing turned out that remarkable the rest of the night, at least from our perspective. Cliff and company took up two narrow tables end to end in the back corner of the room. The significant others of the band were in tow this time, creating a larger entourage than usual as well as altering the tone of things for fans to be in Cliff's vicinity.

He was the only one without a date, but that wasn't stopping him from enjoying himself. Between sips of white wine, he laughed so hard he bent his head back at times, and I could hear him talking above the others, his voice distinct. He had always appeared so reserved to me in my limited experience seeing him in these after-show settings. It was the most demonstrative I'd seen him behave.

Sydney got drinks at the bar for us while we watched people at the few tables near him carrying on unaware they were in the presence of someone famous. This distressed Sydney since we couldn't get anywhere near him. It was considered uncool to loiter by his table when it was more of a family event. Even Cliff had his limits as far as fans were concerned.

Sydney took a double sip of her drink. "This is going nowhere for us. We might as well head back to the city."

"You don't want to try and catch him when his car picks him up afterward? Get a full hug this time?" I surprised myself with the suggestion, and Sydney too.

"Look at you, getting into it." She high-fived me. "But no, not with all those other people around, the girlfriends. They hate fans like us."

"Really?"

"Not hate, but I'm sure they find us annoying. We'll wait for him another time. It's not meant to be tonight."

"You're the expert." I finished my screwdriver. I was willing to stay for whatever she wanted to do, but I could feel my eyes getting heavy. Going back earlier would make my workday better.

We paid our bill. As we left, we passed Paige and Evvi and the new girl arriving. Sydney let them know it wasn't a good scenario for Cliff fun, and they agreed when she explained why. There was discussion on how Cliff had put on a good concert, and then we went our separate ways.

"It's been a while since the whole band gang has been together, couples and all. I guess they were due for it." Sydney stared into the air, pondering. We had moved into the post-mortem part of things. "Usually I have some inkling ahead of time though."

We jostled along on the train heading back to New York with a handful of other people. It smelled like the night, sleepy and lost.

"From where? Is there some kind of underground fan exchange?"

"Not exactly." Sydney shrugged as if it were difficult to explain. "I hear things. Someone might send me a random text. I know Bruce has some relatives in the area. That may have been what sparked making it into a family affair."

"Cliff didn't have a date like the others. I wonder why." I produced a candy bar from my purse, removed the wrapper, and slanted it toward Sydney.

She broke off a piece of the chocolate and suspended it before her mouth. "That's one thing I don't know much about with him. He evades the subject of dating in interviews." She stopped for a minute to eat the candy, crunching a piece and swallowing it. "My guess is he was hurt by someone. You can hear it in some of his songs."

"What about Ramsey's mother?"

Sydney shook her head as if to say the subject was of no consequence. "They aren't together. That was years ago. She was a model, classic beauty, you know, makes a straw hat look elegant." She posed with a wistful expression to demonstrate. "Ramsey is like, thirty-something now." She shrugged again. It was nice to see her so relaxed. Usually on our Cliff Wood excursions she bordered on panic about whether we'd get the information to find him or fretted when our attempts to do so failed.

She offered me her palm for more candy. "There was this girl, Suzanne or Suzette, something like that. Only girlfriend I've known of. She was young. She got mixed up in some of the fan drama. Everyone wanted to be her friend. I think she didn't know how to handle it. I don't know. Maybe she and Cliff ran out of things to talk about."

"He strikes me as the type who likes to be alone." I wadded up the wrapper and stowed in my purse.

"Yeah, a lot of writers are like that."

It was another two weeks before our next concert. Sydney thought there might be a pop-up show at one point but never got any confirmed information. She had several venue websites she regularly scoured for last-minute announcements but hadn't seen any activity regarding Cliff performing.

Though I loved our spontaneous outings, I needed my evenings to work on my article. I had submitted a rough draft to Nina I knew was in no way something she'd think fit the magazine's format. Taking a stab at it had only bought me some time while I tried to come up with something better.

I had also been immersed in my project at the bookstore, not leaving time for much else after work. Marlon had extended his thoughts beyond re-arranging the rear section. He now wanted to transform the whole shotgun space into more of an open layout, an insurmountable idea. He was always so kind to me. I wanted to at least give it a try.

"It's home show week!" Sydney called me in the middle of the day as I flipped through a back issue of the magazine at my desk. "Are you excited?"

I didn't know what she was talking about at first and then realized she meant *Cliff's* home, the concert in Jamestown. "I will be—I am. I've been busier than usual though. I have to set up a last-minute photo shoot for this week."

"You're not going to stand me up, are you? Claim you're too busy?" She laughed, but I detected a note of worry.

"No way. I'm completely in. I do like him a tiny bit, too, you know." I laughed.

"How's the article going?"

"So-so. I'm looking at an old issue right now for more ideas."

"Well I'll let you go so you can focus. I just wanted to make sure you're on board and ready. We're going to meet at Paige's apartment and ride with her. She has a fancy new SUV and keeps it parked in a garage nearby. If we're on the road by three, we can arrive in time to have dinner beforehand."

She had already given me those details in a text message previously but was so hyped about going, she had probably forgotten.

"Tonight I'll send you the outfits I have in mind," she added.

No doubt they would be her usual creations of casual pizzazz. My style ideas were still being inspired by those that would provide warmth due to an early April cold snap. I was so ready for spring to take over. I could be much cuter when I wasn't chilly.

I studied the magazine featuring a cover model in a pair of jeans and a lace top. "Sounds good."

"Okay, get to work! Jamestown is soon!"

Everything went well the rest of that week, no issues with the photo shoot. I had it planned and confirmed to the letter. Nina hadn't replied to the email I'd sent with my draft, a good sign she thought it was a decent first effort. Otherwise, I thought she would have felt a pressing need to provide some feedback.

With Sydney's help, I had figured out something to wear to the concert that was more interesting than usual for me and would also keep me warm. By Thursday, I'd given myself a night off from the bookstore to luxuriate in bed and read. It felt like a gift from the universe to have that quiet time and a Mary McCarthy novel all to myself.

The only kink in my otherwise rare succession of positive feelings was when I'd met my mother for dinner beforehand. I wondered if she realized it was the date of Amelia's death, ten years ago.

I am not one for holding onto the anniversaries of people dying, but Amelia had been on my mind much more of late. She would have been the best source of ideas for my article and getting my creative juices flowing. I knew my mother wouldn't want me to bring up Amelia or the date.

While we ate soup and grilled cheese sandwiches at a deli on 7th Avenue, I held in my misgivings about the unspoken moratorium on discussing Amelia. Instead, I listened to my mother natter about a neighbor's recent cruise to Japan in which I wasn't even faintly interested. A stranger's travel experience wasn't my idea of dinner conversation with my mother. I understood why my dad had left her.

The next morning, the air felt crisp but with a hint of spring as I weaved my way to the subway. It would be a perfect afternoon for our drive to Jamestown.

On arrival at the Grace Building, I sent a text to Sydney confirming I was all set for our concert adventure. She was probably making Paige crazy by re-confirming every minute detail about the game plan.

None of us had ever driven to Rhode Island. Knowing it was a special performance to us since it took place where Cliff lived heightened the importance of being sure everything was on point for the trip. Sydney had even given me instructions on how I was to text her when I got in the cab to head their way, and she would then tell Paige to walk to the garage to get her SUV. The directives were *so Sydney*.

I was glad Paige would be playing chauffeur. I could doze on the drive and catch up on a few missed *zzz*s of late, though I would be sure to remain awake enough to chime in appropriately to Sydney's certain plotting for a Cliff Wood moment after the concert. This was the first time we'd had our own vehicle at a show. I could imagine her suggesting something like circling the venue to look for him afterward. I pictured us all driving around with our faces pressed to the windows. That would certainly be better than standing outside in the cold.

The morning glided by easily with two errands for Nina, one of which had conveniently worked out to be near a salon. A loquacious stylist with long gold fingernails created a sleek finish for my coffee mane and gave my bangs a sideswept effect. Walking back up 49th Street with the sun peeking around the high-rises, I thought about sending Sydney a selfie. She was always trying to get me to jazz up my look.

I decided it would be more fun to surprise her in person later when we left for Jamestown.

In the office, I sat in the breakroom chatting with an intern about her dating woes. The mostly one-sided conversation helped to kill time as I waited to leave early. My adrenaline for the trip had caused me to whip through my task list.

Like a piece to a secret mission waiting to be executed, I'd stowed a canvas bag with my concert attire underneath my desk. My plan was to change clothes in the lobby bathroom right before leaving. I didn't want anyone to ask me where I was headed. I liked to keep my work and fun separate.

But when I returned to my cubicle after my dawdling with the intern, an email had arrived from Nina that changed everything. She had scheduled a mandatory meeting that afternoon to discuss the current magazine issue in production. Impromptu meetings like these happened when deadlines started closing in.

I felt mad at myself for not being more diligent with my article for the issue. I'd spent too much time finding the perfect jumpstart for it. I should have gotten my first draft to Nina faster. Now I knew why she hadn't replied to my email about it. She was saving it for this meeting.

A wave of disappointment bordering on nausea ran through me. I stared at the missive on my computer monitor. I'd read it several times as though it might change if I looked at it enough. It had never occurred to me there could be any obstacles to our concert plans. Sydney's little joke about me being too busy to go was coming true.

Sitting there perplexed and upset about the situation, I realized it was the first time I had felt my own desire to be at Cliff's show versus mainly going to be with Sydney. I wanted to see him sing and strum and smile that radiant yet bashful smile, joke with the audience, and carelessly run his fingers through his lovely hair.

Then on the drive back to the city, Paige, Sydney, and I would discuss all these things and other nuances we'd noticed during the performance. Now I would have to miss it.

The intern came by and handed me a printed meeting agenda. "I saw your name on the email. I gave this to everyone earlier." She shrugged and gave me a sympathetic smile.

I took the paper from her and scanned the lengthy list of items to be reviewed in the meeting, wanting to rip it in half and throw it at someone.

The only positive thing I could think of was how my absence wouldn't derail things for Sydney. At one point, we'd talked about taking a bus to Jamestown and meeting at the subway nearby, but the departure times didn't line up. I was glad our plan had ended up including Paige. Sydney preferred to work with a partner for her after-show Cliff expeditions, and Paige had been around that block plenty of times. Still, I felt I was letting Sydney down.

I went in one of the small conferences rooms to call her knowing I needed to get it over with, let her know I'd have to stay behind. She'd probably be apologetic about my missing out and maybe offer to make a video if Cliff did a special song. I'd tell her to take good mental notes and that I'd wait up for her call to share a full report on their drive back afterward.

Her reaction to the news was nothing like that.

"What? That's ridiculous. Who has a meeting that late on Friday afternoon?" I could feel the sparks flying from her through the phone "You can't miss this, Claudine. You can't."

"I don't *want* to miss it. But there's no choice."

"Tell them you're sick."

"I doubt anyone would buy that." *Would they?* I pictured myself wandering into Nina's office with my hand over my stomach.

"Try to figure something out."

When we hung up, I didn't feel she believed me. That only made things worse. She also should have known by now I loved evenings out Cliff-hunting at her side.

I was so disappointed all the way around. Now I really did feel sick.

Chapter 10

I WAS GLAD NO ONE SAW ME AS I DRAGGED back to my desk fighting tears. I wasn't sure if the emotion had more to do with my disappointment in missing the concert and the fun we'd have coming and going in Paige's fancy SUV or feeling Sydney was upset with me. Maybe it was even due to my feeling of self-blame and lack of ingenuity in devising a way out of the meeting. I was afraid I'd damaged my friendship with her.

In a breakroom on another floor, I hid, stewing until I felt I should return to the magazine's suite and see what I needed to prepare for having not expected to attend the meeting.

I couldn't get my mind to focus as I watched the minutes tick by to the time I would have left and beyond. Then I pictured Sydney with Paige leaving Manhattan and imagined their conversation about me not coming along and subsequently determining to have a great time regardless. Then they'd move onto their musings about the night's set list and plans for after-show activities, forgetting all about me.

Collecting some pens and a notepad, I begrudgingly moved down the hall toward the conference room. I wanted to be sure of a spot at the far end of the table in case I couldn't hide my moping.

I thought I'd arrived early, but Nina was seated at the head of the long meeting table, hair in her usual classic bun, mauve lipstick. She always had an elegant yet matronly look. I hoped I'd have such sophistication in my fifth decade. She sat up straight, her laptop open, a stack of paper nearby along with her phone.

A few others I didn't know had claimed the distant end of the room I had planned to occupy where I could sulk. The aroma of their late afternoon coffees permeated the air. I could have used a cup myself to shift my mind back to work. I pulled out a chair adjacent to Nina. Maybe such a visible location would force me to pay attention and help get my mind off what Paige and Sydney were doing.

Nina fingered the buttons on the jewel neckline of her blouse. "I thought you had someplace to be today."

I stared at her, my mouth hanging open.

Her eyes shifted to the laptop as she typed something at lightning speed and then looked again at me. "Is everything okay?"

"Uh, I thought I was supposed to be at this meeting. I mean—"

She looked baffled. "Oh dear, did I send *you* the email about this? I'm sorry, Claudine. That should have been to our new beauty writer, Claire Stewart, have you met her? Guess I hit return too soon in the address book with the C's. I better message her. I hope she can come."

I gathered my pens and paper in what felt like slow motion. Nina clicked some more. "I got your draft. Keep working on it." The nonchalance in her voice stung as she didn't know how my hanging around for the meeting had wrecked my plans.

I loped back to my desk feeling frustrated and relieved at the same time. I had hoped for more specific feedback on my article, but that wasn't even of issue right now. Paige and Sydney had been gone almost an hour. Did I still have time to get to Jamestown some other way? If I did, I'd be late for the concert. Very late. I twisted nervously in my chair as I thought about it.

I contemplated things, staring at my phone, willing it to offer a solution. I could reach out to Aunt Trudy. If anyone would have an idea of what to do, she would be the one, but I hesitated. I felt bad I hadn't been more forthcoming with her about my true level of interest in these Cliff Wood experiences. I should have told her more about the inside details of running around with Sydney.

Aunt Trudy would certainly have been the type to have seen it for what it was, a fun adventure, a way to cope even.

Going through such reflections right now was a waste of time.

As I powered down my computer, I tapped a text to her explaining things as concisely as I could. Her reply was g*ive me a couple of minutes*. Soon, my phone buzzed in my hand.

"You'll go to Avis Car Rental on 43rd Street. Ask for Larry."

She didn't even say hello or hi.

"Larry?"

"He's my latest beau."

"What happened to Paul the plumber?"

"Oh, he still comes around." I could hear the glimmer in her voice. "But Larry is into Indonesian art. So interesting! And he manages the Avis. He's going to set you up. You need to get moving. You've got a good three-hour drive ahead of you."

I thanked Aunt Trudy with the promise of a thrift store outing soon and then hustled out of the building. There was no time to change into my concert wardrobe. It was still beautiful outside, a streak of late day sun hitting my face as I began tromping down 42nd. I had never been so determined in my behavior, pushing my way through the crowded city's sidewalk, but it worked. Soon, I was on my way to get in motion for Jamestown.

As I neared the Avis, I wondered if I'd even make it in time to see any of the concert. My spirits had done an about-face and were soaring in the change of plans. I considered calling Sydney but decided the situation might only agitate her. If it all worked out, I'd let her know when I got close to the venue. It would be so much fun to surprise her.

"You must be Claudine." A man I presumed to be Aunt Trudy's friend, Larry, stood next to a shiny silver Volkswagen Jetta. He was tall, balding, with a belly. He had kind eyes and a bit of a drawl to his voice, suggesting he wasn't from the area. It was hard to imagine his interest in Indonesian art.

"That's me," I managed, out of breath.

"I've got you all set here. This thing only has a thousand or so miles on it. It's gassed to the brim and ready to go. Don't worry about filling it up when you come back. That's on me. I just need a driver's license. You have one?"

I chuckled as I reached for my wallet. Many people who live in New York City don't bother with learning how to drive. Ubiquitous taxis and the subway make it unnecessary. But I'd gotten a license years ago as I fantasized about weekend getaways, meandering on my own, something I still enjoy.

I handed the license to Larry with my credit card.

"I'll put the Visa on file just as a formality. This is on me, too."

"That's really sweet. Thank you." I could see why Aunt Trudy liked him.

Feeling an ache of hunger, I remembered I'd used my lunch window for my hair appointment. Beyond Larry, I saw a customer enclosure with snack machines, but I felt I couldn't spare the extra minute to check them out.

I tossed my bag onto the backseat and then plugged my phone cord into the charging jack.

"You're going to Rhode Island?" Larry placed a hand on top of driver's side door. I was now seated, adjusting the mirrors, my adrenaline overflowing.

"Jamestown, yes."

"You're gonna hit a lot of traffic on 95. If it were me, I'd probably weave through Providence and then through Preston. Let your phone's GPS pick it back up from there."

"Got it, thank you." I shut the door and started the Jetta. Larry tapped the window, and I pushed the button to let it down.

He leaned in. "Your aunt, Trudy, is really something!"

"She is. I agree! Thank you so much!"

As I eased away, he gave me an encouraging smile and a thumbs up yelling, "Have a great time!" I knew then Aunt Trudy had told him the reason for my transportation needs and probably the distress I was in when I had called her. I didn't mind.

Up the street, a family wearing matching New York City sweatshirts crossed in front of me while

CHAPTER 10

I waited at a red light. I searched on my phone for the Blue Bay Room in Jamestown.

The route that came up would take me exactly where Aunt Trudy's Larry had told me not to go. I knew how to wing things enough to sidestep the GPS, and when the light changed, I took a right to begin winding my way out of Manhattan and beyond. Then I kept moving until I was headed for Providence, hoping Larry was right, and this alternate pathway wasn't making things worse on my timing.

Being behind the wheel of a car felt strange, but the Jetta provided a smooth and tight ride with its positive steering, the wonder of German engineering. I realized I hadn't driven since back when I'd lived in Mississippi. It seemed like eons ago now.

I'd had a beat-up Mustang. Maroon. Cost me $2000 and needed new tires. The joy of having my own car and being able to roam at will along back roads whenever I wanted was probably the best thing about my time there.

I'd bought the muscle car from a brown-eyed guy named Chase. We'd had dinner together a couple of times. For a moment, I pictured him and wondered why I hadn't wanted something more to happen. I couldn't remember.

The late day sun spread across the road before me. I was thankful for daylight saving time and knowing I'd only be making the last section of the trip in darkness. To pass the time, I thought about my design for the bookstore. Marlon liked what I'd done so far. I had told him I'd be in tomorrow, but that was before I had become my own chauffeur.

I was already planning to suggest I follow Paige back after the show. I would need some caffeine to get through it, but I'd worry about that later. I still had a ways to go but was feeling rejuvenated knowing I'd get to be with Sydney and see Cliff Wood perform. Aunt Trudy was such a perfect aunt.

My mind zoned in and out with a parade of classic eighties tunes provided by a local radio station. I let my GPS take over the route at the point Larry had suggested, and soon enough, Rick Springfield's hit 'Jessie's Girl' ushered me past an illuminated "Welcome to Jamestown" sign in the shape of a fish. I'd made it.

Piloting the Jetta into the venue's lot, I coasted into the first space I saw. The show had long begun, and no parking attendants remained to direct me. It felt so good having pulled off the surprise, and I couldn't wait to send a text to Sydney.

I hurried through the parking lot toward the entrance while haphazardly attempting to write her a message at the same time. *Guess what, I'm here! Come get me outside,* I managed.

When I made it to the doorway, I hit send and prepared for her excited response. I didn't even care how the dampness in the coastal city had already confiscated the warmth I'd enjoyed with the car's heated seats.

I waited. And waited more. A minute felt like an hour. Two minutes. Three. I realized she was probably engrossed in the concert. As I proceeded through the doors, I sent one more text. *I'm inside now.*

Surprisingly, no one asked me for a ticket right away. I wasn't worried about it since Sydney could present mine as soon as I could find her. Any second now, she'd reply, and the fun would begin.

I ventured further into the room. There was Cliff perched high on a stool, guitar on his thigh, plucking away as beams of light above accentuated his silver-streaked locks.

I didn't know the song, didn't take time to listen closely or even think about it. For now, the music was a sound in the background as I looked around for Sydney.

The place was so softly lit it made it hard to see much less locate anyone. I figured Sydney was probably making a video and planning to give me the story on the song later as well as whatever else I'd missed. Normally, I could spot her jagged hair from a mile away. That or either find the shortest person in a line of people standing. But this venue was different. Instead of rows of chairs, the place had a more formal setup.

Round tables with white tablecloths peppered the room. A votive candle stood on each with a tasteful coil of greenery. It looked more like a wedding reception was taking place.

A wall of ceiling-high windows framed a view of the bay, the water only evidenced by boats lingering upon its surface. As I considered the setup more closely, I saw a few of the tables had dishes on them and realized it was some kind of supper club-cum-performance hall. I wondered if I could still get something to eat.

"May I help you get back to your table?"

An usher stood beside me. His white hair lay perfectly parted and combed to the side. A nametag on his coat read Walter.

I looked at my phone. Still nothing.

"My best friend—she has my ticket. I'm not sure where she is. Could I stand in the back and wait for her?" I gave him my best look of misfortune as I realized it was the first time I'd referred to Sydney as my best friend.

"The show is almost over."

"I know. I was stuck in traffic." That was an easier explanation. "I came from New York."

"That's a long drive for a concert." He looked around for a moment. "We're not supposed to do this, but that seat over there," he pointed, "has been empty the whole evening."

I crept over to the table and joined three others who didn't notice me. The centerpiece candle had been reduced to a minor ember.

Cliff was now thanking everyone for coming. His gracious smile with that cute dimple was wide and obvious even from my distant view. He apparently had some special guests and invited one of them, a local guitar player, back to the stage to join him for the last song.

The extra musician freed Cliff to sing without playing his guitar. He wandered about, touching hands with people at the rim of the stage before starting the song.

Now was the best time to locate Sydney. I considered snaking my way up to the front knowing it was where she was likely to be, but the tables with the chairs pulled out and people standing made it difficult to navigate.

Ignoring Cliff's performance, I scanned every direction. No Sydney. Or Paige. Or anyone I'd met at other concerts. Not even Alternative Kyle.

Cliff didn't usually do an encore at his solo gigs. As everyone waited, hoping he might deviate from that norm, I tried to think of other reasons why Sydney wouldn't be responding to my messages. Maybe she'd taken too much video, and her phone had died. Maybe she was truly mad at me for not finding a way to come in the first place.

I didn't know what to do. It was such a letdown to have made it there after such a travail, only to be unable to find her.

Back outside in my rental, I watched, hoping to see Paige and Sydney leave the building, but it was too dark with too much confusion what with the frenzy of cars getting lined up to exit. I didn't know what Paige's SUV looked like, model, color, or anything. Not that it would have helped as I waited my turn to back out in the jam that inevitably comes to pass in the exodus of a packed parking lot.

I looked at my phone. *Sydney?* I wrote. I didn't have any expectation she'd reply.

Now I would have to drive back to New York in the dark by myself, hungry and disappointed. It wouldn't be safe, I knew. On my phone, I searched for hotels and tapped for the directions on the first one that came up. I just needed a place to rest and something to eat. I'd sleep off this whole mess and head back in the morning. Maybe somewhere in there, Sydney would call and tell me what I'd missed.

That was the best I could hope at that point.

Chapter 11

THE CHARMING, COASTAL TOWN OF Jamestown, Rhode Island is awash with cute restaurants and scenic shopping areas, beautiful architecture, and picturesque views over Narragansett Bay. A lot of moneyed people live in the historic city.

I couldn't see much of it in the dark.

The quaint inn where I landed felt more like someone's grandmother's house than a hotel. It even smelled like warm cookies. As I climbed a staircase covered in soft green carpet leading to my room for the night, I realized I didn't have any pajamas. Or a toothbrush. Not even a used paperback to keep me company later. It was going to be hard to fall asleep despite how tired I felt.

At the top of the stairs, I waded down a hall across more of the comfy carpeting to locate my accommodation and used an actual key to open the solid wood door. A faint aroma of cleaning agent mixed with the scent of lemons greeted me as I tossed my canvas bag on a light blue chenille bed-spread and sat down.

I couldn't stop checking my phone for a message from Sydney. I felt like I could cry. I'd been so tearful lately. First at work earlier when I thought I wouldn't get to come to the concert, and now this. My body and mind were telling me I needed to take a break.

Leaving my phone behind to keep myself from checking it every ten seconds for a response from her, I trudged back down the stairs and stopped at the front desk to ask about nearby places to eat.

"Well let's see." An elderly innkeeper wearing pearl earrings and a chiffon scarf stared beyond my shoulder as she considered things. "Do you have a car?"

I nodded.

"Then the Happy Catfish would probably work. That's about a mile from here. I can call and see if they're still open. It's big with young people. And then there's this one mostly outside place. It's by the water. Course, you might catch a cold this time of night, and I don't think the parking is—"

"What about a place I could walk to?" I hated to cut her off. She was trying to be helpful, but aside from feeling like I was starving now, I didn't want to rely on my own sense of direction. I needed to go by foot so I could leave my phone be. All my continuous checks for Sydney to reply were only serving to make me feel bad.

"Oh yes." She brightened. "Halstead's is right around the corner. A lot of our guests go there. It's more on the costly side, but— "

"How do I get there?"

If she hadn't described it to me, in the darkness I'd have never come across the local dining place hiding on the other side of the inn.

Inside of a minute, I was walking through a parking lot of broken seashells crackling beneath each step I took and happy knowing I'd quickly be back out of the cold. A row of overhead beach lamps provided a path to a sturdy wooden ramp leading to the restaurant's entrance.

A maître d' greeted me. The sight of his vest and bowtie made me worry I was under-dressed, but of course, I'd never had a chance to change out of my work clothes.

"Good evening. Are you looking to dine with us?"

"Yes. It smells great in here." I looked around.

"The dining room closed at ten. You can still order food at the bar though. Will that be okay?" He leaned slightly forward awaiting my reply.

A table to myself had been more of what I had pictured, but my appetite was calling the shots. When I agreed, he said I could get a menu from the bartender and pointed the way.

I headed over to the bar where small round tables were occupied with groups in conversation over mojitos and martinis. The only empty spot was at the bar between two other diners. After I took off my jacket and got settled on the high back chair, the couple next to me paid their bill and departed leaving space between me and another diner to my left.

I heard his voice before I noticed him.

"What kind of wine is this anyway?" The question was followed by a low laugh, one I'd heard enough times to recognize, often after telling a humorous story about a song's origin. It was a voice that had sung me to sleep through my earbuds lately.

"The expensive kind, your favorite." The bartender laughed as he answered.

It might have been due to being famished, but I suddenly felt lightheaded. I wanted to look over and confirm what I already knew—that I'd stumbled across Cliff Wood, alone—no Bruce, no fans—but I couldn't bring myself to do it.

"What? This is *not* expensive wine." I heard him take a sip and swallow it as I sat there trying to process the situation.

Now I regretted leaving my phone behind. Sydney and Paige couldn't be that far away yet. Knowing them, they'd hung around the venue after the performance, probably found the backstage door, and waited for Cliff to exit. I hadn't thought about that earlier when I was trying to locate them. If I could text Sydney Cliff's whereabouts now, she probably wouldn't be mad at me about not coming to begin with.

"What can I get for you, young lady?" The bartender, late fifties, wavy grey hair, stood behind a tray of beverage napkins, straws, and other restaurant accoutrements. "Do you need a menu?"

"Yes I do, please."

He gave me one already in his hand. "We're out of the shrimp fettucine. The name is Atlas. I'll be right here when you're ready."

When I'd arrived, the idea of anything edible had sounded good. Now my anxiety about Cliff's presence overrode my sensation of hunger. As much as Sydney and I had tried to be in this exact situation, I didn't know what to do now that I was in it without her. I was surprised by how nervous I felt by his presence. The menu quivered in my hand. I lowered it to my lap.

Atlas brought me a set of silverware wrapped in a linen napkin along with a sweaty glass of water. His timing was perfect. My throat felt like the Sahara Desert, and I immediately drank most of it. I could still feel my hands shaking as my fingers clutched the glass.

My reaction seemed a bit much. I'd sat next to Cliff Wood once before in that private room after the pop-up show and had even been on stage with him the first time I'd seen him perform. But that was before I'd become involved in going to his concerts and discussing him so much with Sydney. The idea of him now seemed much bigger to me. He was no longer just a guy *I sort of remembered.*

I scanned the menu in my lap. I knew I should eat. It would hit me later if I didn't get some nourishment and would also give me something to focus on as I sat there feeling out of sorts and duplicitous, pretending not to recognize him.

When Atlas looked my way after serving other guests, I lifted the menu to call him over. "I'll have the Mediterranean salmon salad." I sounded tense, as though I were requesting something out of the ordinary.

He took the menu from me. "One Mediterranean salad. With salmon. I'll get some bread for you."

My discomfort furtively filled the air. If I'd been a smoker, this would have been the point I'd have lit a cigarette. Atlas refilled my water, and I nursed it to keep myself from fidgeting.

"While you're waiting on your food, try the wine. You can give us your opinion on it."

Oh God, it was Cliff. Talking to *me*.

I felt his gaze as he set down his wine glass. "If you don't like it, Atlas here will be buying. He picked the label."

I played through the last time I'd sat next to Cliff Wood, barely able to speak and uncomfortable with all the fans around, especially Evvi and her friends eyeing me from across the table. I needed to be more conscientious this time and not say something inane like *I enjoyed your concert*. I eyerolled to myself inside my head.

CHAPTER 11

I noticed how relaxed he was now, on his terms and in his own environment. The times Sydney and I had located him in our post-concert hunts, it never felt as if he embraced the excitement of the fans who had gathered for a glimpse of him. He was cordial but reserved.

Now, he presented like a social coordinator trying to include the newcomer at the bar.

When I didn't respond to his remark, he added, "Seriously though. Let me buy you a drink. Doesn't have to be this so-called *expensive wine.*"

His voice was comforting, a note of concern in it, perhaps because I was by myself. The gesture made me feel reassured after the upsetting evening I'd had.

I knew I was going to have to get up the nerve to look at him and at least acknowledge his offer. It would be rude not to. I scanned the others sitting nearby. Were they oblivious to his identity and presence? Slowly, I turned my head to look at him and fixed my expression into one of nonchalance, ready to politely decline his offer.

Instead, face to face with him, my concentrated indifference fell by the wayside. I took a deep breath as my eyes met his. "Wine sounds good. I'll have the expensive one." My remark sounded flirtatious. I hadn't meant for it to be.

"Atlas—get our friend some of this." He raised his glass as if an illustration were needed.

I sat back feeling relieved I'd said something co-herent. But I still needed to play things cool. It was important I handle the situation right and make the most of it, the way Sydney would direct me if she were there. I pictured her critiquing my moves later as I recounted them blow by blow. I wanted her to feel I'd made the best use of this propitious scenar-io I'd landed in without her.

"Is it okay if we sit here?" It was a man and wom-an, late twenties. They were dressed as though they'd been to a formal event like a wedding. They wanted to claim the two open spots separating Cliff and me. I waved my hand in the air palm up to give them the go-ahead, but Cliff intervened.

He pulled one of the chairs toward him posses-sively and invited me with a nod of his head to move over. "She was just about to scoot down."

The couple stepped back as Cliff lifted my jacket off the chair and relocated it. I felt dizzy as I moved into my new spot even closer to Cliff Wood.

The wine he'd ordered for me arrived, and I needed it. I rested my fingertips on the base of the glass as I let the idea sink in that after all the calcu-lated efforts Sydney and I had made together, I was now hanging out with Cliff Wood, on my own.

My hands had stopped shaking, but waves of nervous energy galloped through me. I began to tuck the same section of hair behind my ear every few seconds. Hair fidgeting was a gesture I'd picked up from Sydney, I knew. To make myself stop, I reached for a napkin and held onto it in my lap.

Cliff smelled like the perfect mix of a wood fire and sea air, rugged and inviting. Given the stress of my day, it was tempting to throw my arms around him and submerge myself in the pleasing aroma.

Instead, I extended my hand to him. "I'm Claudine Davis." *Was that weird?*

I was trying to act as if he weren't who he was. I thought he might appreciate the feeling of anonymity. Plus, I thought it would make *me* feel more comfortable talking to him like a normal person, not as the rock star Sydney and I traversed New York and other cities to see.

"Cliff." He set his glass down and clasped my hand. His grip felt measured and his skin warm.

"I know. I—I heard the bartender call you by name earlier." *That was close.* I hadn't really heard anyone say his name.

But letting on I was a fan of sorts, yes *of sorts*— not like a fan at Sydney's level of fandom, which I felt made things different—would be a bad move, even if I explained the "of sorts" part the way it was in my mind. Clearly, I was over-analyzing things, as usual.

I needed to start drinking. After a mouthful of wine, I pretended to thoughtfully swallow and evaluate the flavor. I didn't know anything about wine, and I didn't know if what I'd just tasted was of the high-priced variety, but it did go down smoothly. I would have felt that way about anything helping to take the edge off at that point. I took another sip and another before leaving it be, lest my anxiety out my knowledge of the rock star next to me.

"It's good, thank you." I gave him a confirming look.

"Red wine is supposed to be better for you, but I find most of it to be bitter."

I wasn't sure how to comment. I knew Sydney would want me to get something more useful for us from the conversation. What would she say to him at this point? As I thought about subtle segues, he was the one who kept the conversation going.

"Do you live here?" *God, that voice.* Even in a simple question it had a seductive quality.

I tucked my hair back once again while mentally vowing I'd stop the nervous twitch. "In Jamestown?"

He nodded and shifted his eyes to me temporarily. Beautiful dark eyelashes surrounded his unassuming expression. I was jealous.

"I came to visit some friends."

He mockingly looked around. "Where are they?"

"They had to head back home." I knew that didn't make sense, but he didn't press.

Atlas brought my salad and set it before me with a sheepish face. "I forgot the bread. Do you still want it?"

"No, this is fine. Thank you."

Cliff watched as I unrolled the silverware and cleared my palate with the water. He pointed to nearby salt and pepper shakers. "Need these?"

"Um, the pepper, yeah." After he'd set it by my plate, I added, "And I guess the salt, too."

He put the saltshaker within my reach and took a napkin from the extra stack behind the bar and set it next to my plate.

"What are you, like, secretly on the wait staff or something?" I had a wad of lettuce in my mouth causing my sentence to come out garbled but still decipherable. Cliff found it funny, his laugh soft and light-hearted.

"Or something." He winked at me. "How's the salad?"

"It's doing the job." I stabbed a tomato and black olive with my fork. "It needs more salt."

He pushed the shaker further, so it now touched my bowl. "I'm having another glass of wine. You in?"

"Sure." Given what was happening, that I was casually eating dinner with Cliff Wood and would probably be wide awake thinking about it later, I knew I'd appreciate the sleep aid the alcohol was sure to provide.

Cliff briefly consulted a wine list laying atop the bar. "Let's try the Zenato Pinot. Sound good to you?"

I scanned the list, clueless. "Sounds good." It did sound good to me because I would drink it in

Cliff's company. I liked how he wanted to consult me—even though it seemed plain I didn't have much to offer about it.

Atlas looked up from the mixed drink he was making. "Coming up."

Cliff leaned back in his chair. "So, tell me. What about you? What do you do, aside from visit friends who ditch you and leave you in bars with strange men?"

I ignored the *strange men* comment and waited until I swallowed my current mouthful of salad. "I work for a small fashion magazine. I'm a writer. I mean, I want to be." I wished I hadn't said it that way. I felt stupid.

"If you put words on paper and express your thoughts, you're a writer. I'm a writer too."

"Yeah, but you're—" *published,* I almost said. I'd finished the sentence as, "you're more confident, in your ideas. I can tell. You probably know your writing voice."

"Sometimes." He lifted his wine glass to his lips and stopped short. "It changes depending on what I'm working on."

I assumed he meant his songs verses his books. I was hoping he'd volunteer more on the matter. I pushed away the salad bowl. I'd gotten through half of it and didn't want to eat in front of him anymore. I feared being asked a complex question just as a piece of lettuce got stuck in my teeth. I felt bad about the times Sydney and I and others had stood on the sidelines in restaurants watching him have a meal. I realized how intrusive it must feel.

"Who are your favorite authors? And don't say Kerouac. Guys who wear leather jackets and faded jeans always go there." I looked at him with a sardonic smile and awaited his reply.

He smirked and chuckled as his head fell forward. A thatch of hair tumbled onto his forehead. He casually glided his fingers through it. "Oh, let's see. Plath. Woolf."

"That's pretty dark." I wondered if he was trying to name writers he thought might start a conversation. I tried to imagine him reading *The Bell Jar*, a difficult picture to conjure given I knew he wrote westerns.

He raised his eyebrows. "What about you? Who do you like?"

"Camus. Emerson. Diski." I could have named a dozen. *Wood.*

"Diski?"

"Jenny Diski."

The new order of wine arrived. Atlas set each of our glasses before us and removed the other ones. Mine still had enough for another swallow or two while Cliff had drained the last of his moments before.

He pulled his new glass close and held onto the stem. "Fiction is the lie through which we tell the truth."

I swiveled to look at him feeling both astonished and impressed. "I've never heard anyone
quote Camus."

"I've never heard anyone name him as a favorite."
He lifted his glass to touch mine. "A toast to our
mutual good taste—and to good books and great
writers. And I want to name one more since you
had three so it's only fair: Charles Bukowski."

I swallowed the wine swirling in my mouth and
then clinked my glass to his. "Hmm, a bit graphic for my taste. What do you like about him?" I
wasn't just making conversation. I truly wanted
to know.

"Mainly that he didn't limit himself. And didn't
try too hard. It makes his dialogue real. Grabs you,
makes you think."

That's the way I feel about some of your songs, I
wanted to say. But I wouldn't have dared interrupt
the intimacy and enjoyment of our discussion about
writing and authors in the crowded bar. And especially not to derail the experience by saying I was a
fan or a *sort of fan*, a new one.

"How's the wine?" Atlas returned holding a bar
towel and wiped the area before us.

Cliff gave a thumbs-up. "It's perfect.
Very *expensive-tasting.*"

We all laughed, loud and buoyant. Cliff said,
"Is it too late to get some fries?" And then to me,
"Would you eat some of them?"

I said I would even though I wasn't hungry anymore. At least my nerves had calmed down. I felt I should ask him something Sydney might want to know. I was about to see if I could pivot our conversation to that end when two women in sparkly blouses were suddenly next to us. I had seen them sitting at the other end of the bar and suspected they were *concert types* by their attire. When they strutted over, I knew what was about to happen.

"Hi, we loved your show," enthused one.

"Well, not just the show either—we've loved you since we were sixteen," the other one said, perky eyes, completely captivated by Cliff. "Would you take a photo with us?"

Cliff didn't have time to answer before they had posed next to him. The first woman handed me her phone with the camera ready to go and was already thanking me for my help as I took it from her.

Suddenly conscious he hadn't given his consent, I met Cliff' gaze. "Is this okay?"

He smiled as though he both appreciated and thought it was cute I'd thought to ask. "Sure, it's fine. Take a couple."

As I tapped the device to get the shots, I thought about saying something like everyone say, 'Let's Go' which was a song title of his, but I hadn't yet admitted I knew who he was and didn't think this was how I wanted to do it.

I handed the phone back to the elated women. They admired the image and then copiously thanked him as they walked away sharing giddy whispers.

Alone with our wine again and the backdrop of the purr in the room growing with patrons, a feeling of awkwardness set in. I wondered if Cliff found it strange I hadn't questioned why someone would want a picture with him. I'd obviously also heard their declarations about loving him since their teens and mentioning his concert. It was time to confess.

By then I was sitting to the side in my chair, our faces close. I took in a breath and looked at him squarely. "I almost saw your show tonight, too."

The words came out like I'd shared a deep-seated secret. I cringed. I wondered if he now felt uncomfortable I'd known who he was all along.

"Almost? Changed your mind?" His expression was one of curiosity, not discomfort.

"No, it wasn't like that." It hadn't occurred to me he'd think I purposely missed the show. "I drove from New York but didn't make it in time. There was a snafu at work. I got a late start."

Cliff rested an arm on the bar and took a sip of wine. "Snafu. That's a word you don't hear often enough. What happened?"

I felt embarrassed about it for some reason. Maybe because the whole thing with getting held up and thinking I'd miss the concert with Sydney and Paige had felt like such a big deal at the time. But it had turned out not to matter considering I was now sitting there talking to him, an experience infinitely better.

"I got pulled into something at the last-minute. I was meeting my best friend and another friend over here. Then I couldn't find them when I arrived. That was the even bigger snafu."

He laughed at me using the word again and then his expression turned to perplexity "When did you get here?"

"In time to hear two songs, maybe. I'm not sure."

"That's a long drive for *maybe* two songs and no one awaiting you." He studied me.

I shook my head as if it weren't an issue. "Can't win at everything I guess. It was a nice drive though. It gave me some time to think. That part was nice."

"You needed to think?"

I nodded.

"I like drives, too. Me and the road. Solitude."

"See, I knew you were a Kerouac fan." I felt my face light up as I said it, and his did, too.

Our fries arrived. Atlas put them between us and presented a bottle of ketchup as though it were wine. "This is a great year. Tangy, sweet, with a warm rich body. Enjoy."

As we began eating, Cliff was approached for another photo, this time by a man and woman, mid-forties. The man described how he'd enjoyed the night's concert and then gushed about growing up with Cliff's music. It made me think of Amelia. I don't know why the women wanting the photo hadn't activated her memory. Maybe because they were so bubbly, nothing like her.

I squelched the sad thoughts and watched as Cliff listened good-naturedly, even obliging the couple a joke or two along with a photo. He didn't comment about the interruption when they left, and neither did I. It was clear this was routine for him.

"I feel tired." I picked up one more fry and dragged it through some ketchup before poking it in my mouth.

"You're not driving back tonight, are you?" Cliff's concern was more obvious this time.

"I've got a room near here. I'll head back in the morning."

I reached for my bag I'd hung on the back of the chair. It had been a surreal experience getting to talk to him, but I mainly wanted to get back to my phone and see if Sydney had responded.

When I produced my wallet, Cliff lightly pushed it away.

"I'll get this, Claudine. Your salad too."

"What? No."

"I have to. You only got two songs, if even that. I owe you." His eyes were set in a shy warmth. "Really, if you came to see me and didn't get the full show, then a few fries and some lettuce are the least I can offer to make up for it."

"And the expensive wine," I joked.

"Yes, and that."

"It's been so nice talking to you. That was a gift on its own." I put my wallet away. Now I felt timid. I had purposely kept myself from being long-winded but wanted to say something more about how it wasn't just the talking. It was his kindness, his attention, his interest—how those things had made the drive worth it, concert or not. "Thank you for the drinks and dinner," was all I could get to come out.

I stood up and put my handbag on my shoulder.

Cliff started to get up, too. "I'll head out with you. Hey Atlas, put this down for me." He motioned at what was left of our dishes.

"You got it, Mr. Wood. You both have a good night."

We moved through the congested bar area. I'd unconsciously set aside the idea of the celebrity he was, but now as I heard a few shout-outs to him, and even some applause, it hit me again, and my heart drummed. I was being escorted outside by *Cliff Wood*.

In the quiet of the parking lot, I thanked him once more and turned to walk back to the inn. I wasn't sure what I was going to tell Sydney about the evening. Thoughts about how to approach it were already spinning in my mind as the cold air pervaded my jacket.

"Claudine, where are you staying?" Cliff's voice sounded like an echo in the darkness. With the help of the moon's luminous cascade, I could see his strong silhouette.

"I think it's called Lambeth's."

"I know Lambeth's." I heard his footsteps over the broken shells. "I'll walk with you. Is that okay?"

"Sure, as long as you walk fast. I'm a wuss about the cold."

"I can do that."

We made small talk about the area on the way. He told me he'd lived in Jamestown for fifteen years and had a chalet in Colorado where he hid a few times a year, his own writer's getaway. His preference was to be near water though. I didn't have time to say much more than that I'd grown up in Greenwich Village and still lived there.

"When will I see you again?" he asked.

The question caught me off guard. It had a romantic quality to it I wasn't sure he intended. And in what capacity was he asking to *see me?*

We stood under the awning outside the hotel's entrance. Even in the glow of an exposed yellow bulb, his inviting features stood out. I'd had time to get used to them up close at the bar, but now I was taken in by them again.

"I don't know," I said. In my mind, I ticked through the list of his shows Sydney and I had reviewed the night in the secret Chinese restaurant. I couldn't remember where we were in the line-up.

"I want to make it up to you with tickets to whatever concert you want of mine coming up for you and your friends or whoever you'd want to bring."

"You don't need to do that. You bought me dinner *and* expensive wine, remember?"

I expected him to laugh. Instead he said soberly, "It wasn't enough. You can look at the tour online, or on my site, or wherever and let me know."

Wow, he knew where his concert information was listed? That struck me as unique, funny even.

I pawed inside my bag searching for my room key. "That's a really nice offer. I'll have to think about it." The key was in a side pocket, and I held it up for him to see. "All set."

Standing there with a faint smile and piercing eyes that looked as though they held a thousand secrets, he didn't say anything. My heart began to race again as I headed inside.

Chapter 12

SOMETHING ABOUT THE DARKNESS AND night and being alone has a way of igniting contemplation. I was far too familiar with those things at that point in my life.

I sat on the edge of the unfamiliar hotel mattress as the tips of my fingers absently grazed the textured bedspread. I thought through what had happened at the restaurant. It felt like an abstract dream, me eating French fries with Cliff Wood while casually chatting about authors. Sylvia Plath, really? She was one of his favorites? Sydney and I hoped something like that might happen for us *together*, at least as far as getting to have some one-on-one time with him. But outside of that, I was never fantasizing about it for myself. It was all so unexpected.

Especially how he had made me feel he was genuinely interested in everything I said. His attention alone had been worth the drive.

I couldn't wait to talk to Sydney and figure out what concert we'd see with the tickets he'd offered. If I knew her, she'd need to do an evaluation of his tour schedule including venues and a myriad of other factors before deciding. I also hoped she'd have an idea about how to notify Cliff once we figured it out. I hadn't thought to ask him about that part.

Removing my phone from the nightstand, I saw a stream of her replies to my messages. Finally. In the last one, she said to call her no matter how late. I settled against a pillow in a frilly sham as I made the call.

"Claudine?" Her voice sounded like a nervous mother anxiously waiting to hear from a teenager out past curfew. "Where are you? Are you in Jamestown?"

"Yes! Hi! I'm in a hotel. I'm too tired to drive back. Where are you?"

Silence. And then, "I'm in New York on my couch with Lyric. You're in Jamestown?" she repeated. "How did you get there? Did you go with someone else? I thought you couldn't go."

Her giving me the third degree accompanied by a fractious tone quickly doused my eagerness to tell her about my time with Cliff or any other details including his offer of the complimentary tickets. I explained to her about the debacle at work with the meeting.

"My aunt helped me rent a car, and I headed over, but I couldn't find you. Did you and Paige leave the show early to wait outside for him?"

"No. We weren't even there. We never made it. Paige's SUV crapped out on the way."

"Oh. How come you didn't tell me?"

She drew in a long breath and let it out so forcefully it felt as though it had penetrated my phone's speaker. "I was incredibly bummed. I was already upset you weren't coming. Then when Paige and I couldn't even get to Jamestown... It started with the traffic being backed up like crazy and then the SUV went haywire."

I sat up and moved a pillow onto my lap. "Are you okay?"

"I'm fine. We had to pull over. All the controls in the car went crazy. Then it wouldn't start. Her husband had to come get us." She sighed.

"I thought that SUV was brand new."

"It is. Her husband thinks it's some bug in the electrical system. You should have seen her dashboard. It looked like the Rockefeller Christmas tree with extra voltage."

"Well, I'm glad you're okay."

"How much did you get to see of the concert?"

"Not much. The last two songs. He had a guest performer."

"I saw that. Someone posted a video clip in the fan group. Oh gosh, it's going to make me nuts if he sang 'Any Word from William?' I haven't seen anything about that. I was hoping he'd do a few of the slower cuts from the last album. Did you go behind the venue after?"

I stiffened. "No. It was too cold. And I was looking for you."

She was quiet, no doubt processing her disappointment in missing out and what seemed to be my lack of interesting information given I'd ended up going. "Jamestown is a small place. We probably could have found him or maybe driven by his house. Paige has done that, a quick drive-by. I thought he might bring his motorcycle to the venue, and we'd sneak a picture with it. It would have been such a fun night."

"Cliff rides a motorcycle?" I found the detail odd given the conversation he and I'd had. It felt like it didn't match his persona.

"I don't think he would really bring it to a concert. It was just something I was hoping might happen. Anyway, I'm sorry you drove over for nothing."

Her last comment was the entry to talk about what had occurred in the restaurant, but I didn't think she could handle hearing about it. It would add insult to injury, and more than that, I didn't want to risk how she might react to the idea I'd had one-on-one time with him. It would be better to tell her in person. I changed the subject, reiterating, "I'm glad you and Paige are okay."

After we hung up, I lay awake continuing to think about the evening and re-create parts of the conversation I'd had with Cliff.

Earlier, I had paused the thought of Amelia and now imagined what it would be like to tell her about how it felt talking to Cliff Wood and the way he had provided an unforeseen comfort after such a stressful afternoon, missing his performance, and then feeling let down after getting myself there and not finding Sydney. I felt horribly guilty things had turned out so well for me in the end. In my mind, Amelia told me not to worry about it.

***

The sun's rays whispered through the blinds the next morning. I had slept so soundly that the phone clanging on the nightstand jolted me awake. When I reached over to answer, I knocked the whole unit onto the floor. After I pulled the curly cord to the receiver toward me, I heard a voice say, "Ms. Davis? Are you there?"

I rested back on the pillow. My eyes felt unready to face the light. "Yes, hi. This is Claudine."

"I'm calling from the front desk. You have a guest."

It had to be Sydney. I wondered how she'd found me, but with her finely honed detective skills from her Cliff Wood pursuits I should have expected such. It was so her to head over, to want to salvage what she could of the failed concert excursion and maybe do that drive-by past Cliff's house she'd mentioned. I'd have to find a way to discourage the idea.

I rubbed my eyes and eased myself onto one elbow. "You can give her my room number and tell her to come up."

There was a pause. "It's a Mr. Wood."

That put me wide awake. I sat up to evaluate the situation. Seriously? He was here? I had slept in my clothes, and without even looking, knew I had the worst bedhead. I pulled my hair to one side and raked my fingers through it. The sleek blow-out I'd had the day before wasn't even of note.

"Ms. Davis?"

"I'm here. Tell him I'll be down in a few minutes."

In the bathroom, I wiped my face with a cloth and then scrounged in my purse eventually finding a God-only-knew-how-old mint and some lip balm. It was the best I could do. Thank goodness I wasn't so much wanting to primp as to merely be somewhat presentable.

From the top of the stairs, I could see Cliff near the front desk. He looked out of context being offstage as he browsed a rack of souvenir t-shirts. His hair wasn't its best either. He'd rejuvenated it with a bit of gel perhaps. It looked glossy, and a section of it refused to stay in the right place. That aside, he wore black jeans and a green and black flannel shirt.

Rock star, morning edition. For a moment, I saw him as an ordinary guy.

"Hi." My one-syllable greeting sounded overly chipper. He hadn't noticed me coming down the stairs. I felt I'd startled him.

"Sleep well?"

"I did actually."

In one hand, he held a paper cup of black coffee with steam rising from it. I looked around, thinking he might have gotten it when he arrived. It would have hit the spot.

"You needed it after that long drive. I was wondering if you might want to grab some breakfast. They have great pancakes here." He motioned with his coffee toward the innkeeper.

Pancakes, really? What was happening? I looked away. I thought about the invitation as if it required the same level of decision as buying a house.

He tilted his head, eyebrows raised. "You don't like pancakes?"

I showed him the keys in my hands. "I do, but I have to return this rental car. I think they thought I'd head back last night and bring it in first thing this morning."

That was mostly true except I knew Aunt Trudy's Larry wouldn't hold me to it. But really what I wanted was to get back so I could bring Sydney up to speed on everything in person. Plus, Marlon was expecting me to be at the store later.

"You were going to drive back after the show?" He sipped his coffee. I could tell it was too hot given the way he squinted after he swallowed it.

"I was going to follow my friends."

"The friends you never got together with."

"Yes. They didn't ditch me. They were supposed to come to your concert, but I found out their car broke down. I talked to my friend later last night. She's beside herself. She thinks she missed a song she was hoping you'd play."

He started to sip the coffee again but stopped. "What was the song?"

"Something about William. 'Where's William?' maybe."

I could see he was suppressing a smile, amused either that I wasn't familiar enough to be sure of the title or that he *had* played it. Discussing the concert and his music with him now morphed him into rock star Cliff in my head. My anxiety went into gear.

And then it hit me. I didn't need to discuss the comp tickets he'd offered with Sydney.

"I know what show I want the tickets for you offered: the one with your daughter." I couldn't think of her name.

"You know about Ramsey's show?"

Ramsey. Right. "It's sold out. That's the main thing I know." I also knew it would make Sydney ecstatic if I got tickets for us.

"It's not 'til June. That's the one you want?"

"Yes. My friend was disappointed we couldn't get seats."

I stepped over to the innkeeper and set the room key on the desk. "This is a great place. My credit card is on file."

Cliff followed me outside, and we stood by the silver Jetta. I couldn't wait to get back on the heated seat. I opened the door and tossed my handbag inside. "I'm sorry I can't stay."

"Next time then." He winked at me and had a swallow of coffee before taking a few steps back.

It took me a minute to get settled, fasten my seatbelt, and run the windshield wipers to clear the glass of ice that had begun to melt in the early sunlight. When I glanced up, he looked like he hated to see me go.

After I backed up he raised his coffee in a parting gesture. I started to think I should have stayed for the pancakes.

Chapter 13

I DON'T KNOW HOW TO DESCRIBE WHAT I WAS feeling as I drove away.

So much was circling in my mind. I wanted to be happy and lose myself in the thrill of my time with Cliff, being with him at the bar, the ease of our conversation. I'd never expected to feel such a closeness to him that had nothing to do with his music. I thought we'd just have a meal, and that would be it.

Discomfort over what the encounter meant for my friendship with Sydney swirled in my mind like a tornado. I felt like I was stabbing her in the back and was starting to dread telling her about everything. I knew she would act as if she were happy for me but inside would be deeply jealous. One of the first things she had told me when we met was how much she'd like the opportunity to chat with him.

On the drive back to the city, I practiced aloud having the conversation with her explaining how helpful it would be for both of us to have an in with Cliff and the possibility of us getting those coveted tickets to the special performance with Ramsey. I hoped those things would help. I knew it was going to be an upsetting thing for Sydney to hear no matter how I presented it.

At the rental place, Larry greeted me. "Soooooo, how was it? Did you have a good time?"

"It was great." *More than great.* It was noon on the dot. I insisted he charge me for some gas and handed him a twenty-dollar bill if for nothing else, a tip toward his kindness

"Trudy wouldn't forgive me if I accepted that." He reached for the keys in my hand instead.

I was too tired to do anything at the bookstore and called Marlon to beg out of coming in. The time I spent there was always up to me, but I wanted him to know that helping him was still a priority to me. I loved that little bookstore. It was my oasis on many days when I didn't know what to do with myself. Sometimes, I'd sit in the back on a stool out of sight and thumb through books by authors I'd never heard of. It was great therapy, and Marlon never interrupted me. I wanted to give something to it, to Marlon. But that would wait.

At home, I made a peanut butter sandwich and sat on the steps outside. The day had gotten warmer, giving me hope that spring might soon take over. I called my mother. We hadn't been in touch much lately. I missed her and was looking for anything to distract me from my mind's incessant evaluation of how I would approach sharing with Sydney the full scope of my visit to Jamestown. I'd heard her enough times describe situations of other girls who'd only had minor exchanges with Cliff and how it bothered her to know that a whole evening of talking to him and then his coming to the inn the next morning would send her over the edge.

She'd already sent several follow-up texts to ask if Cliff had made any unique comments during the show or if I'd seen Evvi or any other regulars there. She'd also been updating me as she pieced together the set list based on videos she'd found online. The whole thing made me uneasy.

When my mother told me she and Aunt Trudy were getting together to make jewelry, I asked if I could come hang out with them. I knew it would make her happy to see me, and I owed Aunt Trudy an update on my excursion after she'd come to my rescue with Larry.

"Well, look who's here. You look gorgeous." It was Aunt Trudy in a purple shirt with ladybugs on it, a wrist of bangle bracelets, and a black beret made of synthetic felt. The outfit made me laugh though I was used to her eclectic attire. She kissed me on the forehead.

For the remainder of the afternoon, I had slept and then taken a hurried shower before heading over. I'd clipped my bangs to one side with a child's style metal barrette. I knew I didn't look gorgeous by any means, but it was her way to make over me. I loved it. There was simply nothing like having a doting aunt, and Aunt Trudy fit the bill and beyond.

"I brought pizza." I set the box from Brunetti, my mother's favorite pizzeria, in the kitchen and the scent of the Italian spices took over her apartment.

A lone bottle of gin with no cap stood next to a stack of napkins and a shot glass. It appeared they'd concocted some manner of adult beverage.

"Hey, I want one of those." I studied the bottle as Aunt Trudy joined me, let me taste hers, and made another for me.

Being with them was just what I needed, having a drink, sifting through the jewelry charms as they talked. Tonight, they were all about their great aunt, Edna, trying to remember her pound cake recipe and laughing about things she used to say to them as children.

It felt good to be in a familiar place.

"What have you been up to lately?" My mother reached for a container of tiny beads. She lifted a green one with a pair of tweezers at the card table where the three of us sat.

"Yes, tell us, Claudey," Aunt Trudy chimed in. "What fun things have been happening?"

I could easily have lied about my Jamestown adventure, and my aunt would have understood I wanted to keep the details to myself, but I had no reason to hide it. I brought them both up to speed on what I'd been doing with Sydney and the concerts, and when I shared how things had played out the evening before with Cliff, it was cathartic to verbalize it all without editing parts of it the way I'd probably have to when I told Sydney.

"Mom, do you remember him?" I looked at my mother after I'd finished describing everything. "Amelia loved Cliff Wood. She had this one poster on the back of her door and—"

She cut off my sentiment before I finished. "You kids were into all sorts of things I had no idea about." Bringing up Amelia had caused her to become vacant and heartless. She stayed focused on the bracelet between her fingers as if she hadn't heard what I'd really asked, had not heard how I still thought of Amelia. It hurt enormously. Sometimes, I just wanted to talk about my sister. The fact she couldn't was painful.

Aunt Trudy glanced at me with a warm smile as if to say, *I understand.* "I remember him, Cliff Wood," she said. "He's a handsome guy. Sounds wonderful to me, Claude. I'm glad you had such a good time."

I returned to the kitchen feet away and helped myself to the pizza along with dips and pretzels the two of them had been snacking on before my arrival. Mentioning Amelia had altered the tone of the evening, and I was sorry I'd said anything about her or Cliff.

"Brownies in the oven, Claudine, and some spray cream in the fridge. There's also a tin of mint fudge in there somewhere." My mother pointed as if I wouldn't know where to go.

Joining the two of them with a full plate and a side of brownies, I stayed quiet as they fell back into family stories. My heart was still with Amelia, wishing I didn't have to keep her suppressed.

The next Cliff Wood concert Sydney and I had planned to attend was three weeks away, but since she'd missed the one in Jamestown, she didn't want to wait that long.

A text message from her came while I was sitting outside the Grace Building that Monday during lunch, happy for higher temperatures, no longer needing a coat.

Let's see the show in Maryland this weekend. You game for it?

Originally when we'd reviewed Cliff's tour schedule, she'd ruled out the location due to the venue being an outdoor amphitheater. Now she didn't care about that. She just wanted to be at a Cliff

Wood concert. Anywhere. I think she was hoping I'd encourage the idea, but I gave neutral replies.

Another message from her read, *Solomons Island sounds like a cute place. Doesn't it?* It was clear she would keep sending these texts until I said I was in. It was kind of annoying and kind of adorable at the same time. I did love Sydney for her effervescence, that sparkle that wouldn't stop—as she had no clue how to dampen it—until she had you on her side with whatever her latest plan might be.

I was about to look up the coastal Maryland town on my phone when her name popped up on the screen calling me. I had avoided talking to her the rest of the weekend. I'd spent hours in contemplation and decided to wait until I heard back about the tickets for the show with Ramsey before telling her about the whole Jamestown thing. I'd also decided what I did tell her would be an abbreviated version, and there would be no mention of the invitation for pancakes, pancakes for which I still wished I'd stayed.

"Hey, can you talk?" She sounded bright and energized when I answered.

"Yes, I'm on lunch now."

"Okay, so what we'll do is fly into D.C. and then we'll have to drive a couple of hours to Maryland. I think that would be better, you know, to stay near the venue. You won't have to miss work because we'll leave Saturday morning and come back on Sunday. The main thing we have to do is find seats to the show. I can put some feelers out and check the group online. If we don't come up with anything, we'll have to suffer it out in the general admission section."

"General admission? Is there anything else?"

"There's a VIP section up front. They cost like, three times as much, but don't worry, it'll be on me if we come up with a pair since I'm the one who's pushing us to go."

"I can pay for my own ticket and flight."

Her buying me pricey concert tickets would heighten my guilt about the whole Cliff thing. It was all getting to be a bit much, and the trips would become a burden if I didn't fund mine for myself. Thankfully, she didn't try to change my mind.

"I'll let you know what I find and send you the flight details."

On the elevator heading back to the magazine office floor, I felt unsettled. Another concert already. I would have to skip working on the project at the bookstore again on the weekend. Marlon was going to hate me. Not really, but I felt bad about it.

At the show, would Cliff recognize me? Why wouldn't he? That was a new issue to consider. It might present a problem if we got the tickets in the front section. My mind went into overdrive picturing all the possible outcomes. I tried to tell myself it didn't matter, that none of it mattered and was a much smaller issue than I was making it out to be.

In the hallway, I passed Nina as she came out of the boardroom. She was dressed in a cream pantsuit with a red scarf tied at her neck, phone to her ear, walking purposefully. I envied her focus on being so committed to the magazine's success. I wondered if I would ever feel such a clear passion toward anything and find my way to it.

Chapter 14

I'D SPENT SO MUCH TIME WORRYING OVER things with Sydney I hadn't allowed myself to enjoy thinking about the evening with Cliff.

Sitting in the bath later that night with my arms framing the tub's edges and the scent of eucalyptus taking over my bathroom, I remembered what it was like being next to him at the bar—his relaxed demeanor, no rock star bravado. Simple conversation and some laughs. It had felt natural being in the moment with him. He was so down to earth and engaged.

That was going to be the hard part to share with Sydney, describing the personal quality of it. I hoped if I got the tickets to the show with Ramsey that Sydney's excitement for going would override any misgivings. I ran a warm rag across my face and held it against my forehead as I thought about it all. Cliff hadn't mentioned how he'd get in touch with me. I wondered how I'd find out the status of the tickets.

———

In D.C., Sydney and I arrived to overcast skies and a twenty-percent threat of rain at Dulles airport.

One of Sydney's reasons for avoiding outdoor shows was that she enjoyed getting dressed up for Cliff's performances, and bad weather could hinder that fun. She'd insisted we wear mini-skirts and midriff tops to the concert, an eighties throwback motif she'd picked up for us at a vintage boutique in Soho. I felt I'd look ridiculous in such a getup and brought an alternate outfit. She impressed me when she didn't let the weather issue bother her although she suggested we find a place to buy some ponchos along the way.

We'd taken the earliest flight and were in a rented Chrysler Sebring riding along with sodas and a giant bag of chips as *Atlantic Memory*, Cliff's second to the latest album, played at a low volume from Sydney's phone. It was an apropos choice given we were crossing waterways leading us to Solomons Island, and the song was about a trip over sea to find an old flame. I had listened to the album one evening while cleaning my apartment right after Sydney and I met.

She sang along with every song while I happily looked out the window, cars whipping by in a blur.

I appreciated she didn't hound me to join in. I liked paying attention to the lyrics, thinking how in some way I now knew the person singing and imagined Cliff in thought as he crafted them.

"Did you have enough to eat on the drive? Maybe we should wait to get food until after the concert. We could just have a quick snack beforehand." Sydney stood arms akimbo between the beds in the hotel. We had checked in, and she was now acting as concert director, planning our every move as she always did.

"That's fine with me."

She began to rummage through her suitcase. "I'm so happy we're here! All week I've been upset about missing the concert in Jamestown. I wish we could have a do-over, but I'm glad we made it to this one together."

"Me, too." Though being in Jamestown would have been a memorable time with her and Paige and whatever mischief we'd have gotten into, I wouldn't change how it had all turned out.

I walked into the bathroom to assess my hair and decide whether I wanted to take the time to wash and style it. Already disheveled from sleeping on it the night before, it had been made worse on the plane when I'd napped.

"Do you ever feel like you're in love with him?" Sydney called out.

What? My brain screamed inside my head. *Where did that question come from?* I swallowed hard at her non sequitur, glad I had left the room, my reaction hidden.

"In love with him? I don't even know him." *Yikes. Why did I have to say that?*

She moved to the doorway of the bathroom and leaned against one side of the frame. The two of us were visible in the wide mirror. We looked like such a mismatched pair with the disparity of our height.

"You know, not really *in love* with him, but in love with seeing him perform and the feeling you get when you're watching him?" She looked at me in the mirror.

It sounded like such an off the-wall topic, but I knew she meant it in a serious way. She hovered next to me while I continued pondering. I felt I was taking too long to answer her, so I went with, "No, not really." But I knew what she meant, at least as far as the feeling part went, except my perspective was based on talking to him more than it was seeing him perform, and I couldn't discuss that with her. I wished I could tell her about Jamestown right then and get it over with.

I decided my hair would be good enough for an outdoor show, but I could use a shower to wash away my guilt. I stepped into the tepid spray of water which felt soothing but did nothing to help my contrition. When I finished, Sydney had set out the outfits she'd brought for us on the two beds.

"I hope it's not too cold for these. I checked the high. It's supposed to be about seventy." She held up one of the miniskirts. "Your legs are going to look insane in this!"

"Sydney, really. I'm thirty-five years old."

"So. I'm forty." She shrugged. "It's a concert. Spring is here. It'll be fun to do something different." She sat down on the bed by the window. "I haven't even told you about the tickets we scored. You'll never believe it. We're in the VIP section!"

Oh no, I said inside my head. *No.* And then to her, "How much do I owe you?"

She didn't seem to notice my reaction had been less than enthusiastic. "We'll figure it out later. You rented the car and bought our snacks."

I rather enjoyed Sydney's insistence in wanting the best for Cliff's shows, but I still had the whole Jamestown thing hanging out there. Being up front for the concert at hand might present a problem. But I'd have to go with it.

A poncho over a midriff shirt ruins the whole look of an ensemble, I can tell you. The top was the one thing I'd agreed to. It was cute with white and horizontal black stripes and fitted sleeves to the elbow. If I'd had anything substantial to eat before the show, I wouldn't have been able to pull it off though. The slightest tummy pooch would have ruined the cute factor. When I said I was wearing it with my jeans and not the miniskirt, Sydney made a pouty face but didn't push me.

We decided to get drinks before the concert and found a lounge in the hotel lobby already swarming with fans. Sydney was ready to make her rounds as soon as we got there.

"Would you order a beer for me? If you'll buy, I'll grab the next ones." Then after only taking a few steps, she turned back saying, "I see Alternative Kyle. That's a really good sign!"

Maybe to her.

I knew seeing Alternative Kyle meant Cliff was likely staying in the hotel, too. I'd learned a lot the last few months. I didn't share her enthusiasm, I couldn't. I worried we'd run into Cliff, and he'd acknowledge me by name. My worry over that happening put a crimp in the pre-show fun for me. I was already concerned that any direct interaction from Cliff during the concert might seem odd to Sydney.

The hotel had a rustic look to it with exposed wood beams framing a high ceiling giving the space an open effect. I edged into the crowd at the end of the bar in my midriff and requested Sydney's beer and a screwdriver for me.

A few minutes later, she returned and picked up the beer and took a swallow. "I saw Suede. That's another good sign."

The night in Vegas when we'd tried to sing to Suede for his birthday popped into my mind. That really had been fun, how we'd presented the birthday pie.

Sydney looked distressed. "If we don't see Bruce though, Cliff likely isn't here." She swallowed more beer. "We should leave soon and get into our seats. The general admission crowds can be a little on the crazy side. People will try to come over the boundary rope."

We stayed at the bar until we finished our drinks. Then Sydney veered into the gift shop for some gum. That was when I saw Suede myself. He wore an ill-fitting faded t-shirt with the words *Right Left Right* on it, sunglasses, and jeans. He was talking to Evvi and another girl I'd seen a few times but hadn't met. I only realized who it was when he removed the sunglasses to rub his eyes. Then I heard Evvi ask him, "So where's Cliff?"

Suede shook his head and let out a grunt. "Cliff, shoot. I have no idea. He's not even staying here." I was happy to hear this and felt the tension fall from my shoulders. One less thing to worry about.

"Claudine, let's go." Sydney was already chewing her cinnamon gum and motioning me to head outside and make our way to the amphitheater in walking distance.

It began to sprinkle on the way, and out came the ponchos. So stylish. We'd already accepted we might end up in the rain, so we didn't complain as we put them over our fun outfits.

There were only three rows of reserved seats, and those were the closest to the stage. Sydney explained some of them were used for radio station giveaways and guests of the show's sponsors.

She was right about the madness of the general admission setup. People had circumvented security and had already commandeered our seats. Fortunately, we didn't have any trouble from them when we asked them to move out of our spots which were second row, a few seats to the left of Cliff's microphone.

A disc jockey from the radio station arrived taking center stage to thank everyone for coming and plug the sponsors, a local bank and an energy drink. As soon as he was finished, Cliff's familiar entrance music began, and he sauntered into view to start the concert, legs apart, his blue guitar suspended below his waist. The audience collectively rose to their feet and bellowed cheers of excitement while Sydney, as always, turned into a screaming fourteen-year-old. It was true—Cliff had an immediate magnetic quality. He owned the microphone, the stage, the whole scene. He was a thing of beauty and magic to watch.

I had never felt the same level of elation Sydney did for Cliff at these events, but having more insight into him from my evening spent talking to him in

Jamestown, I had a new appreciation for the rush of joy over his presence, the electricity emanating from his performance, and the way the music folded into it. As I observed it all now, it made sense to me, how Sydney wanted to experience it again and again.

Halfway through the show, Cliff stood in front of his monitor, abandoning his guitar as he revved the audience to participate in a song with the lyric, *We're on fire, fire tonight.* He had the audience repeat the lyric and then playfully commanded them to sing louder each time. It was a fun way of connecting with everyone. Then suddenly, he pointed at me.

"Yeah, you got it. Let's sing it. One more time." He said the words to the beat of the song all the while with the most captivating smile I'd ever seen from him.

Heat washed over my face.

"Did you see that? Did you see that look from him?" Sydney put her hand over heart. "Oh, I'm going to pass out!"

I didn't correct her that I had been the object of his attention. I was actually glad she thought otherwise. But as I nodded my head with the music, I felt a secret satisfying note of glee that Cliff had acknowledged me from the stage. And no harm had come from it.

It rained in the middle of the show, but not too hard and not for long but enough to ruin both our

CHAPTER 14

hair. Sydney could run her fingers through hers with her choppy style and fluff the wispy pieces at her neck, and she'd have a purposeful tousled look.

My hair, on the other hand, separated into sections that looked like the beginnings of dreadlocks. I shook my head, resigned to it, as I viewed myself in a purse mirror. It wasn't worth worrying over.

At least I thought so momentarily.

"I have a surprise!" Sydney grabbed me by the hand at the end of the show and shuttled me away from the seating section, pulling me along like a kid leading mama to the candy aisle. When we were away from the fray of crowd, she looked up at me, her eyes gleaming with delight. "Are you ready? Our tickets include a meet and greet. We're going backstage!"

I nearly fainted. "What?"

"That's why they cost so much because you get to take a picture with Cliff. I was hoping you wouldn't figure that out. It's also why I wanted us to have great outfits." She looked so happy with herself. She ran her fingers through her dark, wet hair once more. It looked cuter each time she did it. And me with my dreadlocks.

"I look terrible though."

"You're fine. We both are. He was in the rain, too. Of course, *he'll* get to spruce up first, but at least he'll understand why we look like this. You're going to your first Cliff Wood meet and greet!"

Sydney beamed. I felt nauseated. This really could get awkward and might even lead to Sydney believing I had been dishonest with her. I hadn't, not really. I just needed to know about those tickets Cliff had offered and the right moment to tell her.

She navigated us through the remaining crowd with her small hand in mine, and we got rid of the ponchos. When we reached the side of the amphitheater, a security guard checked our tickets to be sure they read VIP before letting us through.

My jaw tightened. "I kind of don't feel good."

"Really?"

"Maybe it's from not eating." I touched my stomach for effect.

"We'll get you something soon. It's just a quick picture. These things go fast. You'll barely even get to say hi to him."

She was right, it was all happening fast. Too fast for me to think of a way out. But I hadn't thought about this giving me an opportunity to talk to him. Maybe I could ask about the Ramsey concert tickets sub rosa.

The line was moving and soon we were behind the stage in a makeshift room with what looked like a curtain with the sponsoring radio station's logo printed on it. Various people stood about presumably assisting in some way. A stout man with a Brillo pad for hair barked to keep things moving even though no one was hesitating. They all couldn't wait for their ten seconds with Cliff Wood.

"Oh my gosh, he's right there!" Sydney's enchantment for Cliff never waned.

I looked to where Cliff stood by the backdrop wearing a clean white t-shirt with a grey vest and dark blue jeans. He did look good, very good, refreshed even. It seemed unbelievable this was a guy in his sixties who'd just finished playing an eighteen-song concert with multiple guitar solos. We should all be so lucky with age.

With a casual smile and a relaxed demeanor, he gave each person some minor attention making them feel special. I saw one girl walk away with tears in her eyes. I wondered what he thought about that.

"Are you excited?" Sydney reached up and tried to improve my hair. It was beyond help. Before I answered she added, "Don't worry. He's super nice to his fans."

He is super nice, I thought.

Within a few minutes, it was Sydney's turn. As she scooted toward Cliff, he looked above her at me, and his smile brightened. That was when my genuine fear kicked in, that he might say something to me, something that would expose my night with him in Jamestown to Sydney.

As she fastened her arm around his waist for the photo, I knew I had to duck out. Backing away, I motored to the end of the line and beyond and found a table of sub sandwiches wrapped in cellophane along with some condiment packages and a picked-over bowl of plain potato chips. I busied myself there snacking. Away from Cliff.

A minute later, Sydney returned. She joined me by the table, her face framed in worry. "What happened? Why'd you leave?"

I unwrapped one of the sandwiches. I truly was hungry but not to the point of being sick to my stomach. I stuck to my original story. "The nausea suddenly hit me."

"I'm sorry, Claudine. Are you okay?"

She had genuine concern in her eyes. I immediately felt bad I'd detracted from her enjoyment. "This sandwich will help." I took a bite.

"I think it's probably your excitement to meet him. Talking to him can be unnerving. Do you want to get back in line and try again?"

I was about to offer a new excuse that my hair looked too bad when she added, "I'll wait for you here. I don't think they'll let me back in. They stamped my ticket." She held it out to show me.

That certainly helped. She wouldn't witness my exchange with him. And I knew I'd feel bad later if didn't go. She would want to reminisce about all that happened which would include reviewing how I'd abandoned what she felt was my big moment of formally meeting her idol. I needed to salvage the situation.

"I'm starting to feel better now."

"So you'll go and try again?"

I set down the sandwich. "Here goes! I'm going to meet Cliff Wood!" Geez, my acting was terrible. I sounded ridiculous, but she beamed and even clapped.

When I returned to the line it had dwindled to a handful of people. She was right, it wasn't so much a meet and greet as a hi and bye, like the British queen receiving a bevy of guests she doesn't know.

The whole event had taken only twenty minutes. Gone in a blur. There were just three others ahead of me, and things were winding to a close.

"Look who's here." Cliff's arm was outstretched as I moved over to him.

A wave of anxiety rushed through me. Despite the fact I'd spent time with him so casually at the bar in Jamestown, I felt nervous in his presence. Right now, he was *rock star* Cliff.

To ease my discomfort, I pointed to my hair. "My stylist was off tonight."

"Nice crop top." We both laughed. He pulled me closer to him. The pressure of his arm felt warm and relaxing.

A bearded photographer snapped a shot of us and then checked the camera's display. "That's a good one!"

He was right. It was perfect, both of us with smiles that looked like we were longtime friends.

I'd end up carrying a print of it in my wallet for years.

As I headed back to find Sydney, I realized I'd forgotten to ask about the tickets, but I was happy about my little moment with Cliff, and there was nothing about it I'd have to conceal from Sydney.

When we were back inside the hotel, it was nice not to feel tense. Thanks to Evvi's forward behavior earlier when she'd talked to Suede, I knew Cliff wouldn't be there which left Sydney and me free to enjoy being in the bar instead of being on alert waiting for his arrival. I'd told Sydney about Evvi and Suede's conversation as we walked back after the concert. "Figures," was Sydney's reply.

After we put in an order for a couple of appetizers, I left Sydney so I could wash my hands before the food arrived. I also wanted to take another crack at repairing my hair. I knew Sydney would want to get some selfies to commemorate the trip.

"Are you Claudine?"

Out of nowhere, a man stopped me before I reached the bathroom. He was good-looking, in his late forties, with brown neatly combed hair.

I nodded with suspicion.

"I'm Thomas Yale. I work for Mr. Wood. He wants you to have dinner with him tonight." He spoke as though he were arranging a covert meeting with a top government official.

Behind me I looked for Sydney and was thankful to see she was surrounded by a group of other fans in rapt conversation. "Is he here?"

Thomas Yale didn't answer my question and repeated himself instead. "He'd like to have dinner with you."

"I can't do that. I'm here with a friend."

He looked surprised. "Your friend wouldn't want to have dinner with Cliff Wood?"

There was no way. Not unless I explained the whole Jamestown evening to Sydney, and that was going to have to be a delicate, perfectly orchestrated conversation when it happened. Now wasn't the time. "I'm sure she would, but we're not even staying in this hotel, and we've got an early flight tomorrow." Neither of those things were true, but I needed an out, a quick one.

I couldn't believe how direct I sounded in my response to him, probably out of fear of Sydney seeing us talking. She would have absolutely died if she'd known I had just turned down such an opportunity.

Thomas Yale started to walk away and then turned around. "May I have your phone number?"

"For what?"

"Because if Mr. Wood asks for it, I want to be prepared."

I said my number to him, watching as he tapped it into his phone, and then glanced back to be sure of Sydney's continued distraction. "Um, could I ask you something about tickets?"

He shook his head, his expression flat. "I handle a lot of things for Mr. Wood but not tickets. Have a good night."

Chapter 15

OUR FLIGHT THE NEXT MORNING HAD US IN back in New York by midday. I unpacked and then sat on the stoop of my apartment with a canned drink and an Elizabeth Berg novel I'd started reading earlier in the week. It felt good to be outside, but I couldn't concentrate on the story. I wasn't sure how much longer I would be able to keep such a big secret from Sydney.

I was starting to regret it more that I hadn't already told her about being with Cliff after the concert in Jamestown. I didn't know how to follow up about the tickets he'd offered which were supposed to be my saving grace with her. I had also rejected the opportunity for us to have dinner with him, an event that would likely have erased any misgivings from her about my experience with him as well as my delay in telling her. What could I do about it all now?

It seemed I was becoming a master of missed opportunities lately.

I thought about reaching out to Paige to see if she knew a way to get in touch with Bruce but quickly decided against it. Being so direct with a musician's management might be bad protocol. That was just the kind of thing I could picture Sydney saying. And then I'd also have to explain to Paige why I wanted to talk to him. Would she tell Sydney? The more I thought about things, the worse I felt.

That's the great thing about the city. You can always take a walk anywhere, anytime, and clear your mind.

I set the book inside on the couch for later, slid into a pair of Adidas, and made off into my neighborhood. I could always count on it to give me a reprieve from deleterious lines of thinking. That was one piece of my life I greatly enjoyed, my apartment on Charles Street. It was right in the thick of the Village and even close to water. A fifteen-minute walk could put me in view of the Hudson River at the park.

On this day, the usually energetic vibe dominating the streets had a lazy quality to it though there were still plenty of afternoon strollers. A mosaic of conversations fluttered around me with the occasional bark of a dog as I roamed. A few hours had passed since Sydney and I had gotten into our separate taxis at the airport, and now would normally be a time when I would shoot her a text to say thanks for including me on the concert excursion. But we were beyond that; it was standard practice for me to join her now. I was glad it would be a couple of weeks before our next outing.

Drifting along, I passed a record store spinning the sounds of an old Rod Stewart album, a tattoo shop, and a massage salon where an Asian woman beckoned me inside. I hadn't eaten lunch and stopped for a sandwich at the deli I came to next—cucumber with hummus on ciabatta bread, lots of pepper. It made me feel better as soon as I took a bite. The subtle taste of the cucumber against the tangy spray of spiciness hit the spot. Amelia would always comment it was an odd flavor combination. What was her favorite sandwich?

I couldn't think of it, maybe never knew. Maybe she didn't have one. I bit my lip the way I often did when nervous or thinking too hard about something insignificant.

Eventually I circled back to waft along Seventh, then down Waverly Place until I found myself in Washington Square Park. The sun presented its full set of rays through the trees with leaves in full, colorful bloom as skyscrapers murmured in the distance.

I claimed a bench across from the fountain amid passing strangers' tidbits of conversation. Some NYU students passed by talking about a party they were planning.

Satiated from the sandwich interlude and comforted by the open space, I gave myself permission not to worry about anything further with Sydney. Or Cliff. There was no point in continuing to badger myself about something I couldn't solve right now. I drew in a deep breath and let it out. Maybe I'd find a way to talk to him for a minute at the next concert. Until then I'd let things be. It was best for my distressed psyche. That much I knew.

At the magazine, we were finalizing things for the June issue, two months away. Each day, I received a full to-do list from Nina. I was happy to tackle it. It kept me from thinking too hard. By midweek, it was time for a department meeting to be sure all was on track. No one enjoyed these assemblies. They were filled with intense discussion about the details needed to bring the magazine to a close, and it was easy to see who'd dropped the ball if something weren't ready. For me, it was little more than a big note-taking session.

"Good morning." Nina settled into her chair and opened her laptop.

It was half past eight. Paper cups filled with coffee blends lined the interior of the meeting table like an airway strip, making the room smell like an over-zealous café. Everyone needed their caffeine pick-me-up, including me. I'd gotten mine at the coffee shop I passed every day heading to the subway.

Nina took the lid off her latte to let it cool. "Let's start with photos. Any outstanding ones?"

CHAPTER 15

"Everything has been submitted for approval." The answer came from the opposite end of the table. "Except we're missing a shot for the new rum account. They updated their advertising materials and want the new look in the ad."

"Seriously?" Nina tilted her head, looking above her glasses. "We don't have time for that. That model they used is booked for months. Have them send us a graphic, and we'll alter the photo." She shook her head and adjusted her glasses.

I jotted a note to send a follow-up email and copy Nina, then made another note for myself to check with her later and see if she could talk to me about the latest draft I'd sent to her for my article. If it needed major revisions, I wanted to have enough time to sort them out. I knew she had a lot on her plate.

When I finished writing, my phone lit up with a text message:

Want to visit a museum today? What's your favorite?

At first I thought it was from Aunt Trudy. She adored spontaneity and knew I could find ways to sneak away from work. The last time, she had shown up in the lobby wanting to get street vendor pretzels, and we not only did that but also poked around in a sample sale.

I ignored the text and scribbled another reminder for Nina. The meeting had only been in motion for half an hour, and I'd already filled a page with to-do items. June was a big issue that highlighted all the fun summer dresses and skin products. And apparently new brands of rum.

Nina took a sip of her coffee while she studied the agenda on her computer. The delay gave me time to glance at my phone again and type a short reply. Another text had already come through.

Or we could meet for pancakes.

It wasn't Aunt Trudy.

I slowly turned the phone face-down as if I'd received a lascivious communication.

It may be hard to believe, but when the Thomas Yale person asked for my phone number at the hotel, I didn't think about the prospect of Cliff himself contacting me. At the time, I'd just wanted the guy to go away before Sydney saw me talking to him. Now, an assortment of answers to the current text skipped around in my head making it hard to focus on what Nina was saying. I flipped the phone back over and wrote *I'm in a meeting*. It was the quickest thing to say.

Normally, I didn't pay attention to the clock in these monthly rundowns. They were essential for getting the magazine issue completed so the time spent was moot. Now, all I could think about was replying again to the text and how soon Nina would get through the agenda.

Clearly, the message was from Cliff. How did I get here where a rock star was sending me text messages? I pictured Sydney in the bookstore that afternoon when we'd first met. It seemed like only yesterday, but several months had passed. Cliff Wood had my phone number. And was using it. I wished there were someone nearby I could tell about it.

"Does anyone have a bottle of water I can have?" Nina patted her chest. "My throat is dry." When no one responded, she looked at me. "Claudine, I hate to ask, but would you mind getting one for me?"

Her timing was perfect. The break room was only steps away, but I made a path to her office instead on the other side of the suite passing several interns on my way. She kept her own stash of a brand I knew she'd want. I typed a reply to Cliff as I walked: *At work. I can't leave right now.*

I stopped where I was and waited to see what he might say. No immediate reply. Had I written the wrong thing? What should I have said? My answer had probably come across terse. But it had been the pressure of the moment. I didn't have time to formulate something better.

In Nina's office, I searched inside the burgundy credenza behind her desk where an assortment of water and diet sodas stood at attention in tidy rows. I grabbed the first bottle and began retracing my steps back to the meeting. As I gripped the door handle to go inside, my phone buzzed, long and insistent, the pattern of an incoming call.

It startled me. I drew in a quick breath as I looked at the number. Stepping away from the door, I put the phone to my ear. "Hello?"

"Hey. It's Cliff." His voice was friendly and casual. It sounded so nice.

Still, I felt nervous talking to him. "Hi. Sorry my reply was abrupt."

"It was fine. I know this is short notice, but I'm in the city today, and uh, wondered if you wanted to do something, maybe go to a museum."

"*New York* City?"

He laughed. "Yes, that city."

I paused thinking how strange it felt to be talking to him in this fashion as though he called me all the time. "I'm not sure if I can. There's a lot happening at work." Both were true statements, but I already knew I was going to figure out how to get away. Who wouldn't?

Through the phone, I heard a car door shut in the background against the sounds of traffic and the ubiquitous horns. I pictured Cliff standing next to a black car with tinted windows and the backdrop of concrete and steel towering around him.

"I'll be done around two. You have my number now. If you can join me, let me know. You can call or text me." He didn't say goodbye, and I stood there bewildered for a moment before heading back into the conference room and setting Nina's water before her.

CHAPTER 15

I thought I did well being able to concentrate for the rest of the meeting considering I was mentally planning my getaway to meet Cliff. I had a giddy sensation about seeing him, mixed with uncertainty about why I felt that way. That was the thing. I didn't know what to think. I was thirty-five, feeling fifteen.

When Nina asked me to get an intern to order lunch for everyone, I told her I'd need to leave by 1:30 to take care of something personal. Was it personal? I didn't really know what to call it.

She seemed taken aback and looked at me perplexed. It was clear she wasn't happy about it given how busy and deadline-crazy we all were.

She shook her head, giving in. "Well, that's fine. We've gotten through most of the big items."

I told her I would take it as vacation time as if that would lighten the suddenness of my departure. I had nothing to feel bad about, except that I was adding to the secret I was still holding from Sydney. I was apparently okay with that.

Chapter 16

NEW YORK CITY BOASTS 144 MUSEUMS spread throughout the five boroughs if you count places like The Seguine Mansion and The Grolier Club. If you don't, the number is eighty-three. I've been to maybe eight of them.

When I sent Cliff a text to tell him I'd be leaving the office soon to meet him and asking what kind of museum he wanted to visit, he replied, "One with a restaurant."

I was never much of a museum person. I have no artistic eye, and most of my cultural experiences in the city had been a case of it being someone else who'd wanted to go, same as now.

But when Cliff mentioned the restaurant part, I knew just the one. We'd had the magazine's Christmas party there the year before, and while the place would offer interesting exhibitions to peruse, its restaurant on the ninth floor overlooked Columbus Circle and Central Park. So if I got keyed up, I could just look over and say, "What a great view." Then we could stare at the scenery until the moment passed.

A taxi driver with an Italian accent did his best to bolt up 8th Avenue amid the traffic to get me to the Museum of Art and Design. When we slowed to a stop on 58th where I exited the car, I spotted Cliff standing on the curb with a hand in one pocket outside the geometric building and studying the surrounding structures like a tourist.

Even though it was warm outside, he wore a dark blue lightweight crew-neck sweater, the sleeves pushed up, jeans, and black sneakers. I'd never seen him wear any shoes other than the boots that were part of his concert wardrobe. He looked out of context with no guitar, no stage, no lights streaming down on him. Even if someone didn't recognize him as the famous rock star he was, there was an enticing quality about his look that would make you do a double-take, and if you couldn't place him, you knew he was probably a celebrity.

When he heard my footsteps, he turned around and considered me. "It's good to see you again."

His smile took my breath away, and I saw my embarrassment reflected in his aviator sunglasses.

"Hi, you, too."

He removed the shades. "You found a way out of your meeting I take it?" His eyes locked on mine almost putting me off balance.

"It was already over for the most part."

We walked the rest of the way without talking until we were inside the building. It was good to have a moment to get my head straight. As we waited behind others in line for tickets, he reached into his wallet for a credit card. It was a normal thing but seemed so odd for someone in his position to do.

A minute or so later, a college-aged cashier took his card from him. I watched for her to react to his identity, if not from his looks then from the name on his card, but she simply smiled and explained the current exhibitions as she handed him a brochure. When he fumbled putting the card back in place, I saw it read *C.L. Wood*. A shrewd decoy. I wondered if his full name would have rung a bell for her. I had noticed a contingent of younger fans at some of his concerts, but this young cashier clearly wasn't one of them.

"Thanks for getting mine." I sounded so meek.

He didn't say anything, but I felt he'd heard me. He handed me the brochure, and I flipped through it as we made a path for the elevator. Stopping short of pressing the call button, I turned to look at him. "Did you want to eat first?"

"What about you? You hungry?"

I was and I wasn't. I had only grazed on the lunch items delivered to the meeting. I'd been too anxious about the impending rendezvous, and the feeling still hadn't fully subsided. Maybe a bite of food would help. How long was it appropriate to wait before I asked about the tickets he'd offered?

When the elevator doors opened, a well-groomed man wearing an expensive sport coat and a woman in a leopard print dress with a wide belt—presumably his wife—joined us as we stepped inside. Cliff moved to the back while the woman and I both reached for the button to the ninth floor. Our hands clashed, and we pulled back.

She laughed as she lowered her hand. "Are you two heading up to Robert?"

I knew she meant the name of the restaurant. I exchanged smiles with her. "Yes."

"Oh, it's such a great place, isn't it? Ken and I try to come once a month. It's a standing date. I also like their jazzy martini selection."

"Hope they have pie." That was Cliff's contribution as he stood with arms folded next to me.

The doors opened, and we all trailed out, Ken and his maybe-wife going first and then Cliff and me. We were rounding the corner toward the maître d' when the woman stopped and faced Cliff. Her body language was formal as if she were about to make a public speech. She moved a notch toward him, and I suspected he knew what was coming.

"*Bright Lights* is one of my all-time favorite albums. And I've listened to the song 'Lonely Friend' more times than I can count." She put her hand over her chest as she finished. "And you look fantastic. Continued success to you."

Cliff responded with a polite nod followed by a quiet "Thank you."

"Enjoy your afternoon." She smiled at him as she walked away.

———

In the dining room, scents of lavish ingredients filled the air. Cliff sat across from me, a look of relaxation on his otherwise chiseled face. I wondered what he thought about the woman's declaration. He didn't comment on it, the same as he hadn't the night the two girls had approached him for a photo at the bar in Jamestown. He kept his ego in check if he even had one. I couldn't have put my finger on the concept right then, but his humility was a factor in what attracted so many to him both when on stage or off, for me included.

Being that it was past the lunchtime rush, only a few guests shared the room, and it felt as though we had the place to ourselves. We had been given a table with a marathon view of both the city and verdant plants of Central Park. I looked at the expansive layout of it and forced myself to start a conversation with the rock star before me. It was too early to use the "what a view" line.

"So, why are you here?" I placed a napkin in my lap and tried to survey the menu, a means to manage my nerves. It was hard to believe I was with him and alone again.

"I had a meeting with my publisher." Cliff withdrew a pair of glasses and put them in place. On most people, glasses age them, but on him they added a studious tone to his features making him even more handsome.

How exciting that sounded to me, the idea of meeting with a book publisher. I wanted to ask him a hundred questions about it. "How did it go?"

"I have a first draft for something I want to try, and there was some discussion about it."

As soon as he said the word draft, I clamped my hand over my forehead, my face contorting as I realized I hadn't mentioned *my* draft to Nina. I knew I had forgotten something earlier.

Cliff raised his eyebrow and scowled playfully at me. "You okay?"

"I remembered something I meant to do at work."

"Need to call someone?"

"No, it's okay."

I felt frustrated with myself for shirking something important to sneak away for this outing that was mainly about squaring things away so I could confess to Sydney about Cliff. Regardless, there was no way I'd have missed the opportunity to talk with him again.

A waitress arrived. She had an old-fashioned vibe about her like she'd been working in restaurants for years and could do the job without thinking too hard about it.

"Welcome to Robert. I'm Freda. How are we doing? I can bring you some water while you make a decision about your order."

Cliff set his glasses aside. "I'm ready. I'll have the crab cakes." Then he looked at me expectantly. "Wanna share?"

"Sure, that's fine."

"We'll have some fries, too."

"Got it. Fries. Anything else?" Freda held her pen in mid-air.

Cliff pushed his menu toward the edge of the table. "And some pie. Any kind except cherry. Surprise us."

Out came the electric smile of his, and Freda blushed. I wondered if she'd be sharing her favorite album of his, too, or perhaps asking him for an autograph later.

After she left, Cliff adjusted his watch and considered me. "Thanks for coming. I wasn't sure if you would."

"Why?"

The edges of his lips curled faintly, a timid expression in his eyes. "You barely talked to me at the meet and greet in Maryland. And you turned down my dinner invitation afterward."

I looked at my lap and toyed with the napkin. "It wasn't because of you." Now I felt timid. "My best friend was there. She was one who didn't make it to the other show. She sprung the whole thing on me with the meet and greet. She's a really big fan."

"You're not a fan?" The shyness in his eyes was now replaced with curious delight.

"Well, not like that. She's the kind who has all your albums, even the special editions, knows the words to your songs, reads everything out there about you. My sister could be like that some-times. She—"

"You have a sister?"

I was glad he cut me off. It was a stream of con-sciousness that made me bring her up. I wouldn't have done so otherwise. I nodded.

"What's her name?"

"Amelia."

"Older or younger?"

"Older."

I wanted to say something about him having a sis-ter, too, but then it would have only been fair to tell him Amelia died, and we'd inevitably have to talk about how we'd lost each of them. It made me un-comfortable. I was used to sidestepping these kinds of conversations, but right now it was harder to do.

In my mind, I imagined Amelia sitting on the blue shag carpet in our bedroom with a giant poster of Cliff taped to the back of the door nearby. I'd seen it so many times. Cliff's hair was complete-ly dark back then. He wore white jeans, a black sleeveless t-shirt, and his fingers tightly gripped his guitar. He stared into the camera, brooding and sexy, the epitome of youth and rock and roll. Now his features had been massaged by time with a layer of reserved wisdom part of his visual landscape. He was more attractive at this stage of his life to me. I hadn't thought about it until now.

I realized I was staring at him with too much scrutiny as all these things swum around in my head. "But, my friend, Sydney, she—"

"I offered you some concerts tickets for you and her."

It was good he cut me off again. Besides the downpour of thoughts about Amelia, I was trying to find a way to describe the complexity between my spending time with him and the Sydney aspect of it. It would have been too weird for him to under-stand all the nuances of the relationship between fans and the fan ethos. Thankfully I didn't have to explain any of it. His bringing up the tickets was a useful non sequitur.

"You still want to go to the one with my daughter?" He took a sip of his water.

I nodded. "That one is important to my friend."

"Need to talk to Ramsey about it. It's really her show."

"It is? I thought she was joining you to do a few songs or something." At least that's what Sydney thought.

Cliff circled a finger counterclockwise in the air. "It's the other way around. I'll do a song or two. A duet. The rest will be her stuff."

"My friend said she's talented."

"She is. She's a good songwriter." The look of a proud father took over for a moment, and then, "What about Amelia? You want a ticket for her, too?"

It felt so weird hearing him say Amelia's name as though she were someone he knew. I had to swallow before I could answer. I looked toward the tree-filled park. "She wouldn't be able to come."

I thought I might start crying. It was a sensation I had mastered suppressing or thought I had.

Freda saved me, arriving with the French fries resting on a red platter. She described the pie she had in mind for later, giving me the break I needed to compose myself. When Cliff reacted with a smack of his lips at the thought of the impending dessert, I genuinely laughed.

"I got a Jenny Diski book." He picked up one of the fries and bit half of it.

"Yeah, which one?" I picked up a fry too except I put the whole thing in my mouth.

"*Stranger on a Train.*"

"Oh, you'll like it," I said between chewing. "It has a Sylvia Plath vibe to it."

Freda delivered the crab cakes and asked if we needed anything else.

Cliff slid a crab cake onto his plate and one onto mine as well. "I already do. I like the introspective feel to her writing."

"I think that's why I like her. I can be pretty introspective, too."

He speared a bite of crab cake, and his eyes met mine. "I already know that about you."

When it was time for the pie, he insisted we each get our own slice, saying he wouldn't share; but we both ended up eating his piece, pushing the plate back and forth between us like it was something we had done together many times.

I took my slice home at his suggestion. I'd carried it around in an elegant bag from Robert later as we browsed one of several exhibitions in the museum, a display of 1940s art jewelry.

"I'll check on the tickets for the show, but don't worry."

Those were his parting words to me after we'd had our fill of museum meandering and exited the building. Manhattan's noise returned in surround sound.

He had said what I needed to hear. No more clandestine meetings with a rock star. I could tell Sydney about everything.

Chapter 17

ON THE WALK ACROSS COLUMBUS CIRCLE going to the subway entrance, I felt such relief. I could give Sydney the good news about us getting to see Ramsey's performance, and moreover, let her in on the way it had come about. I had planned what I would say in my head—that I'd hung out with Cliff in Jamestown by accident, how he'd felt bad about us missing his concert, and he wanted to make up for it with tickets to another show. It felt easy enough. I dialed her as I walked.

"What's going on? Are you okay?" Sydney sounded out of breath when she answered.

"I'm fine."

A song I couldn't place but with a familiar melody pulsed in the background. I pictured her wearing her Cliff Wood t-shirt with a close-up of his face on the front. She'd slept in it on our Vegas trip.

"Sorry it took me so many rings to answer. I couldn't find my phone. It was in a drawer! My bestie is here from Boston. We went shopping, and now we're having margaritas!"

Bestie? I was standing next to a street vendor and smushed the money I'd taken out for some candied walnuts back into the side of my purse. "Boston?"

"That's where I grew up, remember? Her name's Natasha. I dragged my crate of vinyl out of the closet. We're having an eighties music marathon. Except no Cliff stuff. She's not into him." She said the last part in a stage whisper with a laugh. I could tell she'd had a couple of drinks even if she hadn't mentioned the margaritas to me. "But we do need to talk soon about the Portland concert."

"When is that?"

"It's the weekend after this one. I'll email you the flight information and everything."

That was good news. I'd have a weekend in between, giving me time to work on my project at the bookstore and maybe shop with Aunt Trudy. I owed her an outing.

I started toward the subway entrance again, dodging a gaggle of teen girls taking selfies. I decided it would be best to wait until Cliff gave me a definitive confirmation about the tickets for Ramsey's show. Then I'd fill Sydney in. The timing wasn't good right now anyway while Sydney was busy with Natasha.

While I thought about my line of dilatory reasoning, Sydney chimed back in. "Your picture from the Maryland meet and greet is good. Did you see it? It's on the venue's website."

I had forgotten all about it and hated to say so. The meet and greet had been such a stressful event with my uncertainty about how Cliff would react to me in front of Sydney. Now I wanted to see the photo as soon as possible. That would be my first task as soon as I got home. It was strange to think how only moments ago I'd been roaming around a museum with him.

Sydney jumped back in, "Our pizza order just got here. What were you calling about?"

"I, uh, wasn't sure about Cliff and the Portland show and all."

That was completely true. I knew we had a concert soon but not the date, and I definitely wasn't sure about Cliff and how I had ended up with him on a Wednesday afternoon discussing art nouveau pendants in between the literary accomplishments of Graham Greene and Carol Shields. Had Sydney not been buzzed, she'd have realized she had brought up Portland not me and may also have been able to detect the anxiety in my voice.

For much of the call, she'd a been whispering innocuously to Natasha. *Can you turn it down a little?... Just two minutes... There's some cash on the desk.* Her distraction had worked to my advantage.

On the subway ride back to the Village, I played through the time I'd spent with Cliff, how we'd moseyed about the museum as though we'd been on similar outings together. At one point, I'd studied him thinking how familiar he felt to me, his look, his voice, while at the same time acknowledging I didn't really *know* him. To be fair, he was a stranger, someone I'd watched sing and perform on stage. Now I was getting to see the person he was outside of all that and feeling some shared bond with him in our conversations.

I wondered if that was what Sydney had sought in the times we'd tried to find him—the hope of having a connection with him and getting to be more than just someone in the audience. I vowed to share what I'd learned about him with her once things were out in the open about my time with him.

The week finished in a haze. I spent Friday night at the bookstore, happy to be immersed in my layout project for Marlon. After several hours whipped by, he and I prepared to shut down for the night. The paperbacks I'd shuffled about in my reorganizing were everywhere. I loaded them into a few crates in no order. My phone rested at the top of one of the stacks, and when I picked up the device, I saw a text alert. I had set up Cliff's number in my phone after I'd left the museum, adding a special code for him: RS, for rock star. Now the two letters stared at me. I unlocked the screen.

Enjoyed lunch. What are your weekend plans?

Next to a bookcase in the narrow hallway at the back of the store, I thought about my reply. Perhaps he wanted to tour the Center for Book Arts? Walk the Brooklyn Bridge?

We'd discussed those things. But what I really needed to do was be at home working on the notes Nina had emailed to me about my article. There were so many. I was practically going to be rewriting it. Also, I had been so absent at the bookstore until tonight. I wanted to devote a good portion of my Saturday to completing my project there.

Before I could reply, he added, *Come to Jamestown. I'll show you around.*

That made it easy for me to answer.

I don't have a car, I typed back to him.

In seconds my phone rang, the initials RS glowing on the screen once more. I inched along the book-filled wall toward the back door, feeling a need for further privacy though I knew Marlon's personality would never permit him to eavesdrop.

"Good evening, Mr. Wood."

I thought my greeting was funny, but he skipped right over it. "What if I sent a car for you?"

"Most people start with hello or how are you."

There was a pause and then, "Hi Claudine." His voice sounded so inviting. Sexy.

What is it about a man, a super-attractive, famous musician saying your name?

My writer's mind imagined him in a pair of black pajama bottoms, his hair ruffled, maybe sitting in a recliner ruminating about these plans he wanted to make.

"I can take care of the arrangements." That voice again.

I was between a *rock star* and a hard place. There was so much I needed to do. Marlon and I didn't operate on a schedule, so I knew anything with him or the store wasn't an issue. And if I gave my article some attention tonight, it would be enough to keep it moving.

But there was also Sydney. I had so much guilt already about the time I'd spent with Cliff unbeknownst to her. If I took him up on his offer, I'd be adding to it.

I told him I needed to think about it, but I knew even as I said such I was going, same as I'd done with his invitation to the museum. I just needed time to work it out in my head. What was one more get-together with him at this point? And Sydney had a lot of plans with Natasha for the weekend. She'd said so in the email she'd forwarded with our Portland flight information. The idea of her having her own fun moderated the guilt.

A black sedan picked me up the next morning at eight o'clock on the nose. I waited outside my apartment in a pair of purple thrift store shorts and a tank I'd been longing to wear. A canvas bag on my shoulder held a pair of jeans and a windbreaker in case I'd underestimated the chill that might come with being near the water.

This time, the three-hour drive felt much more enjoyable than it had the night I'd rushed out in the dark, thinking I'd be surprising Paige and Sydney for the concert there.

I didn't know anything about Jamestown and was looking forward to the tour Cliff had offered. When I arrived, he had his hands in the pockets of knee-length cargo shorts, tanned legs. Even in the casual attire, it was jarring to see him.

The driver looked back at me. "This is it. Hope you enjoyed the ride."

I took a couple of breaths as the car idled next to a sun-drenched marina, the expanse of the bay before me. The picturesque scene gave me an instant feeling of gratitude for being there. I wished I could teleport the special moment to Amelia. I could only hope she was looking down on us, wishing us a fun day.

I tried to tip the driver with a few bills, but he waved me off saying, "It's been taken of."

At the same time, Cliff opened the door. "Thanks, man."

On the sidewalk I stood before him, feeling awkward. I wondered if he could sense I still had him framed in my head as a rock star, a hot, handsome one. I tried to put the thought aside.

He motioned to the area around him. "Welcome back. How was the ride?"

"It was good, great actually. Thank you for setting that up."

"Thomas took care of it. Takes care of a lot of things for me."

I remembered the man who'd approached me in Maryland at the hotel. "Such as asking people to meet you for dinner after a concert?"

He laughed as he took my canvas bag and put it over his shoulder. "Don't remind me of that. I hated you turned me down." He rubbed his forearm. "Ego's a little bruised."

The playfulness of his remark made me smile and helped put me at ease. "Well, I'm here now. What are we going to do?"

We wandered along the dock toward rows of boats gently rocking on the sun-bathed water, the air laced with notes of spring and the calm from the area's intrinsic peacefulness. I watched his feet moving in flip flops next to mine and thought even his toes were sexy.

When we made it down one side of the pier, he stopped. "This one's mine. Thought we'd have some lunch here."

"This one? Really?" I heard myself ask. "She's perfect. So pretty." And that was true. She was not at all ostentatious unlike the boastful, *look at me* vessels a celebrity was likely to have. She was medium-sized and cute, more functional than reeking of affluence. Cliff glowed with a smile, seemingly pleased at my reaction.

He went aboard first and then offered his hand to help me as I made the little jump across the gap of water onto the pristine white yacht. Standing on the bow, I shielded my eyes with a flat hand to survey the landscape. As I stood there drinking in the scenery, I couldn't believe this was happening. Being there in the coastal beauty felt so good. The sea breeze danced in my hair, and I knew my face must have been beaming, reflecting the sense of calm I felt. This day was a gift, and so was my time with him. It had been worth staying up until almost one that morning trying to implement Nina's notes.

I wouldn't need the jacket or jeans in the bag I'd brought. The temperature was a perfect warmth. I followed him into the cabin where he set down my bag and then opened the refrigerator. Was I really about to have lunch on Cliff Wood's boat?

"Feel free to look around. Do you drink beer? I've got other stuff, too. Soda. Water. I wasn't sure what you'd want. Oh, and there's *expensive wine*, too, of course."

We both laughed, our eyes meeting. It took us back to our restaurant encounter. It felt surreal that somehow I was beginning to form a shared history with Cliff, already creating memories to look back on.

"A beer is fine if you've having one," I said.

I stood beyond him, scanning the interior. Nothing too luxurious, understated elegance. Black curved couches faced each other on opposites sides of the cabin with a built-in teak wood table in between. In a corner stood a small stereo and a stack of CDs. A picture of a pelican hung on one wall. I peeked through a doorway where a bed draped in a nautical-themed comforter took over the whole room. After I'd lowered myself onto one of the comfy black couches, he handed me the beer.

"Do you spend a lot of time here?" I tilted the can to my mouth for a sip while I waited for his answer. I felt like I was interviewing him. The question itself seemed a little remote.

The room smelled relaxing like the boat itself. I realized a candle was burning feet away in the kitchen, a delicate scent of coconut mixed with lime.

"When I can. I'm out of town so much."

Duh, Claudine.

I drank more of the beer. I needed to finish drinking the whole can and get it together. I seemed to be caught up in this weird bubble of a moment, and trying to process my thoughts about being there was making it worse.

Cliff had been standing in the kitchenette but moved to the couch across from me. "I write here sometimes."

I looked around the cabin again. "Feels like a good space for it. Are you writing anything new right now?"

"Not so much writing but sketching some notes for a future book. What about you?"

I set the empty beer can on the teak wood table. "Sort of. Something for work."

"You don't sound too enthusiastic about it." His eyes waited for me to elaborate.

I shrugged. "It's a fashion piece. The subject is 'pink is the new yellow.' Or 'pink is the new summer must-have.' It's all about pink. And somehow, I'm supposed to tie it to celebrity fashion. I've been working on it for a while. I wish I weren't so disconnected from it. I love words but—"

I trailed off. I knew I was rambling, but it felt good to talk truthfully about my dissatisfaction with my writing opportunities or lack thereof. What I'd wanted to convey was how writing for work differed from writing from my own inspiration and for my own aims. I was self-conscious now having already filled the air between us with more of my own voice than seemed polite. Another beer would have helped.

Cliff eased back onto the couch and took a swallow of his own beer, looking momentarily to sea.

"It's hard to write like that, when your heart's not in it, trying put words into an idea you don't feel. Same thing with a song, it's just a different concept, writing feelings into a melody. It has to be in you." He patted where his heart would be. "If not, the song won't resonate with others. So, I know exactly what you mean."

Wow.

My brain stirred with admiration. Cliff had picked up my sentiments without my even fully giving voice to them. Was I imagining that? I was sure I hadn't said anything about having to *feel it.* I loved his explanation and that he'd volunteered the part about the songwriting.

It was my turn to share again. "I know. I went to some writers' workshops. I thought being around other creative people in a controlled environment would help. I wanted to write a book. I *still* want to write a book—books— but it's starting to feel like a hopeless dream. I can't write just by planning to write, you know? I have to feel it, like you said. And there's so much to sort out."

"About what?" He looked at me like he genuinely wanted to know. Maybe it was because he didn't have that issue. His life was on solid ground.

About myself. That was the real answer, *and there's so much.* But what I really said was, "How to make it all work—the balance of my regular job and everything else. It's hard to make time for

CHAPTER 17

it. And there are so many dead ends, maybe ones I've created."

Clearly I was getting more comfortable with him. The only person to whom I spoke from my heart in such a way was Aunt Trudy.

He got up and retrieved another beer for us both, finally. He opened one for me and set it on the table. "Claudine, forgive me," and then, after thinking quietly for a moment, "I do have manners."

"Forgive you? For what?"

He pointed. "No glasses. I have no idea why I didn't ask if you wanted a glass. Do you?"

At the time I thought he was being facetious, but later I'd realize he was trying to bring the tone down in the space, seeing and hearing the frustration and notes of sadness as I talked about my lack of ability to get to my dreams. Looking back, it was so like him to want the day to be fun and memorable for me.

"A glass? No, I think I'm good." I picked up the new can of beer and tossed back a couple of swallows.

"Well that's a relief. I'm often around people who can't just go with things."

We stayed on the subject of writing a little longer. Cliff's eyes lit up when he explained he wrote western novels in memory of his dad. Those were the kinds of movies they had always watched together, usually on Sunday afternoons, he told me. All his

249

book titles were subtle nods to things his father had liked. He wanted to try his hand at science fiction because it would challenge his creativity.

It was all so mind-blowing. When I'd ridden over in the car that morning, I didn't know what was in store. I thought our conversations at the bar the night we'd met and then in the museum were something to celebrate. Now we had traversed a new plain.

Hearing him talk about writing in such a personal way made me even more motivated get to a point where I could experience the magic of creating something important and interesting with words.

I told him I wanted to write about relationships, not romantic ones, but about what made people connect and how they secretly hurt each other. I could tell when I said the last part he wanted to know more. But he was giving me the courtesy I'd given him earlier when I hadn't pressed for more details after he'd talked about songwriting.

He stood up. "We've been talking all this time, and I haven't even shared the menu."

Then he looked around as if searching for someone. "Waiter!" he called out and then paused. "Seems my crew have mutinied."

I laughed so hard, barely able to swallow the sip of beer I'd just ingested. He held this comedic side back on stage. I loved having a ringside seat for it. Everyone was missing out.

I didn't care if we ate at all. I didn't want the easy back-and-forth to stop, the simple but meaningful conversation.

Cliff took the few steps over to the kitchenette that featured a miniature sink, about two feet of counter space and a slightly larger than dorm-sized refrigerator. I joined him. Observing his hands as he set out boiled shrimp, potato salad, and then gathered plates and silverware, I couldn't help but think about the number of times I'd watched his fingers move intricately along the neck of a guitar. It was a strange feeling, seeing them do something so ordinary as prepare lunch.

He turned to me. "Full disclosure, my neighbor helped me out and made the salad. She's always wanting to do things for me, but this is local, fresh, shrimp I cooked last night."

When I reached over, peeled a shrimp, and started to take a bite, he held up one hand, "Wait, you need cocktail sauce." In a second, he pulled an unopened bottle from the cabinet nearby, quickly twisted the lid, and poured a generous helping into a bowl. "Okay, now you're ready."

We ate for a few minutes standing there without talking and eventually took our plates to the bow of the boat. I could have spent that whole afternoon watching the water and feeling the sun caress my face, happy to be there with him. It felt so good, a special kind of goodness that goes all the way to your core.

After we'd eaten and cleaned up the few dishes, we headed over to the local market area for our favorite things starting with mine, a used bookstore where I found a novel written by a 1950s actress, Ruth Chatterton. It was on a sale table outside for a dollar. Cliff announced he would pay for it, joking it would be my souvenir of the visit instead of the Jamestown t-shirt he had planned on.

But he got me one later to be funny. White with a sailboat on the front. I wore it to shreds.

Side by side, our bodies sometimes touching, we perused more of the books piled on tables and then drifted in and out of a handful of stores before settling in the back of a café. A generous piece of chocolate cream pie rested on a plate between us.

Passing the dessert back forth like we'd done in the museum restaurant was how we'd end the day. It was so crazy to think how one minute I was on stage with him as rock star Cliff Wood at a concert I had no plans of attending and the next there I was, sharing pie with him a couple of miles from his house. I was getting more used to being around him. We never had a silence that felt uneasy.

That night in my bed under the covers with my new used book, I reminisced in my mind about the day. I realized I hadn't thought once about Sydney or worried about the status of the tickets to the concert with Ramsey the whole time I was with him.

To my surprise, I didn't feel bad about it.

Chapter 18

MAINE TURNED OUT TO BE ONE OF MY favorite places, especially the hidden coves and back roads.

A week later, Sydney and I arrived in Portland. I'd never been to Maine and wished we'd have some time to explore the area, but our concert travel for Cliff never allowed for such. We were always too busy evaluating his potential after-show agenda, devising a plan to infiltrate it with the hope of having a moment to talk to him. Sydney kept a list on her phone of topics in case we succeeded.

It had been a rough week in terms of flying under the radar, not mentioning anything to her about the time I'd spent with Cliff.

As was our way, the days leading to the show we sent multiple text messages planning our concert attire right down to the earrings. We had decided to go with a rocker glam look: ragged jeans, wide double prong belts, earrings shaped like lightning bolts, and orange t-shirts featuring a motorcycle Sydney had picked up for us, hoping the tee's graphic might get Cliff's attention.

Sydney had heard he had arrived the night before and thought he would have been sequestered long enough in his hotel room to venture into the lobby restaurant versus getting something delivered to him, his typical routine. But I knew he hadn't arrived early and was, in fact, being picked up by car around the same time Sydney and I were boarding our plane. By the time she and I landed, he would still have about an hour to go before getting there.

During the week, he and I had sent text messages, mostly basic check-ins, *how is your week going,* and such. We'd talked about possibly getting together for dinner after his performance, but I'd summed things up by saying that doing so might present some jealousy issues with my friends since we'd had the concert trip planned for a while.

He offered to provide some backstage passes for whomever I wanted to bring if it would help the situation, but I turned him down. If Sydney had known, she'd have strangled me. She would want to later regardless, but I figured there would be other times to cash in his offer. It was so much to navigate—communicating with him and having inside information about his whereabouts and plans. I would be so glad when I didn't have to keep it all to myself.

When I'd left Jamestown after my visit with him, the same driver who had brought me over picked me up that evening as well. Cliff had tried to surreptitiously hand him a fifty-dollar bill as he gave instructions to get me home safely. I had seen the bill in his wallet earlier. I liked that he was generous with those who worked for him.

"Let Thomas know when you get her there," he told the driver.

Right before I had gotten into the car, I felt like I should hug him or maybe give him a light peck on the cheek, some little act of appreciation, but I wasn't sure if he'd view it as being forward. It didn't occur to me the number of women who'd probably impulsively kissed or touched him through the years.

Instead, I thanked him for a great time, and when I rolled down the window to add a final word of gratitude, he softly touched my chin with a look of endearment. I thought about that tender touch for much of the ride back to the city and often in the days that followed.

In Portland, I knew the hotel where he would be staying, no pre-show hunting was needed, though I would still have to go along with the pretense of the search ritual for Sydney's sake.

It was a solo performance, so the band wasn't along. Thomas Yale had sent me an itinerary of the day and evening's rundown starting with a two o'clock sound check. I had determined that when Cliff performed alone, Thomas was at the helm of things whereas Bruce played a bigger role for concerts with the band. Also, Thomas was the one connected to Cliff's personal world. I wondered if Sydney had figured out this distinction.

Though it would turn out not to make any difference, I steered Sydney and myself clear of the hotel on the itinerary Thomas had given me. It was such a duplicitous thing to do, but I didn't want us to run into Cliff. I'd have to deflect any acknowledgement from him, which there undoubtedly would be. I could picture the whole thing—Sydney and me casually wandering into the hotel's entrance and Cliff coming out of nowhere, changing his course to say hello and me awkwardly pretending not to see him, inventing some emergency to head in the other direction.

I was glad Cliff had told me rehearsals with Ramsey would begin soon. That meant he would be in closer communication with her and could get a firm answer about the tickets. Then I could finally bring Sydney into the know. That moment couldn't come soon enough.

Sydney had heard from one of her insiders that Cliff would be staying in a boutique hotel off the beaten path, a place called the Mercury, but it was completely booked. It didn't matter anyway as the information wasn't accurate. He was actually going to be at a hotel a few blocks from the venue where the lobby housed a large bar, a place we'd all end up after the show. The place where things would go south.

For now, Sydney and I settled into our room after purchasing bottles of water and snacks in the hotel's gift shop and doing a walkthrough of the lobby for any Cliff-related people or key fans.

I wanted to rest. We'd taken the earliest flight as was our custom in case there were any delays. Lying on the bed atop the covers, I closed my eyes. The TV played at a low volume in the background, and Sydney spread out our outfits on the other bed. Then she took the spot next to me rolling up on her elbow, her face close to mine.

"I wonder if he'll do anything new tonight. What do you think?"

"New? Like what?" I purposely tried to sound drowsy. I needed some quiet time. Being tired from the flight was one thing but having to be on guard with every move I made or thing I said was a different kind of fatigue involving endless mental acrobatics.

"Songs. You know, something we don't get to hear. Like the time he sang 'Out of the Blue.' Major oldie. That was great."

"'Out of the Blue?'" I repeated it to make her feel I was listening.

"He did it at a pop-up show once at this cool bar called Arlean's Grocery. I have a pick from that night."

"He'll probably do something like that at the one with his daughter."

"Ramsey." Sydney clarified the name, probably frustrated thinking I still didn't know it. "Not that *we'll* be hearing it. I looked at some aftermarket sites for tickets, nothing. A lot of people want to go."

I yawned. "Things always work out for you and the concerts. It'll happen somehow."

"I hope so. We should get dressed and go eat before we go to the venue."

"Only if I get to lie here and nap for a little while." I turned away from her.

"Deal. I'll grab a quick bath, and then we'll wander around some more because I'm pretty sure this isn't the hotel where we need to be later."

I wondered how she had figured that out.

Sydney filling the tub sounded like a waterfall and would have been a pleasant backdrop for my somnolent activity, but my mind wouldn't stop with the Cliff and Sydney gymnastics. I so wished we could skip the search process for him, but I knew that would be ludicrous to suggest. Even if she knew our efforts likely wouldn't get us anywhere, she enjoyed the quest.

My mind flashed back to that first night we'd looked for Cliff in Times Square. I had felt honored she included me in her adventure. Now, here I was harboring his number in my cell phone with the question of where he was or the songs he planned to sing a phone call away.

Inside my mind, I flinched. My nap was doomed.

———

We both got salads and ate them on a nearby restaurant's patio after trekking once more through the common areas of our hotel as well as the one next door. I could tell Sydney was getting anxious the way she went quiet after our unsuccessful discovery of Cliff or anything Cliff-related. She wanted to go ahead to the venue, a place called Aura.

"Let's get drinks. There's a bar connected to the same building."

It seemed like a great way to stop her manhunt for Cliff.

When we arrived, the room was already littered with fans. Thomas Yale was in conversation at the bar holding what looked like a martini. I did an about-face pulling Sydney by the arm and forcing her to turn around and look up to face me.

"Maybe we should check one more hotel and cover our bases? We didn't even check the Mercury to see if it has a hangout spot for afterward." I was grabbing at straws. Thomas had only seen me that one time when he'd delivered Cliff's invitation for dinner, but I didn't want to risk it. Sydney would find it so odd for him to know me by name.

She considered things for a moment. "Well, Paige is also checking things out, and she's with Evvi. Evvi is relentless. So, like you said, it'll work out. Paige will tell us."

We ended up crowding into a circular booth with some of Sydney's fan friends. I could never keep up with all their names and backstories and the shows where they'd met. I kept my head turned to the side as one of them talked, not really listening. The position kept me out of Thomas Yale's line of vision, and when I peeked over after a while, I was happy to discover he'd left.

The trip felt like it was more about dodging bullets than going to a concert, a concert I was eager to see, having a greater interest in Cliff's music as I had started to know him beyond the stage. But there was so much at play now, and being with Sydney was making me tense.

"I guess these are okay." She examined our seats in the venue after we'd left the bar.

I stood beside her in the aisle. "I think second row is great."

"On the venue map they looked more in the center." She scooted past several people as I followed.

In the row ahead of us were Evvi, Paige, Doreen, and Lorie, all of whom I'd met at the first pop-up concert.

Paige turned around. "Oh hey!" And then with a note of satisfaction she whispered, "Alternative Kyle is in our hotel."

Sydney leaned in and held onto the back of Paige's seat. "Any *other* sightings?"

"Nothing so far, but there's a big bar in the middle of the lobby. You can see everyone coming and going. We're planning to stake out a spot right afterward."

"We'll meet you there." Sydney sat back, pleased with the plan.

I felt pleased, too. In fact, it eased my mind. If Cliff did make an appearance or decide to come to the bar, I knew I'd have time to make an escape to sidestep the situation. I was sure he'd invite me over if he saw me, and if I avoided that, all would be fine.

My seat was right behind Evvi giving me a view of her brunette tresses lying in fresh spirals. Her height provided a convenient shield to keep Cliff from easily seeing me from the stage. I had been to enough concerts to know he liked to make eye contact with those he recognized, and though Sydney didn't have any reason for suspicion about him and me, I didn't want to risk sounding a silent alarm. I'd already cut things close once at the Maryland show when Sydney thought he was interacting with her and not me.

Soon enough the lights dimmed, and there it was, the collective sigh from the audience amid applause, some whistles, and the usual extended cheers as Cliff arrived on stage. When he reached the center, someone yelled "Cliff, I love you so much!" A declaration like that always surfaced at his performances.

He usually didn't respond, but this time, he briefly put his hand on his heart. It was sweet.

That small acknowledgement wasn't the only thing different about him. Instead of his typical ensemble of a black or other muted colored t-shirt, underneath his leather jacket he wore a pink button-down collared dress shirt tucked into his jeans. It took a moment for it to register with me.

Sydney knit her eyebrows together, puzzled. "What's up with the pastel?"

I shook my head as if I were similarly perplexed. I had to suppress the urge to smile. To glow. To hide my happiness.

The applause continued as Cliff surveyed the room, the spectators thrilled by his presence as always. Now, I wished Evvi and her hair weren't blocking me. I wanted to share the moment with him, his secret nod to our conversation on his boat about writing and my magazine article.

As luck would have it, Evvi leaned down for her purse giving me enough time for one stealthy moment to engage with him. When my eyes caught his, I watched his smile change into a bigger electric one causing more noise from the audience as every nerve in my body exploded in joy.

"So weird." Sydney sounded frustrated. "Something must be up."

I shrugged again, continuing the façade. I knew we'd have to stay awake to discuss the change in his wardrobe later, and if not then, on the plane, probably both.

The set list started the same, nothing new as Sydney had hoped. "He's being lazy," she said at one point. "There are so many songs on his last album we haven't heard live."

I didn't comment as it didn't matter to me what songs he played. All I could think about was the pink shirt. Did he already own it? Did he dispatch Thomas Yale or some stylist to pick it up for him?

I couldn't wait to share my appreciation with Cliff. Writing about a rock star wearing pink wasn't going to save my magazine article, but the gesture had put my spirits in overdrive. In my mind, I began composing the text I wanted to send to him about it and was anxious for a moment alone to do so.

Sydney wasn't into the show as much as usual. She liked the ones better with the whole band where Cliff moved about the stage playing his electric guitar, allowing him to have more interaction with the audience. It didn't help there was a large gap separating the seating area from the stage which detracted from the intimacy his solo shows usually offered.

We were getting to the end of the concert. Sydney had already written it off, feeling there hadn't been anything special about it. She had spent a good portion of the time sending updates to friends about his performance and asking for input about the whole shirt thing. She was anxious to leave and get to the activity of finding him.

Then Cliff said, "I haven't played this in a long time."

Sydney's head bobbed up from her phone.

"This one is called 'Any Word from William?' A few of you might know it."

Cliff strummed the beginning notes on his guitar as he began the slow, somber song. He closed his eyes until he began to sing.

I thought Sydney might jump out of her seat. She squeezed my hand. "Oh my God! Can you believe this?" She put her hand to her chest. "I love this song so much!"

I gripped her hand with equal force. It made me happy, too, thinking how much Cliff had been paying attention in the conversations I'd had with him. I didn't truly know if my influence had played a role in the song selection, but it was likely. Even though Sydney was the one who wanted to hear the song, I felt his playing it was another secret shout-out to me.

The shirt and now the song. I hated I had to keep it all to myself.

Our group walked the ten minutes from the venue to the hotel having left halfway through the encore song to get a head start. When we arrived, we did the usual initial scanning of the bar area. Plenty of high-top tables were available; but Sydney and Paige decided the seats directly at the bar would be the best location believing if Cliff decided to have a drink, he'd be more likely to sit there than out in the open where fans would crowd him and ask for photos.

The key was to keep enough space around us along with a free stool so he'd have an obvious place to go. Evvi volunteered her purse for the task, and we were set. I was set, too. I'd already decided to disappear if Cliff arrived and text Sydney saying the alcohol was getting to me, and I needed some fresh air. It wasn't a brilliant plan, but it would have to do.

Drinks were ordered, and as we tossed back our liquors of choice, there were speculations on Cliff's likelihood of arrival as fans trickled in filling up the tables or joining us by the bar.

Sydney, Evvi, and Paige were a magnet for fans who wanted to see Cliff as it was believed they had some insight into his behaviors for having been on the Cliff Wood circuit for so long. When Alternative Kyle squeezed into the last standing-room-only space, it didn't help matters as he was viewed the same way. More fans gathered nearby. Luckily, Sydney and I occupied the center seats, so if nothing else, the human wall around us provided protection for me from Cliff's initial line of sight, and I could duck my way behind fans until I had an opening to sneak away.

At that thought, I looked beyond our location to evaluate the best route for such an escape, and that's when Bruce came through the lobby doors. Everyone knew his arrival meant Cliff wasn't far behind. The tightly packed group around us loosened as some moved away, readying for Cliff and the hope of a quick word with him or an autograph if someone had thought to bring something for him to sign. I stayed put as Sydney swiveled for a better vantage point.

That was when the trouble started.

A girl I hadn't noticed was suddenly before me. She had pretty eyes, just the right amount of smokey eye shadow, and flouncy brown hair. I guessed she had been at a nearby table or standing close to our group. I thought she was going to ask us to flag the bartender for her, but instead she looked at me squarely, her eyes inquisitive but kind.

"I'm so sorry to bother you ladies, but I've been watching you all evening trying to place where I've seen you. You're the girl who had dinner with Cliff at the bar in Jamestown, right?"

Sidney's head spun around exorcist-style as her body pivoted a beat behind it.

I had thought, or hoped at least, she was so fixated on awaiting Cliff she hadn't heard the girl's comment. No luck on that as Sydney's eyes were now glued to mine with flames in them.

Game over.

I ignored the flouncy-haired girl and stood up, motioning for Sydney to come with me. If I was going to tell her everything now, I wanted to do it privately. I thought she'd appreciate that. I would be honest about it all and take her through it step by step from the moment I'd first heard Cliff's voice that night in the restaurant, including all the tidbits I'd learned about him, and how he was working on getting us tickets to his concert with Ramsey.

In my mind, it was all going to be fine, but as I reached for her wrist to encourage her to come with me, she yanked it away.

"Claudine, just answer, is she right? Are you *that girl*?" Her voice sounded so pejorative. I thought she might erupt like a tiny volcano.

The handful of other fans in earshot stared at me as though I were on trial. They no longer cared about Cliff's potential arrival.

"What do you mean, *that girl*?" I repeated.

Sydney set her drink down as if it were part of the problem. "I'm talking about the girl someone posted about on the fan page—the one who hung out with Cliff after the show in Jamestown. Was that you?"

"You—never mentioned that to me." I hated feeling so put on the spot.

"No, Claudine. I wouldn't. I don't talk to you about all the hardcore fan stuff. You're not that deep into it! You don't even know much about his music!"

WHEN I REMEMBER YOU

Her last statement stung the most. True, I didn't
know as much about Cliff's music as she did, but I
had my own connection to it, to him.

I felt my hands shake. I clasped them together to
reduce the sensation. "Sydney, come on. We don't
need to include everyone here in this, do we? Let's
go back to our room and talk, just you and me."

"I can't believe this." She sounded so angry, disgusted. "Answer, Claudine. Was it *you*? It's all I
need to know—a simple yes or no."

If she had mentioned about the issue of someone
being with Cliff coming up in the fan group when
it happened, I think I would have come clean right
then and told her I was the one, but I didn't want
something so personal on display. It *was* personal,
to me, my friendship with Cliff. And it was personal inside my friendship with Sydney, too. Everyone
didn't need to know the details.

I sat there feeling at sixes and sevens. In all my
thoughts about how she would react to my experience with Cliff I had never imagined such venom
from her. Thank goodness she didn't know anything about the time I'd spent with him beyond that
first evening—the museum and being on his boat. I
wasn't sure now whether I'd ever be able to tell her
about those things.

With everyone waiting for me to say something,
I took a slight breath. "It was me, but it was an
unexpected evening, and I enjoyed getting to talk

with him." That was as much as I would offer. If Sydney wouldn't meet me halfway to discuss the matter elsewhere, I wasn't going into specifics.

The woman who had started it all by recognizing me clinked her glass to mine. I'd forgotten she was even there. "Good for you, girl. He looked really into you."

Great.

Chapter 19

EVERYTHING HAD FELT SO GOOD WHAT with Cliff wearing the pink shirt at the concert and playing the song Sydney had been wanting to hear until things went awry afterward. It was all beginning to feel like a bad dream.

One minute, we had been taking selfies in our glam rock outfits in the bar, and the next, Sydney was questioning me as if I were a murder suspect.

When I returned to the hotel room, I changed clothes and then sent Cliff a text telling him I was in bed and didn't feel good. It was true and not only from an emotional standpoint. I was feeling bad all over as though my body had been bruised, a symbol of sorts of the verbal blows I'd received from Sydney. Cliff called within seconds, my two favorite initials RS lighting the phone's screen.

"Hey—what's going on?" The sound of his voice alone was a panacea.

"I'm just tired I think. We had an early flight this morning." I adjusted myself against the pillows trying to find a comfortable position while I talked him.

"You sure?"

I imagined him relaxing in his bed, too, bare sexy feet, the TV on mute. The simple fantasy vision helped my feelings although I felt burned out and dispirited.

"Yes, I'll be okay." *But when? How?* I wanted those answers for myself.

I let my mind drift back to the concert and realized I'd never sent him the text I'd planned.

"I can't believe you wore that pink shirt during the show. Everyone was talking about it. And you sang the William something song."

"I wanted to surprise you."

"You did. And my friend was overjoyed," though she'd abandoned me, something I wouldn't tell him. "I admit it's not a song I'm familiar with, but I can tell it's about loss."

I heard him swallow, probably having a late drink or more likely a piece of pie he'd had delivered to his room. "Most songs *are* about loss in one way or another, Claudine. You haven't noticed that?"

Speaking of loss—

I considered telling him some version of what had transpired with Sydney, but I didn't want the subject of fan drama to have a history in our conversations. It was so embarrassing—grown women acting like catty teenagers. And I certainly didn't want to tell him he was monitored so closely by many of them to the point our dinner in Jamestown had been a topic of discussion in their secret online group.

Sydney was right. I wasn't into it the way she was. The concerts were fun, and I enjoyed going to them with her, but I was more interested in Cliff as a writer, both in his books and his song lyrics. I wished I'd said so back in the bar. I had been caught so off guard.

As I played through it all again, I felt I might start crying. I told Cliff I wanted to get some sleep, but when we hung up, I lay there in the darkness for hours, waiting for Sydney to come back.

Around six the next morning, a knock came at the door. I dragged myself out of bed, relieved she was finally ready to talk, or so I assumed. But when I opened the door I found Paige instead, a look of worry on her face.

She held out a bottle of water for me. "I'm sorry for waking you. I don't have your number."

I held the door open further, inviting her inside as the scent of her recent cigarette floated in the air. Though I was disappointed she wasn't Sydney, I was happy to have some company, someone who was acquainted with what had happened.

"Sydney is riding back with us. She asked me if I'd come get her bag. I'm really sorry." Her pool blue eyes held genuine empathy.

"It's not your fault. Don't feel bad." My voice quivered. I pointed to the open suitcase on the floor. "It's right there." The handle lay to the side with a guitar-shaped luggage tag with Sydney's initial suspended from it alongside Cliff's logo.

Paige squatted and began organizing the haphazard clothing nearby. Her cropped blonde hair was askew as if she'd rolled out of bed and didn't care about it although she had taken the time to apply lipstick and large hoop earrings. She held up a pair of boots to confirm they were Sydney's before tucking them away. After she zipped the bag closed, she stood up and turned to me.

"Are you okay?" She laid a hand on my shoulder. "I can stay for a few minutes."

I pushed one side of my own askew hair behind my ear. "I don't know what to do." My voice wavered again.

Paige rolled the suitcase to the door and returned, taking a seat next to me where I'd landed at the foot of the bed. She lightly touched my back. "She'll cool off eventually. That's just Sydney. She's so caught up in everything that has to do with Cliff."

"Isn't everyone? Aren't you?"

She thought for a moment. "No, it's not the same. I like to go to the concerts. It's fun, it's a getaway from my family—not that I don't love my kids and my husband—but when I can't go or make it to the bigger Cliff Wood events, I'm okay with it. Sydney—not so much."

I remembered that first day I'd met Sydney, how she'd arrived in the bookstore breathless and desperate to find the tickets she'd lost. It was true, going to Cliff's concert had seemed like a life-or-death matter to her. Thinking about it made me wonder how late she and everyone had stayed in the bar after I'd left and if Cliff made an appearance. I never saw him after Bruce arrived.

Paige toyed with her hair and then looked at her watch. I realized she was wearing pajama pants, blue with snowflakes, as she rested her hand on one thigh. "You know how Cliff does the thing with 'Come Home With Me' where he brings someone on stage? I've done it a few times. Evvi has. You've done it, but Sydney never has."

I had wondered about that, whether me having that experience had bothered her. "We never talked about it. I thought it was because she was used to that part of the show and didn't think it was a big deal."

"Oh, it was a big deal. It was a big, *big* deal." Paige shook her head slowly as she spoke.

I got up and removed Sydney's phone charger where she'd left it plugged in by the bedside lamp and handed the cord to Paige. "I wonder why he's never picked her?"

"Honestly, I think it's robotic. He's been doing it for years. He just grabs someone and does the song."

I didn't agree with that. I'd been around Cliff enough to know his kind nature wasn't robotic in the least. It hadn't felt that way when he picked me that night. I made a mental note to tell Cliff I'd been one of his singing victims and see if he remembered.

Paige stood up and moved back toward the door. "So. It's really about resentment. She wants the opportunity to connect with him. And she's tried, a lot. We all want it. I want it, too, but for Sydney, it's different, goes much deeper."

She held onto the door handle. "You'll get to the airport okay?"

I nodded. I didn't even know what time the flight left and dreaded ambling through the airport on my own. It made the situation feel even sadder.

She produced her phone and asked me for my number. After I gave it to her, she said, "I'll send you a text so you can contact me. Let me know that you make it home, okay?"

Her kindness made me feel I wasn't a complete outcast among the few fans I had befriended. But I still felt like crying and did once she left.

———

Starting a work week with what was happening with Sydney hanging in the balance would normally have made it hard to focus, but the current issue of the magazine was closing. That meant back-to-back meetings and follow-up tasks leaving little mental space to obsess about anything else. I'd sent a few text messages to her saying I would wait until she felt like talking, but she hadn't responded to any of them. I went about my work with a knot in my gut, desperately wanting to make things right with her.

My 'pink' article didn't make into the magazine. I'd taken Nina's suggestions to heart and also written it several different ways. But I couldn't find the right angle, one that fit the readership and had the right amount of spark. Even with Cliff's attempt to provide inspiration with his wardrobe surprise, my words came out stilted and mediocre.

When I'd spoken to Nina privately about it, she said she'd already determined it wasn't the right assignment for me, and we'd look at other opportunities down the road. I hoped that was true, but I couldn't help feeling she had doubts about my writing talent. Though I'd tried my hardest, I had my doubts, too. I knew I had also been heavily distracted, nowhere near as focused on the task as I should have been. I felt bad about this as well.

Everything was falling apart. I wasn't sure which was worse, feeling like such a failure in writing something I thought might propel me into even a small literary career or feeling like a

failure in a friendship that had made such a difference for me.

———

Cliff had been in Nashville and returned home on
Friday afternoon. When I'd waited at the airport
alone in Portland, he had called to tell me he'd be
rehearsing with Ramsey for the week and staying
at her apartment. I was so tearful about how the
weekend had gone sour that I'd lied and said I was
about to board the plane, when really I was sadly
sipping on a cola near my gate. I hadn't talked to
him since then. Now he called me again when he
landed, this time asking if I had any Saturday plans
and wanting to know if I'd come knock around
with him in Jamestown.

The invitation surprised me. I figured he would
want to relax, or make notes about the set list, or
whatever he did by himself, but it was a relief to
have somewhere to go. I was tired of being in my
apartment. Though the days had been busy at the
magazine, I'd spent the evenings alone in a funk,
missing Sydney and planning our concert excursions. I wondered if we'd ever get back to that. For
now, I knew it would be good to get out and take a
break from the analysis.

That next morning, I packed a bag with fruit and
nuts, a light jacket, and a swimsuit before heading

out in the car I rented through Aunt Trudy's Larry again, her longest beau so far. A few CDs of Cliff's music kept me company along the way. So many of his songs I hadn't explored as Sydney had so publicly pointed out to me.

Each time I thought about the exchange with her in the bar, it made me feel both angry and melancholy. But as soon as I saw Cliff, I felt better, even with the familiar starstruck sensation I had yet to shake.

"You made it." Dark blue shorts, black tee, disarming smile. He waited on the wide stairs leading to his house, a structure of weathered cedar shanks and windows framed in teal. From afar the place looked like it was made from driftwood. A backdrop of lush greenery and calming water outlined the area behind it. I'd learn the place was called Mackerel Cove.

I parked near the detached garage and surveyed the landscape from every angle, a panorama of peacefulness. If I'd thought the marina was a relaxing place to be, this was paradise.

I headed toward him. How strange it was to be watching him performing one minute and then walking up his driveway.

When I'd made it up the stairs, he motioned me to follow him inside. We trailed across an immaculate hardwood floor through a galley kitchen and into a room with a voluptuous white sectional and a wide window showcasing the water. On the adjacent wall, a fireplace awaited frosty nights with recessed shelves housing the best in stereo equipment. A few wildlife paintings provided the only wall decoration. I looked for a nod to his profession, his platinum albums or Grammy awards. Nothing. I wondered where he kept them.

He stood to the side with his hands in both pockets encouraging me to examine the place. I moved to take a closer look out the window. I had always felt a pull toward the water, the serene nature of it. As much as I enjoyed the city and its offering, the ocean provided instant solace. I felt like I could look at it for hours, its presence a way to help me escape the things that normally stayed in the center of my mind and discouraged me about my life.

As I thought about it, I imagined Cliff watching me and then heard him take a few steps. "It's even more beautiful at night."

"I don't know how you ever leave it. I'd be holed up, napping, reading, watching movies."

"Maybe you can do that sometime. I'm not really in here that much. I like to be outdoors."

"On your boat?"

"Among other things."

I wondered if I were being too intrusive. I'd thought about that on the drive, wanting to maintain the right boundary with him. Though he had asked me to come, he was a celebrity and probably still wanted to guard his privacy to some degree.

I looked around the room trying to visualize him there on his own, perhaps half-burrowed in the soft cushions of his couch with a book in hand, reading glasses perched on his nose. I liked the idea of imagining him alone in the quiet, the same as me on so many nights.

We moved to the kitchen and I set my bag by the sink. "Thanks for asking me to come. I needed to get away. It's been kind of a bad week."

"In what way?"

I wanted to take back my comment. I shouldn't have said that. I was only making conversation. I couldn't discuss what was going on with Sydney. How much did he know about the subculture of his fans? I wasn't going to be the one to describe it to him. Plus, I hated to point out how much I knew about it.

"Work. We closed the upcoming issue," I said instead, "and my article isn't in it—the one involving pink. It just wouldn't come out right despite me working on it forever."

I could tell he was about to console me. I jumped back in to stop him. "It's not a big deal. I'll have another chance later in a future issue."

He looked like he was deciding whether to let it go and then disappeared returning with his sunglasses. "I thought we'd take a ride. You got any kind of pants in that bag?"

I looked down at my yellow shorts that fit me perfectly. One of Aunt Trudy's finds. "No. But aren't these cute?"

"Very cute, but they won't work for what we're doing." He motioned me to follow him, and we landed in a spare bedroom where he opened the closet inside to the right. "These are Ramsey's." He stood back so I could see the hangers of clothes. "Grab a pair of her jeans. You're about the same size. She won't mind."

"Are you sure? Most women wouldn't want someone to meddle with her clothes."

That made him laugh. "I'm sure. Ramsey's different. She's a free spirit. It'll be fine. She knows all about you."

"How does she—?" I began, but he'd already left the room, shutting the door behind him.

I looked around, still wondering where he kept his platinum albums and hoping to see a Grammy up close. The room was plain, holding a bed with a red and blue plaid comforter, some neatly stacked books. I slid into a pair of well-worn Levi's. They were a tad tight but would suffice. When I returned to the kitchen, I realized he'd gone outside.

I found him in the garage wearing jeans, too. He walked over to a motorcycle parked in one corner. It looked as if it had taken him on many a jaunt.

"It's a cruiser." He patted the bike's seat when he saw me.

I joined him next to the metal force. Though Sydney had mentioned him having one, it surprised me to see it. "I've never been on one."

"You're about to." He reached for a yellow helmet on the shelf above him. "Jeans good?"

"Pretty good. I know they look snug. She must be petite."

"They're fine. You have nothing to worry about, you look great in anything." He wasn't even looking at me when he said it. *Did he really see me that way?* He examined the helmet before handing it to me. "This is hers, too. I thought she said it had a crack in it, but I think it's fine, functional anyway."

I warily studied the bike. To me, it looked huge and powerful, forbidding. "I'm a little afraid of them actually."

"You won't be scared riding with me. I promise. A ride is good for the soul, very freeing." He stared at me for a second, seemingly testing whether his brief statement had made a difference and then took the helmet out of my hands seating it on my head. "Does that feel okay?"

"I think so."

While he held onto the thick fiberglass gauging its fit on me, I peered through the plastic shield. Standing only inches from his body, it reminded me of the time I'd been on stage with him that first night, how electric it felt to be in such proximity, seeing every minute detail of him. Now I stole a closeup glance of the cut of his face, the soft thatch of hair dangling on his brow, and his thoughtful eyes. He was gorgeous in so many ways, not only his looks. I felt dizzy for a moment.

We were becoming friends, but I hoped the butterfly sensation of his presence would never subside.

Chapter 20

IF YOU HAVEN'T HAD A TOUR BY MOTORCYCLE of a coastal town, I recommend it.

Cliff was right. I felt safe with him. With my arms clasped around his trim waist and my helmet occasionally knocking against his, we sped along roads adjacent to vibrant landscapes of both waterways and wildlife as the sun saturated our path. For over an hour, the cruiser beat the ground before us while the highway melted into the distance. It was like watching a movie of the best parts of life, an experience that made everything seem good and possible, like a newly blossomed flower.

This was a fantasy made for Amelia, strapped to her first crush, no plans, open to whatever nature offered, the more uncertain and adventurous the better. For a moment, I felt as if I were channeling the excitement of it to her and imagined her reaction of delight and pride. Pride for her little sister coming out of her shell, embracing unexpected exhilaration, and for finding friendship both with Cliff and with Sydney after so much time spent in sadness, hiding behind books and other people's stories when I so needed to find a story for myself.

I had no idea where we were. Most of the ride had been a watercolor blur of trees and flowering vegetation the names of which I didn't know. We parked outside a café that had appeared out of nowhere nestled off the path we'd taken. A few cars parked nearby were the only clue to its presence.

Cliff pulled off his helmet and ran a hand through his compressed hair. "Well? How was it?"

"Oh my gosh, that was incredible! Amelia, she'd have—she loves—" I heard myself stumble, unable to finish the sentence. I pretended I'd lost my train of thought as I tucked my hair behind my ears.

Cliff dismounted the bike and steadied it as I did the same. "She likes to ride, does she?"

"Yeah." *Or she would.*

When Amelia's name came up again I had decided I was going to tell him the truth about her, but the timing was bad. It wasn't a two or three sentence conversation and not something I wanted to do in a parking lot either. I was mad at myself for mentioning her.

"I'm glad you weren't scared like you'd thought. I knew you'd be fine," Cliff said.

"I think I'd feel different surrounded by cars, but being out in the open like this is wonderful." *Being with you is wonderful.*

He winked at me with a simple, inviting smile. "Let's go get something to eat."

As we headed toward the building carrying our helmets, I lagged behind him to be sure I'd evaded any emotion over Amelia. Aside from it being the wrong time to talk about her, I didn't want something sad to interfere with our fun.

We took a window seat and inspected a menu written in chalk on the wall. The place was part market, part deli, also apparently specializing in house-made cookies given the pleasant aroma of warm chocolate chips hanging in the air. After a couple of minutes, we joined the deli line and ordered sandwiches on seeded bread. Then we browsed shelves of specialty grocery items while we waited.

When our number was called, we picked up our order and headed back to our table. Cliff had also added a half dozen of the house-made cookies unbeknownst to me. He opened the bag and held it toward me suggesting we go ahead and taste them.

"Um, these pants are already tight." I batted his hand away jokingly. "Maybe later."

He laughed as he picked up the bag of chips that came with his sandwich and immediately popped one in his mouth.

"So what brought you here? To Jamestown? I've lived in New York most of my life, and I didn't know about all this." I gestured toward the window with my freehand, my sandwich in the other.

He finished chewing and skimmed a napkin across his lips. "Gwen. My sister. She used to rent a little vacation home here in the summers."

My question was meant to be an innocuous conversation starter. I didn't want to bring us back to the subject of family which had the propensity to go in too many uncomfortable directions. That aside, I wasn't sure of the protocol when it came to the personal things I had learned about him from Sydney's Cliff Wood vault or the bits I'd found in the online searching I'd done right after the first couple of concerts. Was I supposed to pretend I didn't know anything about his background, *his* sister?

Truthfully, I didn't know much other than the song he'd written about her. I wouldn't forget how the lyrics had reached inside of me that night he sang it at the Bowery Electric. Sydney had said it was a song he didn't perform often, and I understood not wanting to summon such pain. I didn't want to right now either.

"We were seventeen years apart in age, and our mother worked. Gwen took care of me growing up. She's been gone about twenty years now. She had congestive heart failure. Young for it. In her sixties."

His tone was matter-of-fact talking about his sister's death as is often the case when decades have passed after a loss. But I remembered how his eyes had glistened when he finished the song. He had not yet resolved Gwen's loss, and I doubted I could ever resolve Amelia's either.

He bit into the sandwich and chewed. "I figured I'd be taking care of her by now, returning the favor, you know?"

I started to ask him if he'd had any chance to give his support to her or say something about the difficulty of losing a sibling but stopped myself. "'When I Remember You' is a wonderful tribute to her." That was a safe reply.

"You're familiar with it? I had already started writing it before she died. I don't sing it much at my shows. Sometimes it just feels cathartic though."

Familiar? I'd listened to it for days after I'd heard it that night. It felt like a close friend. "I could sing it by heart."

He reached across the table and squeezed my hand. This would have been the perfect segue to share about Amelia, but I didn't want to make the moment about me or ignite melancholy.

He went on to talk about how he wanted to write more and tour less and why he did what Sydney and I called pop-up shows. Sydney had been right about that, how they were like therapy for him. He enjoyed casually getting to strum his guitar, and relax, and be with people.

He told me about his son who was the product of a relationship with a girl he'd met young in his career. That was what inspired the song 'Any Word from William?' Now in his forties, William barely acknowledged Cliff. And his name wasn't really William. The name fit better in the melody for the song, but more than that, Cliff didn't want to risk upsetting his son with such a public presentation of their distant, strained relationship.

"His mother and I weren't ever close. It was kind of an on the road thing. That's a terrible excuse, but when you're twenty years old with stars in your eyes, you aren't thinking straight or about others." He looked away, and I could see a thought pass over him. "You live in the now, and the now, back then, brought William—Louis. That's my middle name."

I knew that look, a veil that tried to disguise a troubled heart. I felt I'd invented it.

"I don't think I'd want to be twenty again unless I could keep all the things I've learned. My middle name is Seraphina."

He lifted his drink. "Cheers to that Claudine Seraphina."

I laughed as I picked up my water and touched the glass to his. I didn't ask him to elaborate, and after we ate for a few minutes, he circled back to the topic.

"I wonder if he's forgiven me or what he thinks about who I am. I'm still hoping to find out someday."

"I think you will. I don't know why, but I think it will happen for you." I gave him a reassuring smile as if I could transmit a positive outcome to him for the future. It was meant to be a moment of encouragement, something nice to say. I thought he'd respond with *why do you think that* or some such. I wasn't expecting what he said next at all.

"You're beautiful."

I'd bitten a potato chip. The pieces crumbled inside my mouth while I processed the statement. Men didn't refer to me as beautiful. Attractive maybe. Occasionally pretty. But not beautiful. I moved the food around in my mouth, crunching, trying not to let my discomfort show. After a sip of water, I made myself look at him. I felt my teeth latch onto my lower lip. "Me?"

"I don't think you realize it. It's a soft, simple kind of beautiful."

I didn't know why I doubted his veracity. Maybe because it had been so long since I'd been given a compliment, and coming from someone like him it felt much bigger, more meaningful.

I savored the moment, accepting he'd meant it, and eventually weakly said, "Thank you."

When we finished eating, he collected some of the items from the browsing we'd done while we'd waited for the sandwiches. Anything I had expressed interest in earlier he added to the cart. Bagel crack-ers. Assorted teas. Salted pecans. Chocolate-dipped pineapples among other things. While he paid, I wondered how we'd get it all back to his house.

The cashier handed him a receipt. "We'll have this to you by six tonight, Mr. Wood," she chirped. She probably wanted to touch his hair, too. I wondered who she thought I was—his too-young girlfriend? A daughter?

We began to wind our way back to his house exploring along the way. We veered down side roads to see what we might find and stopped in hidden coves to admire marble water waltzing with rocky shorelines.

Sitting there on the motorcycle with Cliff in such peaceful scenery, I felt I could solve any problem that might come my way, and anything that had ever hurt or derailed me didn't matter. Even the recent upset with Sydney didn't feel as heavy right now. She and her anger at me had been swept from my mind by the warm wind and Cliff's company and the wonder of this day. I tried to memorize how it felt to have the clarity and control of my own thoughts versus being preoccupied with all that didn't seem to be right for me.

At dusk, we coasted into the detached garage. Cliff navigated the bike to the back corner across from his white Jeep Hawkeye. I got off first as he held it in place.

"I enjoyed that so much. Really. Thank you for showing me those places. It was kind of magical." I removed my helmet.

He was off the bike now, too, and slid off his helmet revealing his disheveled hair. "Soul-hugging."

"Yes. That's a great descriptor."

"I'm glad those jeans worked out for you. Ramsey isn't here much. She probably doesn't know what she has in that closet." He reached for my helmet and set it on a workbench with his. "Speaking of Ramsey, I forgot to give you the update. The venue is small—I can't remember the name—"

"The Bitter End."

"That's it. Kind of miserable, isn't it? The sort of place to go after a bad divorce." We burst into laughter. "Anyway, she's made promises for the comp tickets. There aren't that many because of the size of the place. But you and your friend can watch from backstage on the side. She says you'll have a full view of everything."

I was just about to say how great that would be when he added, "You can bring more than one person, so maybe you can invite Amelia."

I felt flush hearing him say her name and was glad his back was to me while he searched for something in a toolbox. I wasn't expecting her to come up again so soon. It was time. I had taken too long to come clean.

I licked my lower lip briefly biting one side of it and then took a step toward him facing the ruffled hair above his neck and t-shirt damp with sweat. "No, she really won't be able to go. Amelia."

He lifted a wrench from the toolbox considering it and then walked back to the motorcycle. "You don't want check with her first?"

That was awkward. Did he believe I was being mean to my sister, not wanting to include her?

I hated to drop such a bomb on him.

"I can't. I really can't ask her. She died when I was in my twenties."

Cliff let go of the wrench. I heard it clatter as it hit the work bench or his toolbox or something. I wasn't sure. I didn't react. I had to keep going now that I'd started.

"It was a car accident, but I'm pretty sure she made it happen." I heard the sad lilt of my voice and the wobbly cadence of my words. At the same time, all my muscles felt like they'd been drained of their strength, as though I were hearing this information myself for the first time.

I had never made that pronouncement aloud about Amelia, that she'd taken her own life. It had circled in my mind for years and my mother's too I suspected. As I tried to fully launch my words, I now believed I understood why my mother never wanted to talk about Amelia and what had happened: the talking made things real. And it felt awful.

Even so, being silenced in such a way had affected us all so much, my dad especially, never being allowed to discuss his daughter, how she was in life, or his grief over losing her. This was why he'd left. He couldn't accept it as a verboten topic with my mother. I pictured him for a moment at his place in Hoboken. I owed him a visit.

As I continued speaking, I tried to sound straightforward like Cliff had when he'd talked about Gwen earlier. "She had a broken arm at the time from a rock-climbing trip a couple of weeks before. It was late and foggy. Everyone said it was just one of those terrible accidents—that she couldn't see her way out of a curve on the road and didn't have the reaction time with her bad arm. That's what everyone—well, my mom—likes to say. That way we don't have to discuss it. But I've pieced together some other things I remember and some conversations with her friends afterward."

I pursed my lips hoping to stifle the urge to sob, but everything was sloshing about in my head. This was the most I'd let myself think about it all in a long time. Whenever I did, I only allowed fleeting thoughts and stopped them before they could develop. Never the details like I was voicing now. I'd learned to keep it all at a distance. Now I couldn't stop the thoughts or the parade of tears in full formation. I smeared them from side to side as they spilled down my cheeks leaving my eyes soaked and blurry.

I felt Cliff's arms wrap me against him. The strong and supportive sense of his body was like a human brace to my faltering spirit. It felt like the hug I'd been needing all my life, a perfect mix of understanding and comfort. I pressed my face into his neck breathing in the soothing sea air and raindrop aroma of his skin.

"I'm sorry, Claudine. God, I'm so sorry. I thought maybe you were having to choose between your friend and your sister. That was the second time I did that. I'm sorry."

I had reached the point of complete sobbing, but it started to die down, thankfully. "It's okay. *I'm* sorry." I sniffled. "I wanted to tell you earlier when you were talking about Gwen. It's just, I don't talk about it. I mean—" I let out a sigh, feeling frustrated by my inability to speak succinctly though I knew I had to make myself say what I kept hidden in my mind. "The thing is, I'm so ashamed I didn't notice something was wrong. She was hurting. She was my sister, and I didn't even realize." His arms tightened around me, and I took in a breath. "I didn't do anything to help her."

"Claudine. It's okay. Don't beat yourself up. You didn't know."

I held onto him, not saying anything, feeling his warmth and knowing he was right about easing the burden I had placed on myself. But it was nice to hear someone say so, to give me permission. It made me feel it was true—that I hadn't been aware enough of Amelia's hidden hurts to have intervened. I was thankful I had the good luck of knowing someone like him who could see it from a clearer perspective.

We walked back to the house. I changed out of Ramsey's jeans and set them on the bed. It had been such a perfect day except for the emotional scene in the garage. But even that part had been good. Telling Cliff the truth about Amelia had taken a weight off me.

I couldn't stop thinking about the motorcycle ride and how invigorating and good it felt. I imagined Sydney falling all over herself at the thought of me describing it to her, but I knew that wouldn't— couldn't— happen. Even if she weren't mad at me, I couldn't share it.

Jealousy aside, it would be so unsettling for her to think of me hugged up against Cliff half the day, having intimate conversations where he talked about his personal life including the origin of the song Sydney liked so much about William, or Louis rather. But the part about watching the concert from the side of the stage and getting to hang out beforehand, seeing him and Ramsey interact— maybe tuning their guitars or something? I still wanted her to be part of that.

When I walked into the kitchen, Cliff was unbagging the items delivered from the café. "You okay?"

I nodded. "I put the jeans on the bed. I can take them home and wash them."

He waved off the idea and faced me. "Stay with me tonight, Claudine." His voice had a husky, seductive edge to it.

I tried to imagine what it would be like to be naked in his arms. *Was that what he was asking?*

As if reading my mind, he took a few steps and lightly smoothed my hair. "I know what the route is like to the city. I don't want you driving back in the dark by yourself."

I knew he was worried after what I'd shared about Amelia. I had cried so hard. When I didn't say anything, he added, "I want you to be safe. Here with me."

Truth be told, when I'd put my things together that morning to head his way, I'd thought about packing more of an overnight bag but had envisioned us having a late dinner, a long conversation, and me getting a hotel room afterward without telling him.

This was better.

Once again, I found myself invading Ramsey's stash of clothes. My shorts were fine having been replaced for the bike ride by her jeans, but my shirt smelled like the heady mix of exhaust fumes and the road. I flipped through the handful of tops in the closet deciding on one with a yellow hummingbird on the front. It must have been a favorite of hers as the material was worn and soft.

After slipping it over my head, I found Cliff on the living room couch with a beer in hand. He'd set most of the gourmet snacks on a nearby tray and looked to have already made a dent in the salted pecans. I loved this about him, how he was so easygoing, so relaxed whether in his own home or someplace else. No pretensions.

"How 'bout a movie?" He picked up the remote control nearby. "I've got a whole set-up but never use it. It's nice to have a guest for a change. You get to choose what we watch."

Sitting next to him, I took a swallow of the beer he'd opened for me, and he handed me the remote. I clicked around the platforms deciding on a black-and-white film starring Katharine Hepburn and Spencer Tracy. Leaning into Cliff, we watched in silence, drinking our beers, sampling the snacks. It felt like an extension of him holding me earlier, the comfort of it, except I was glad it didn't include tears now.

I don't remember the movie ending, but I knew I had been nodding off. Given I'd driven over that morning and we'd spent the day on the motorcycle, I had run out of steam.

In the night, I woke up on the floor with the side of my face pressed against a plush throw rug. After getting my bearings, I reached up to search for Cliff on the couch in the darkness. Following his shoulder to his hand resting across his stomach, I clasped his fingers enjoying the rise and fall of his breathing against our entwined fingers. When I started to let go, he gripped my hand.

"Come up here and be with me." His voice sounded sleepy and slow.

After he turned to the side settling his back against the couch, I folded myself into his glorious body, not waking up for hours and hours.

Chapter 21

SOMETIMES I THINK IF I COULD HAVE MET Cliff earlier in my life and spent a day like that with him—the personal nature of our conversation, his tacit understanding of things with me below the surface, along with the simple enjoyment of his company—then I would have been more determined, aggressive even, in figuring things out for myself.

I'd spent so much time floundering and carrying around a bag of worry believing I had no choice but to accept feeling so troubled and uncertain. But all the bleak things that jogged around in my mind were foreign ideas when I was with him. He made me feel I could overcome them.

Sitting on the edge of his couch, I felt surprisingly good for sleeping half of the night on the floor. I shielded my eyes as the sun sprayed through the large picture window. A pleasant scent of fresh coffee roamed nearby.

CHAPTER 21

I wandered to the kitchen in Ramsey's now wrinkled t-shirt. A maroon mug waited by the coffeemaker but no Cliff. After filling the cup, I turned around to pad beyond the front living room and down a hallway leading into another area of the house. Through a doorway I saw him scrutinizing a piece of paper.

I waited quietly not wanting to interrupt. From what I could see, the room looked to hold the musical aspects of his life: guitars, a keyboard tucked in a corner, sheet music, as well as some of his memories. One was a picture of him with David Bowie. David had vibrant yellow hair, his suit burgundy while Cliff was dressed in black. They were both laughing as though one of them had said something funny. My breath caught at the sight of it, and Cliff looked up, glasses on, clean-shaven.

"There you are." He set aside the paper on the desk before him littered with pens, a notepad, even a few guitar picks, and a small digital clock.

"I'm sorry. I'm not spying on you. You looked like you were concentrating."

"It's fine. I wanted to let you rest." He glanced at the paper he'd just set down. "I'm trying to find an arrangement for Ramsey. She wants to do a song I haven't played in years."

"What's it called?"

"'Your Periphery.' It's from an album called *Heat*. She likes to take things and find a new slant. She gets a lot of latitude with her pop's old stuff."

Him referring to himself as *pop* made me laugh. I didn't think of him as a father even though we had talked about his children. It felt strange, especially given all the times Sydney and I had discussed his attractive body and seductive stage presence. But then, those things had led to children.

"The coffee's good." I lifted the mug toward him in a mock toast.

"I have some breakfast for us, too. We can eat whenever you're ready."

I sipped some more. It was too hot for a full swallow, but the warm cup felt good in my hands. "Is this where you write?"

"Sometimes." He gestured at a closed laptop as he moved from behind the desk. "On the boat can be a good spot for that, too. I may have told you that."

I took a step beyond the doorway. I wasn't sure if he wanted me to come into what looked to be his private area. "I need to set up a better place for writing in my apartment. I usually sit in my kitchen. It's so small though. It can make it hard to think." My eyes drifted around the walls some more. "Whoa! Is that Keith Richards?"

"Lord Keith himself. You can come in and look at it and anything else."

I headed over to the photograph hanging next to a bookcase. "You must have been ecstatic. Did you get to play with him?"

He shook his head no. "When you're a celebrity and you go to someone else's concert, you can almost always go backstage beforehand. My manager set it up, probably so he could meet him, too." He chuckled.

"What year was that?"

"Seventy-six maybe? I'm around thirty there." He tapped the glass.

A photo in the same style frame hung next to it. The guy standing beside Cliff gave him a run for his money. They both had hair made for a shampoo commercial and the handsome fresh faces of every teen girl's dream. "Who is this?"

"That's Shaun Cassidy, younger guy, younger than me anyway. He left the music scene. He writes for television now."

"Oh yeah." Now I remembered. He'd graced the walls of my shared bedroom with Amelia at one point, too. "You've met everyone."

I set the coffee down and wandered about with my arms folded as if I might damage something simply by being there. I still wanted to see a Grammy. I knew he had some. All kinds of things were on display except for awards, including miniature motorcycles, a world globe, and even several cowboy hats on one wall.

I was a little disappointed. I had been thinking of the recap I'd be giving to Aunt Trudy about being with him and had imagined a big finish by telling her about seeing a platinum album or something similar up close. And then I found it.

"I recognize this." I placed my hands on my knees supporting myself as I bent forward to look at a light blue guitar. It was on a stand next to an oversized chair in one corner. A tall, leafy plant partially obscured it. "Amelia was a fan of yours. Have I told you that?" I didn't think I had, but it had been floating in the back of my mind for so long I wasn't sure.

I heard him take a few steps in my direction. He'd already had a shower. A fresh scent of soap further announced his nearness to me. When I turned around, his eyes were kind and inviting. "No, you haven't."

"She wasn't a fan like my friend Sydney, wanting to know your every move, stressing about the right seats for your concerts and all that." He pressed his lips together in a muted smile, and I went on. "She played your records a lot and read the magazines with you in them. She had a poster of you on the back of our bedroom door. It had a dark background, and there were some geometric shapes floating around you." I paused as I thought of our old room with the twin beds, the picture of Cliff feet from us, and Amelia dancing nearby. "I think that's the guitar you were holding in the poster. I saw it every day for a couple of years. Do you know the one I'm talking about?"

He moved past me to lift the guitar out of the stand and then held it face up so I could view it more closely. He squinted and shook his head. "I'm not sure. I know we did a lot of photo shoots with this one." He sounded like he hated to disappoint me.

I felt the guitar's finish and then ran my fingers lightly down the strings of the neck. "I hope you're not upset I hadn't mentioned her being a fan. But I was afraid I'd have to get into, you know, what I told you when we got back from the ride last night."

He put the guitar against his torso in position to play and then stopped short of strumming. "I understand. I'm glad and honored to know Amelia was a fan, a dedicated one it sounds like. I wish I'd known her." He always knew what to say.

"Thank you. You would have liked her. She was the motorcycle-riding type. She was all about exploring and finding adventure. She also would have wanted to see your Grammys and so do I. Where are they?"

All of that was true, and I wanted him to know about Amelia's connection to him, but I was trying to prevent another sad conversation about her. Although as I stood there, I realized I didn't feel sad. It was nice to discuss her with someone like

Cliff who understood and cared instead of having to pretend she didn't still play a role in my thoughts and heart.

Cliff looked around as if he had to think about the Grammys. "Ramsey has them. I've never been into the awards thing."

"Really? How come?"

"When I write, the feeling I get from giving life to my thoughts and others having an interest in them—that's the meaningful part to me. I don't need an accolade."

I found his answer surprising. It seemed to me national recognition in the entertainment world was the ultimate thing for a musician. I thought about the times he'd appeared on stage, and fans yelled out praises or *I love you* and the like. He always had such a reticent response as though it were too much for him. It made sense now.

I looked at him bashfully. "I've been looking for them since I got here."

He laughed as he brushed past me once more to set the guitar back in place. "No Grammys here, but I do have pie. Let's go have some."

I reached for my coffee mug having forgotten about it. "Pie? It's nine o'clock in the morning."

"That's okay. Think of it like having a pastry, a cinnamon roll. Or a donut. Pie is great any time." He led the way back to the kitchen as I followed sipping the now tepid coffee.

CHAPTER 21

We sat on the back deck of the house each with a dripping hunk of blueberry pie. He told me his neighbor had brought it over while I was still asleep.

"Now this is the kind of thing people should get an award for." He lifted a bite to his mouth. "Seriously, this is a prize-winning meal."

"I don't think I've ever had pie for breakfast."

He winked. "You've been missing out."

I agreed, but it wasn't the pie that had been missing for me. It was how good it felt being with him.

We finished eating and sat for a while not talking. The sky began a transformation with shades of blue bursting into hues of orange. I could easily have stayed there watching the colors unfold, eating more pie, and lingering in the exquisite ecstasy of being with someone in silence.

I knew I needed to get on the road. If I arrived early enough, I could visit Aunt Trudy and fill her in on everything about my visit with him. I so wanted to tell someone about it.

And then there was Sydney. I had done my best not to think about her, but I needed us to sort things out. I missed her. Despite not wanting to leave Cliff and the comfort of being with him at his home, the drive back to the city would be a welcome three hours of focus. I could use the time to think about how I'd talk to her with the right balance of sharing what was happening with Cliff and not exacerbating her anger toward me. And more important than

307

that, not activating the underlying jealousy in her Paige had described to me. Now at least, I had the news about the concert with Ramsey which I hoped would help offset any misgivings on Sydney's part.

I made it back to the city in time to return the rental car, get some groceries, and then meet Aunt Trudy at a Greek restaurant inside Grand Central Station. She was flitting about near there and suggested I come meet her.

When I arrived, her usual flamboyance made her easy to spot. She sat at a booth in the corner of the food court wearing a teal green turban with a peacock feather rising from one side. She looked like a fortune teller but nonetheless Aunt Trudy.

After I described the motorcycle ride with Cliff, the guitar and poster story, and how he'd been so empathetic when I'd told him about Amelia, she said, "You mean to tell me, Claudey, you spent all that time with that man-candy and didn't even get a kiss from him?" Her face fell in playful disappointment.

I told her Cliff had walked me to my car with his arm around me and how he'd placed a careful peck on my side of my head. What I didn't say was that as I'd opened the car's door, I'd thought about turning around, grabbing his head of luscious hair, and pressing my lips to his. I wondered if he'd considered doing the same with me.

Chapter 22

THE NEXT FEW WEEKENDS BROUGHT THE same superb enjoyment of being with Cliff. Time with him was like stepping into a beautiful painting surrounded by gladdening flowers, peonies, lilies, and daffodils. There was so much color and light around when he was nearby.

We'd wander around the main market area of Jamestown, sit on the pier at the marina passing a soda bottle back and forth while our feet skimmed the water, and take walks near his house in the evening. Sometimes he'd tinker with his motorcycle under the fluorescent light in his detached garage while I perched on a crate nearby reading the Ruth Chatterton novel he'd bought for me. My favorite was when I'd share aloud a well-constructed paragraph, and we'd discuss it. Then there would be pie. Always pie.

I thought about inviting him to spend a weekend at my apartment, but it was more fun to be at his place where we could go for rides and be on his boat. We had even slept on it one night, staying up late, watching the moon.

Sydney continued to be distant and unwilling to communicate with me. I rotated between sending texts and emails to her and even stopped by her apartment once while uptown on an errand for Nina. I knew the more time passed, the harder it would be to reconcile things with her. I could feel the divide growing between us.

Initially, there was only the dinner after the Jamestown concert to tell her about and the lunch outing with Cliff at the museum. Now, I wasn't sure how I'd approach all the things he and I had done together and what was happening between us, a friendship bordering on something more.

That following week Cliff's new novel was being released. Sydney and I always spent so much time talking about his concerts, the tickets we wanted, and what we might wear to catch his eye I'd forgotten he had another book in the works.

She had mentioned the new book when we'd first met, but since his novel writing wasn't as big of an interest to her, activity in that aspect of his career didn't come up much after that which was odd because it was so important to him. Cliff himself hadn't even said anything to me about it until a few days beforehand. That behavior spoke to his nature, not wanting to brag, especially knowing how I felt I'd failed with my magazine article.

The day of the book's release he was to appear on a morning television show and then have a book signing. I took the day off for everything. I thought I should be a little fixed up and asked one of the stylists at the magazine if I could come by and have my hair done. The result of glossy tresses spiraling from my crown and hitting my shoulders in a soft bounce came out perfectly.

When I arrived at the venerable television network at Rockefeller Center, an aged man at the front desk asked for my identification and checked my name on a computer before directing me to the elevators. It felt so strange. Exciting strange. I had never been backstage at a TV studio.

In the elevator, I thought about what it would be like to get to discuss, on television or not, creating a story from start to finish and how I'd developed the plot and characters. I wondered if Cliff would be nervous or if he had prepared things to say about the book called *Diamond Days*. It was about a horse named Diamond and the man who took care of him, he'd told me. He'd named the main character after his father.

When I reached the right floor and stepped into the corridor, I was welcomed by a young girl who I assumed was an intern or other entry level employee.

"Are you here for Cliff Woods?" She wore her hair slicked into a bun, no doubt an attempt to make herself look sophisticated.

"Wood." I corrected her. She didn't seem interested in the mistake she'd probably been making all morning.

At the end of the hallway I could see Thomas Yale with Bruce in conversation along with a woman wearing a red suit and sporting a smart page boy haircut. She was Cliff's editor, Jane, who I'd meet momentarily. Next to them, the tallest, was Cliff, his hair styled with just the right amount of product. He wore black pants, a burgundy European cut dress shirt with his sleeves rolled up, and the silver bracelet he often wore on stage.

When I started to move toward him, the bun-wearing intern stopped me. "You'll have to wait in here." She stretched her hand toward a doorway as though she were offering a prize.

"Can I just say hi to him?" I felt like a child asking for permission though I was easily ten or more years older than the girl.

"The contest winners will only be in the audience. If there's time after his segment, and if Mr. Woods wants to, you may be able to be part of a group photo with him." She sounded so matter-of-fact but also forced herself to speak with a suitable level of cheer.

"It's Wood! And I'm not a fan. I mean, I am a fan, but I'm not a part of *those* fans."

"Really, Miss, you have to wait in here."

"But I'm NOT a fan. I'm—"

I could tell the girl was getting frustrated with me as a tight smile took over her expression.

312

Then I heard, "She's allowed," in a voice deep and commanding. Cliff had moved toward us and motioned for me to come his way. "She's with me."

"Yes, I'm with him!"

I still remember how glorious it felt as I headed toward him, my arms sailing around his shoulders, the touch of his hand gliding down the length of my freshly styled hair as he whispered, "I'm so glad you're here."

And even though I had known him a while by then, it still felt like a fairy tale to be able to say I was with him and knew him personally.

We went further down the hall and around the corner through a set of heavy doors where the broadcast was in full motion, one of those live mid-morning shows where the bulk of time is spent on soft news items usually involving celebrities, movies soon to come out, a new clothing line, and such.

"Whoa, honey, whoa! Look who's here." The program's host, an elegant woman of color, left the set during a commercial break. Her shoes clicked on the polished studio floor as she headed over to meet Cliff.

Her name was Shana, and she wore a fitted royal blue dress and heels that put her eye level with him. She had the same look of mild shock everyone had when seeing him up close, then commented about his luck in the aging process. With a shy smile, he vaguely said it was kind of her to say.

The on-air piece with him lasted about five minutes. I was glad Shana had gotten her fawning out of the way and concentrated on questions about his new book. She then segued into his music career, and Cliff said he already had some songs in the works for his next album.

From my vantage point in the wings with Jane, I scanned the audience for Sydney. How was I to react if I saw her? Luckily, I didn't have to decide. A contest would be beneath her level of fandom. I knew that much about her ways of thinking. She was probably already at the bookstore, front of the line, awaiting Cliff's arrival. If things had been different, I'd have been there with her.

When we left the studio, I joined his entourage aboard a Mercedes limousine. Seated next to Cliff in the luxurious vehicle, I still couldn't believe I was there. When he had asked me to come to the book release events, I'd expected my presence to be more in the background, getting myself to and from the locations, and maybe having a spot saved in the audience at the show. That would have been special enough to me. I hadn't imagined being so on the inside.

"How did I do?" Cliff looked over at me as we coasted along Park Avenue making our way to Union Square. His face was relaxed, his eyes their usual comforting gaze.

He and I were the only ones not held hostage by our phones. Jane, in the front, was confirming the details of a book signing event for another author.

"You did great." I touched his hand. I wanted to say something more specific, but I hadn't paid complete attention what with having been thinking more about Sydney's possible presence. I felt bad about it. "Are there really some new songs?" I wanted to demonstrate I'd been listening.

"A couple. Not finished yet."

I wished I could tell Sydney. She would love getting a direct confirmation like that about potential new music. Everything was so bizarre now. Here I was riding right next to Cliff in a limo, and I wasn't communicating with her. It was hard to accept this reality about a friendship I'd wanted so much.

"I hope I said enough about the book." Cliff broke through the cloud of my thoughts. "The music always comes up. Can kind of get in the way." He hadn't noticed my mental absence.

I decided to be honest with him. "She was a good interviewer, but I didn't hear everything. I was busy looking for someone."

His slight laugh said he was both amused by and appreciated my honesty. "Who would that be?"

Now we were getting into uncomfortable territory. "A friend. A friend who's a deep fan of yours." I didn't go any further. This was his day. I wouldn't let the nonsense with Sydney and me interfere.

At the south end of Broadway, the sun streaked through the front windshield as we arrived at the Strand, a landmark bookstore.

The line of people waiting for Cliff folded around the building. Sure enough, Sydney was among the first dozen. She had lightened her hair. Caramel highlights popped against the rest of her dark layers, and the small shaved section above her ear on one side had grown out. The standard gang, Paige, Evvi, Doreen, Lorie, and Jerry, were part of the same front cluster by the entrance.

As we waited for Jane to alert the store of Cliff's arrival, I tried to think of what to do. I didn't want my getting out of a limousine with Cliff to be the first time I saw Sydney. It would crush her.

"Is this where you'll go in?" I looked beyond Cliff through the tinted glass.

"Guess so."

"I think I'll let you get situated and come in after."

"No need for that."

"You're not worried about all those fans wondering who I am?"

He leaned close to the window. "Not really." He looked a moment longer. "Is it something to do with the friend you were looking for at the show?"

"Maybe, but this is your day, okay?"

He teasingly bumped my shoulder. "I'm sharing it with you okay? Which one is she?"

I leaned across him to locate Sydney, having lost sight of her, so easy to do with her diminutive size. Then Evvi moved, and I could see Sydney in profile. She had a messenger bag grazing her hip with a worn baseball cap tucked in the side of it. "The one with the hat." I pointed. "That's Sydney."

"What's the deal with her?"

Now I bumped his shoulder the way he'd done to me. "Come on, don't' worry about this! I'll figure things out with her. It's just a little falling out."

"I hope it wasn't over me."

When I didn't say anything, he knew the answer. I saw Jane coming back, phone to her ear. I knew it was time.

You'd have thought I was walking to a death sentence what with the nerves I felt as we exited the limousine. I did my best to trail behind Cliff knowing all the onlookers were taking photographs and videos of us. Even before he had stepped out of the car, I saw all the phones poised in the air, ready to capture the first glimpse of him.

The usual shout-outs and cheers erupted, and when we got close to the entrance, Thomas Yale held the door for us. I lingered a step trying to catch Sydney's eye. I didn't want her to think I was ignoring her or rubbing the situation in her face, but had she taken any of my calls, I'd have brought her into the know ahead of time. She might even have been in that limo with me.

She wouldn't look at me though. Instead, she fixated on her phone. Paige gave me an enthusiastic smile while Jerry and Lorie were supportive with a thumbs-up.

Admittedly, I did feel special being in Cliff's entourage. A few people took pictures of me, probably to post in a group later and speculate on my identity or role in Cliff's world. I knew how those things went from Sydney's deliberations in similar situations. I couldn't do anything about it and figured Cliff must have accepted this public aspect of his life long ago.

Inside, he was led to a table displaying his new novel with hardcover copies propped on small easels and a stack at each end in a decorative fashion. He picked up one of the books with a green cover, a speckled brown and white horse in the background, and pretended to read it. When he caught me looking at him, he feigned an expression of intrigue, making me laugh and forget for a moment the tension and sadness I felt about Sydney.

A text message from Paige. *You arrived with him!? Wow!*

At least someone was communicating with me. I sent her a smiley face and found a place to the side next to Bruce and Thomas while Jane spoke to the bookstore employees about the game plan before letting everyone inside for their moment with the iconic rock star.

It felt so uncomfortable, knowing Sydney was nearby and had completely disregarded me. All I could figure to do was distance my thoughts about the situation. I wanted her to enjoy her moment with Cliff. I knew how important those experiences with him were to her, to all the fans waiting to meet him.

I considered looking around the store until she was gone, but not only did I think my disappearance would be rude to Cliff, I also wanted to experience everything that happened with him. Plus, Marlon's bookstore was too small to hold signings. The event itself was something unique for me.

When the long-waiting fans were invited to enter the store, I saw Sydney had moved and was now further back in the line, probably a means to keep me at a distance or not have to see me too soon. The store's manager made an announcement welcoming Cliff, and after the applause died down, the first woman approached him.

She had blond hair parted down the middle, her cheeks blushing, and looked to be Amelia's age. She handed her book to Cliff. "Oh. My. Gosh. Hi. This is so fabulous! I wasn't into westerns until I came across your novels. I grew up with your music."

Cliff flipped to the title page as he gave her a subtle smile. "Thank you. What's your name?"

"Alyson."

"Hi Alyson."

She looked as though she might absolutely pass out at the sound of his voice that was equal parts kind and sensual, even heart-stopping when you weren't used to him saying your name. Then he did his trademark flourish of a signature that barely looked like it read Cliff Wood other than the *c* and the *l* and maybe part of the *w* in some cases.

"Um, could we, um, do a picture?" The girl took the book from him and turned to hand her cell phone to Jane, now the official photographer for the event.

And so it went.

"Hi, what's your name?"

"Sylvia."

"Veronica."

"Kristina"

"Josephine."

"Suzanne."

"Victoria."

"Jessica."

"Eileen."

After getting the autograph, each girl leaned over the table trying to get as close as possible to Cliff for the photo. I completely understood. He smelled like the sway of palm trees that day, or something refreshing anyway. I couldn't put my finger on it.

Then it was Sydney's turn.

She had run her hands through her hair a few times, I could tell, the misplaced strands loosely falling to one side. Where I waited out of range, I watched as she handed her bag to Paige and then said something, which knowing Sydney, was precise instructions about getting the best candid shots.

Cliff used the moment to glance back at me. His face paused into a brief smile as he stood up and stepped over to a separate table holding bottles of water. After twisting the cap off one, he tipped it to his lips and carried it back to the signing area a few feet from where Sydney waited. Except he didn't sit in the chair. He positioned his perfect buttocks on the edge of the table and pulled her under one arm, his other raised in a peace sign. It was such a cute pose that everyone applauded.

After the picture was taken, he took the novel from her as he said, "It's Sydney, right?"

"Yes, with a 'y.' Two."

Her gleaming smile could have been seen on the other side of the earth while Paige captured an album full of photos during the ten seconds.

In normal circumstances, as in not trying to avoid me, Sydney would have stayed to watch the rest of the event all the way through to the moment Cliff left, waiting for him by his car. But this time, as soon as her turn was over, she left the store.

That's when I made my move.

"Sydney. Wait!" I followed her outside and hurried along the sidewalk. Cars buzzed down Broadway as a taxi's horn drowned out my voice. Either that or she was continuing to ignore me. "Sydney, wait. Please!"

She finally stopped and did a slow turn-around, her eyes low and to the side. She wore heavier make-up than usual, shimmery neutral eye shadow and thick eyeliner, looking her best for Cliff. I didn't notice it in the store.

"Look, I wanted to—um, did you have a good time?" My teeth caught my lower lip's edge. I hadn't considered what I would say to her.

"Is that why you came out here? To ask if I had a good time? Yes, I had a good time. Anything else?" Her dismissive tone caught me off guard even if I hadn't expected any warmth.

"Your picture with him was cute."

I thought the comment might soften her anger, but she continued in the same caustic manner. I felt stupid for trying. Maybe I deserved it despite having the best intentions all along.

"Well as you saw, he knows *me,* too. Just because I wasn't the one who got to have dinner with him doesn't mean he hasn't ever noticed me. And what, you're his sidekick now? You think you're a star because of that I guess. Whatever."

Wow, this was teenage stuff, and Sydney was forty years old. I remembered she'd told me how some fans think they're better than others in the Cliff Wood zone. Something along those lines was probably afloat in her head right now. But I wasn't like that, and she knew it.

She had her arms folded with her freshly signed novel clamped under them as she eyed me. I had hoped she'd had time to cool off since the show-down in Portland and maybe seeing me would trigger something in her—our shared memories for one—to resolve things between us. Obviously that wasn't happening. I decided it best not to react to her mordant comments.

"Sydney, I wanted to tell you I'm sorry about what happened in Jamestown." Well, not sorry about how it had turned out with knowing Cliff, but sorry for what it had done to our friendship. "That's why I'm out here. Finding Cliff was an accidental thing, and I really wish it would have been you. I can't change that. But do you want to go with me to the concert to see Ramsey next weekend? There aren't any tickets, but Cliff said we could have standing space and—"

"With you? No thanks. I'm already going."

"You are?"

"Mmm hmm. With Natasha."

"I didn't think she liked Cliff."

"She does. In a different way."

"Well, Cliff said I could bring an extra person, so if you—"

"I don't want to go with you, anywhere, Claudine. Not anymore. Especially to anything involving Cliff Wood."

I was stunned. And sad. I licked my lips, unsure of what to say other than, "Okay. I guess I'll see you there."

As I walked away, she called back, "I hope not."

I wondered what had happened to the Sydney who had thought me to be a good luck charm because it had turned out to be true. And I wanted her to share in it.

Chapter 23

THE BOOK SIGNING WENT ON FOR AT LEAST two more hours. When it seemed things were wrapping up, more fans would arrive. Cliff dutifully and happily stayed until each person had their moment with him. I hadn't expected such a prolonged event and kept thinking Jane would come along to intervene and announce things to be over causing some stragglers to be turned away, but that didn't happen. Cliff showed no signs of wanting to close the session either.

My conversation with Sydney had left a bitter taste. I was disappointed to say the least. I hadn't expected she'd come running into my arms, but I did think she'd at least want to repair things with me to some degree. Did she care anything about our friendship? About me? Her behavior moments ago hadn't said so. I thought about the beginnings of our time together and couldn't stop my mind from its desire to reminisce. I thought of how we'd get a meal and then end up drinking and talking and not wanting to go home.

I knew Cliff so well now I could call or text him anytime. It would have been fun to share that with her, no more having to figure out his whereabouts after his concerts. That access had been one of the first things to cross my mind as I'd started getting to know him.

"Where can we eat? I'm hungry." Cliff was always hungry. His voice knocked me out of my haze in the biography section.

For the last twenty minutes I'd been traipsing among the rows and running my finger along the colorful spines. It felt so reassuring to be among books right now, immersing myself in the words, desires, and pages, imagining all the long hours spent by the authors as they pored over their manuscripts, searching for the right verb or character name. It made me feel better after the encounter with Sydney.

I turned around to face Cliff. "Pizza maybe? There's a place we could walk to nearby. I mean, I could, maybe not you without being accosted, Mr. Songwriter-Novelist."

But we did walk. All of us. Cliff and me first, leading the way, Thomas Yale and Bruce close by, Jane on her phone, and a handful of others including Paige. I was glad she had hung around until the end so when Cliff said to invite some friends, I could motion her and her group to come along. I assumed the limousine had been dismissed; I saw it gliding away as we left the Strand.

What was so enjoyable about the atmosphere once we got to the restaurant was how it didn't feel like we were there with Cliff Wood, *rock star*. It was just a group of people having a good time. Four or five different pizzas. Pitchers of beer. Conversations. Laughs. No one asked him for a photo or an autograph.

I was happy getting to share the joy of being with him, though I wished as always Amelia could be there, and in the corner of my mind, Sydney, too. Cliff made a point of engaging everyone during the meal, something out of character for his reserved off-stage persona. When he spoke to Paige, her words came out as a statement of fact rather than sounding like an enraptured fan.

"I've been into your music for so long. All your writing has such a meaningful quality." She clasped my hand under the table as Cliff gave her one of his warm smiles, a tacit thank you.

I loved how he was so understated. He was respectful to everyone he met—to waiters and cleaners, bar staff and receptionists. It struck me as unusual for someone in his position. But that was the real Cliff. He saw everyone as his equal.

There wasn't a bite of pizza or drop of beer left when the table thinned out. I hadn't noticed who had left or when having spent a good portion of the time talking with Jane about her work in the publishing world.

Now it left Thomas, Cliff, and me, the three of us heading out as well.

"Are you coming with me or getting back on your own?" Thomas turned to Cliff after reaching for a toothpick by the cash register in the entryway.

"I'll be fine. Appreciate your help today." He gave Thomas a manly pat on his shoulder.

Thomas pushed the door open. "It was a great turnout. Gonna be a bestseller. Good to see you, Claudine."

Outside Thomas flagged a taxi. My mouth swirled with the taste of pizza crust, green onions, and mushrooms. I reached in my purse for a stick of gum and pushed it into my mouth. "Did you enjoy that?"

"Enjoy what?" Cliff had his hands in his pockets, aviator sunglasses in place.

"Being with fans like that in a casual way."

"Sure." He shrugged ever so slightly as if his answer were a given. "Were you upset your friend didn't stay and come with us?"

We took a few steps, not really knowing where we were going yet. "It's kind of complicated. I appreciate what you did, getting up for the picture with her and all." I didn't want to discuss it beyond that and sully the moment of happily ambling along after such a pleasant day.

I changed the subject. "We're not that far from my apartment if you want to see it. It's just a quick subway ride."

The sun wasn't strong enough for Cliff's shades, and he moved them atop his head. "I like the subway. Let's go."

On the train, we slid onto the orange plastic bench across from a woman carrying a day's worth of shopping. Most everyone else was head down, mystified by their cell phones or otherwise adrift in thought. Someone's stale perfume hung in the air.

It occurred to me there had been a time when public transportation would not have been an option for Cliff with his face too recognizable when his songs had been at the top of the music charts. Though he still had a respectable following, it was unlikely he'd be identified now, especially with mostly twenty- and early thirty-somethings aboard.

We took the R Train for one stop to 8th Street NYU and then walked through Washington Square Park. When we arrived in my part of the neighborhood, I watched as Cliff paused to survey the landscape and building facades. He looked solemn, the gears in his mind turning. I figured that must be why he was so good at writing songs, the way he thought about everything so deeply, always examining his environment. Inside his mind had to be such a creative and interesting place. Though he'd shared a lot with me, I knew there was much more to learn about him.

"This is a great area. I like the small venues around here. They have a lot of character." He had the expression of a tourist taking in the scenery as his head turned side to side.

"I went to your show near here, at the Bowery Electric. I saw you in the hotel's lobby beforehand. It freaked me out."

He looked over at me. "And now here we are. Friends."

"I grew up around here. I like it. I like being in a place with its own special vibe." I motioned to a sign in a window that read, 'Free the people. Free instantly. You are your own Venus.' I'd never figured out what it meant.

A breeze swept his hair across his forehead, and he brushed it to the side. "I can see a writer like you being happy here." He looked at me, serious.

"A writer like me?" I lightly put a hand to my chest. "I'm hardly a writer. I couldn't even eke out one basic article about fashion. Even when the guy I like tried to inspire me by wearing a pink shirt." Mentally, I questioned if the *guy I like* part was too much.

"I bet there was a lot of talk about that shirt."

"Oh, there was. And probably some I didn't even know about."

We made it to Charles Street and stood on the sidewalk below the square archway framing the door to my apartment. The day was winding down, and the street felt empty. To the south, the sun had begun its goodbye.

I felt a sensation of the excitement of the day come over me, being part of Cliff's entourage at the TV studio and book signing and then being the catalyst for other fans to hang out with him afterward.

Those experiences aside, he'd given me so much, making me feel I could share private things aloud to him. He had activated something in me that made me want to try harder to figure things out for myself. I memorized all that goodness. Then he added to it.

"Claudine, please listen to me. That article wasn't you. I can't write a whole song on a sentiment that isn't me either. Well, I *could*, but it wouldn't be a good song in the end, you know? It'd just be a song."

The last bit of sun burned from the distance like a whisper through the trees along the street. The subdued tones softened his face and made him look younger. I reached up and briefly lay my fingertips on the side of his chin.

He stopped and looked at me for a moment as if trying to make sure what he was saying was sinking in. "We talked about this before on the boat. You knew going in it wasn't something that was grabbing you. You tried, and you were true to yourself as a writer. That's how it should be." He was so eloquent, so thoughtful about the explanation.

I felt shy. I'm never sure what to do when someone says something so heartfelt like that to me. It didn't happen often and was even more touching coming from him, and unreal, and everything you might imagine it to feel like if someone famous you admired said something helpful to you, something to make you feel better. I half expected a crane with a movie camera to come into view and hear, "Cut!"

My inclination would normally have been to react with tears, but instead, that was when I slipped my hand into the back of that hair I'd been wanting to touch and collapsed my mouth into his. The immediate sensation of his lips mounted on mine felt exotic and exhilarating. It was like standing on a mountaintop and realizing all the enchantment you'd been missing from the view.

The times I'd imagined kissing him, I'd pictured it taking place somewhere more poetic like on his boat or at the end of a motorcycle ride, but the tranquil end-of-day stillness of my street worked fine.

When we broke apart, I couldn't tell if Cliff had experienced the same sensation I'd had—this kind of falling and not caring if or where you landed. Realistically, he probably hadn't. Who knew how many women he'd kissed through the years?

He pulled me against him, and my face fell into his neck. I could still taste his lips on mine as he lightly rubbed my back. It was as if he were trying to tell me what I'd done was okay but didn't want to endorse my behavior. I thought about how he had characterized us as *friends* moments ago. That wasn't a bad thing, but I wondered if he could ever see us as something more.

We didn't say anything as we took the wide stairs up to my apartment door. I mentally admonished myself for being so impulsive, but honestly, that kiss hadn't been entirely spontaneous. I'd thought about it more than a few times that day as I watched him maneuver his television appearance and book signing with such finesse like it was just another day. His laidback ways made him that much more attractive.

It took less than a minute to give him a tour of my apartment. I had a red, velvet couch—a giveaway of Aunt Trudy's, some random wall art consisting of mosaics with ceramic pieces, and of course, my collection of expertly chosen books. I wasn't really into decorating.

In my kitchen, I offered him some water, and we found a place on the couch and kicked off our shoes. I suggested we watch a movie and queued one I'd recorded featuring a 1960s Elizabeth Taylor. During the opening credits, he murmured he'd met her once.

He scooted closer, arranging his arm around me, and I folded my knees against his thigh.

I set the remote aside. "I had a Liz phase. I liked to think I resembled her in that natural yet striking kind of way. But really it's just us both being brunettes with blue eyes. She wrote a whole book about how much she loved jewelry. You wouldn't think something like that would offer much, but she filled it with humor and poignant thoughts." I looked around the room trying to remember if I still had it.

Cliff stared at the television screen. "You're doing it again. Showing your depth and experiences, the way you talked about that. You've got writing in you. You just need to find it."

I let out a sigh. "Thank you. I appreciate all the things you've been telling me." I wanted to kiss him again but squeezed his hand instead.

As the movie neared the end, I felt my eyes drooping. The flurry of the day had caught up to me. Cliff had a long trek back to Jamestown in the dark. He was probably tired, too. I didn't want to waylay him, but I wished he could stay longer.

"This couch is pretty comfy. I won't give you anymore surprise kisses if you want to stick around." My comment was a way to test the waters about his interest.

Cliff stood up, stretched, and reached for his phone on the nearby table. "I've got a hotel room in Midtown. I have to get up early for some radio interviews tomorrow morning." He checked his phone. "I'd ask you to come, but you don't need to miss more work for me." He made no comment on the kiss.

"But I would, you know."

He smiled with a charming sparkle in his eyes. "Let's meet for lunch before I go back. Next week I'll be tied up getting ready for the show."

Outside, the smell of the city hung around us as I waited with him for his car service. I wasn't sure if it was imagined or not, but I felt a shift between us as we stood where I'd made my brazen move with him a few hours ago.

When the sedan arrived, Cliff put his arms around me, bending me into him, his hugs the only good thing each time we parted. I felt his breath against the side of my head and his lips move by my ear saying, "Surprises can be nice."

Chapter 24

I LAY AWAKE THE NEXT MORNING ENTWINED among my blanket and pillows reliving what it felt like to kiss him. Cliff Wood. It had been like a present I'd been waiting to open, the excitement of finding what was in the box. Except now that I'd opened it so to speak, I wasn't sure what it meant, if anything. Of all the times I'd softly fantasized about a moment like that with him, I didn't think I'd ever act on such thoughts.

Now, I regretted doing so. What he'd whispered before leaving had such an ambiguous undertone. Did he mean surprises *can* be nice*, but kissing you* isn't one of them? And more than that, had I put a kink in our friendship?

I once read a quote that said you could spend all your time analyzing a situation or toss the pieces of the puzzle aside and move on. I've always had a hard time with that concept. I prefer to figure things out. With Cliff, I didn't want something tacitly hanging between us that could interrupt the joy I'd found with him. Those puzzle pieces would have to be put together.

The next day, I rode the D train uptown to Columbus Circle and then headed west toward Central Park to meet him for lunch. As I traveled along greeted by the blooming lavender crocus and colorful foliage garnishing the entrances to the buildings framing my path, I decided I would have to find a way to mention the kiss in an offhand way. Then I'd let it sit and see if I could detect anything in the way we interacted.

I mentally rehearsed a couple of ideas for the conversation I would have with him, but all my ideas were immediately derailed when I arrived at the restaurant. He wasn't alone.

It was a small place, as most restaurants are in that area, more deep than wide with a bar to one side but no one seated there. Conversations commingled in the air as waitrons flitted from table to table keeping things moving for the lunchtime rush. One of them passed Cliff's table and then looked back as she walked away. I knew she recognized him.

It upset me he hadn't given any indication it wouldn't be only the two of us for the meal. The day before, we had been surrounded by his entourage and then with the crowd at the book signing. I had so enjoyed being with him alone afterward at my apartment but wanted more. It was an unusual feeling for me to have a sense of entitlement for his time. I didn't like myself for it. It made me feel I was falling into the category of some of his fans who could never get enough attention from him onstage or off.

In the restaurant, I saw he was absorbed by whatever the girl sitting with him was saying. His elbow was propped on the table with his chin in his hand while his eyes registered a look of total captivation. I watched her head move animatedly as she spoke. A glass of water in her left hand jostled with her enthusiastic gesticulations.

Cliff saw me heading their way and half-waved before returning his attention to the girl. When I reached them, I stood awkwardly as though I needed to be invited to join them. Cliff waited as she finished her story and then pulled out the chair next to him. As I took a seat, he simultaneously motioned toward the girl.

"Look who's arrived. Claudine, this is my daughter, Ramsey. Claudine is a writer." Cliff stated this as if it were a concrete fact, and while it felt nice to be introduced in such a way, it seemed a bit misleading. I hoped she wouldn't ask me where I was published or whether I had penned any books she might have read.

Ramsey extended a hand to me. "Oh gosh, it's so nice to meet you! Look at your pretty hair. I've been experimenting with mine."

She had a blond pixie haircut, Cliff's jawline and chin but softer, expressive eyes, and petite lips wet with a pink gloss. When she smiled, I saw she had his dimple, too.

After I'd met Cliff, and we'd talked about their impending concert together, I'd searched for her online and learned she was trying to make it in the indie music scene using the name Ramsey Blossom, perhaps to disassociate with her dad and make it on her own in the challenging music business.

Black and white photos on her web page showed her with subdued expressions, and she had a much longer hairstyle that was layered and looked purposely disheveled. The site had an overall somber tone. I hadn't expected her to be so lively.

She smiled broadly. "I hope it's okay I'm crashing your lunch. I was supposed to get here later, but I flew standby to try for an earlier flight."

"Oh no, of course. Glad you made it. I'm happy you're here. Was it a good flight?" I tried to match her spirited tone.

"I don't know. I slept for most of it!" She laughed, merry and genial, putting her hand over her forehead in embarrassment. "I've been staying up late to learn *this guy's* songs. He has a lot of complicated melodies." She glanced at her father with a cute, pursed smile.

Cliff shook his head in disagreement. "Maybe in my newer stuff, but back then it was the same three chords."

"I wore your jeans." *What? Why did I say that?* My non sequitur caught me off guard. I knew I'd made the remark out of nerves, not because of Ramsey, but because of Cliff and my new internal struggle over my attraction to him.

"For a ride on the bike," Cliff added. He brushed his hand in the air as if the information were insignificant. And it was.

Ramsey laughed. "It's fine! I'm glad you did! I know all about those motorcycle rides."

What did she mean by that?

A waiter arrived setting a glass of water before me and then walked away. The interruption helped distract the awkwardness I'd instigated. To buy myself a few seconds, I took a sip and then tried to get the conversation back on track. "Are you doing mostly his songs?"

Ramsey shook her head, no. "I'm re-working a couple. The rest will be mine. I'm so nervous! I've heard his fans can be super territorial. You're a fan, right? Maybe you can give me some tips on how to manage the audience." She looked at me, hopeful.

"She's not that kind of fan." Cliff pushed his hand against my shoulder. It was a fun gesture that caused me to smile easily and lessened my nerves.

"I'm really not. My best friend tells me all the time I don't know enough about his music. You're right though—it's quite a territorial group. But they can also be supportive of anyone connected to him. You'll be fine. They'll like you. I just know it."

I thought for a moment how I'd unconsciously referenced Sydney in my explanation. We still hadn't talked other than outside the bookstore, if that even counted. I didn't know if we were friends at all now. She was a pile of puzzle pieces unto herself.

Ramsey crossed her hands over her chest. "Oh, thank you! I needed to hear that. I feel so much better! Hey, we ordered a big nacho platter and some guac. You're welcome to share it."

It was impossible not to appreciate the situation, sitting there with Cliff and his daughter, how comfortable I felt as she pulled me right in like a longtime family friend. I felt bad for having arrived with such a selfish feeling in wanting Cliff to myself. I was glad it had resolved.

When we left, Cliff said goodbye to me with a squeeze of my arm while Ramsey hugged me like a favorite teddy bear. She was so uplifting and sweet. I could have melted into her, feeling appreciated and cherished being there, strange, given we had just met.

But then again, I'd had a similar affinity with Sydney our first night after running around Times Square looking for Cliff. Maybe I should have been more guarded. I now wondered if the new side of her I'd experienced had anything to do with her original concert buddy going AWOL.

I wouldn't see Cliff again until the concert that weekend. I envied Ramsey getting to be with him, hanging out in his comfy living room or taking a walk at the marina. Still I was glad for them to spend some time together as it might be all they'd get what with his summer concert schedule or hers for that matter.

He had more book signing events on the horizon, too. My one little kiss with him was probably the least of what was on his mind.

I took care of an errand for Nina after I left and when I returned to the Grace Building, I sat at my desk thinking about the lunch conversation and the way Cliff had introduced me. *A writer*. I didn't feel I deserved to be called such, though I knew it to be my true self at heart. Sentences floated through my head all the time, and so often I mentally described my surroundings as I went about the city. A well-crafted paragraph in a book could make me stop and stare with wonder into space.

I needed to do something about this proclivity of wanting to put words together and stir others' souls with ideas. Maybe it wasn't about having the right amount of thirst. The thirst was there. But I hadn't believed in myself enough. Maybe not at all.

Set against the backdrop of Cliff, I saw how little I had helped my creativity to blossom. Cliff carried his creativity into most things he did in life—writing songs, not worrying about who listened. He did the same with books. Had he thought about whether his fan base was into westerns? Unlikely. And now he was going to write science fiction. That was how it ought to be.

I'd given my experiences with the writers' workshops too much power in my own evaluation of my talent and then not pushed hard enough when I returned to New York in finding a way to satisfy my creative drive. I suddenly felt like I had been wandering around in the dark waiting for someone to turn on a light.

I made a path to Nina's office and found her engrossed by the display on her computer screen, pen to her lip in thought. I tapped the frame of her doorway, and her eyes shifted from her monitor.

"Sorry to interrupt. Do you have a moment? I'd like to discuss some ideas with you." My words felt foreign to me but also like I'd lit a torch for myself.

With Cliff otherwise occupied preparing for the weekend's concert, my time was more free. Not that he took up that much of it day-to-day, but often I'd cut my evenings short if I had some place to go so I could be home to talk to him from my couch or as I nestled in bed. Hearing his voice before I fell sleep was the best of nighttime comfort.

He sent me into dreams filled with softness and true rest. I needed that especially with finding myself waking too early and re-assessing what had happened with Sydney or if not that, mentally reviewing my to-do list for work. Cliff's nightly words made such a difference.

I had dinner with both Aunt Trudy and my mother one evening, and on another was able to spend a chunk of time at the bookstore chatting with Marlon about the latest estate sale collections he'd received. While we talked, I tried to focus on what he said and give some feedback instead of just nodding and letting my thoughts wander to Cliff.

I also completed the reorganization I'd been going about piecemeal for weeks. My tardiness with the project had caused Marlon to move the crates of books I'd been working with to the side. He'd had such patience with my itinerant schedule. He'd also taken care to be sure the spines were visible enough for customers to browse the titles but was careful not to interfere with my haphazard system.

Being in my favorite spot in the snug rows of biographies, romance novels, memoirs and other packaged streams of thought was a great way to forget about how much I missed being in more close communication with Cliff. He had sent text messages in the between time. The first one came a few hours after the lunch with Ramsey, *Hope you're okay,* it said simply. I knew then he had noticed my anxiety. *Sleep well* was another. No matter what he wrote to me, it was a boost alone to see the two initials RS pop up on my phone. He still made no reference to our kiss though which bothered me.

As I continued to go through the crates while Marlon did his administrative work, I found one of Cliff's novels that Sydney had been looking at the first time I'd met her. She had entered the place in such a panic over the tickets for Cliff's concert she'd lost. I thought about her standing beside me right then and wished it could be so.

I carried the book to the counter. The cover was faded like it had spent some time on a windowsill. When I told Marlon I wanted to buy it, I realized I hadn't said anything to Cliff about reading his *new* book. I hoped he hadn't thought it rude.

"I'll put it right here." Marlon patted the space between the edge of the countertop and cash register. "You know I can't charge you."

"Yes, you can. What is it, like four dollars? Dock my pay or something. *Please.*"

He shook his head with a laugh that sounded more like a sputter of air. "Not for you Claude. Nope. Can't do it. Won't."

His simple kindness always made me feel special. In my mind, I said I'd get back to being more present for him so he could leave early to take his wife for dinner or a movie more regularly. I had been robbing him of that recently.

Later that evening as I snaked up and down the streets around St. Mark's place with plans to grab a sandwich and head home, the whole kiss thing with Cliff raced off the sidelines of my brain like a hawk seizing its prey. At work, it had been easy not to let myself dwell on the situation since we'd had so many meetings plus a long and complex photo shoot. But while I was with Marlon, I kept feeling it trying to take the spotlight in my mind.

Walking near Cooper's Square and past Joe's Pub, a tavern where many musicians got their start, was all it took to push me right back into full-blown analysis. What was I hoping for? Was I in love with him, or did I just want some physical attention? I didn't know the answer.

The sensation of Cliff's lips on mine was set on repeat in my head, but the chief thing I kept obsessing over was his reaction to my boldness. I would have expected him to grasp my head, maybe catch my hair in his fingers, and kiss me as if he'd been waiting ages to do so. And then when my mouth was moist from his, he'd suggest we move things forward in my apartment simply by the look in his eyes. Even imagining it now put my libido on alert.

But his reaction hadn't come even close to that. I knew there was information in his behavior. People will show you how they feel, the sage words of Aunt Trudy.

He had shown me how he felt in other ways— his desire to spend time with me, to hear my secret sorrows. I'd never told anyone about Amelia taking her own life and how much I'd carried that thought around with me. He'd handled it perfectly, hadn't tried to solve my grief, only to be there for me and listen.

That wasn't the same as having a romantic feeling or desire for someone though. It meant he was a friend, a true, good friend. Just like he'd said.

While I studied a menu outside a Mexican restaurant, Cliff's novel in hand, I felt disappointed by the conclusion I'd come to. I wished I hadn't scrutinized things so closely. I'd have to find a way to talk to him about it to decisively solve the puzzle. That would have to be much later though— after the concert with Ramsey and the rest of his book signing events. I wouldn't want to distract him from those things. It would be hard to wait, but it was too fragile of a subject to rush.

Chapter 25

THE DAY OF THE CONCERT I SLEPT IN. I KEPT waking, finding I was still tired. When I stopped thinking about the whole kiss thing, reading Cliff's first novel had kept me up. He'd said he wrote westerns, but the story didn't fit that description except for taking place on a ranch. It was much deeper and drew me right in. I shouldn't have been surprised by that.

As I turned over to check the clock, eager sunlight splashed my face bringing me fully awake. It was already going toward eleven. I moved to sit up and felt around for the book in the tangled sheets and uncovered it near my pillow. No bookmark, but it would be fine by me to backtrack a few pages to find my spot. His writing voice had such an intimate feel. I was jealous of his sentence construction. It was as if words fell out of him into thoughtful insights, something I also experienced in him whenever we spoke. He could be so poetic, making the most mundane things sound interesting. I knew that didn't come easily to any writer, but he made it seem that way.

The night before, he had invited me to join Ramsey and him for dinner. They had returned to the city to be rested and ready for their sound check which would be starting in about an hour. He'd also invited me to be their rehearsal audience.

I'd said no to both invitations knowing it was a big day for Ramsey, and I didn't want to be in the way. She deserved time with her father, private time. But it was a relief that my odd behavior when I'd met her hadn't driven him away from sharing her with me.

Over a plate of hash browns I'd cooked in my toaster oven, I imagined the tongue-lashing Sydney would give me if she knew I had passed on attending the sound check. Thinking about it made me smile, picturing her hammering me about it in the feisty Sydney way. I could hear her lecture saying how it would be the supreme roadway to not only having extra time with Cliff but also photo opportunities with him and Ramsey, something other fans wouldn't have and would be impressed by.

On top of that, it would provide the bragging rights in knowing the setlist ahead of time. Sydney loved that kind of behind-the-scenes stuff. Every bit of Cliff-related information I could now access should have been making her do a happy dance. Instead, she had essentially told me not to bother her.

I did agree to a later message from Cliff asking me to arrive early to the venue. After putting my dishes in the sink, I stood before my closet to choose a few outfit options. I wanted to wear something special for the concert but not look like I was overthinking things or trying to be sexy. I knew from Sydney that anyone who saw me with Cliff would make assumptions about my presence with him.

I didn't want to be perceived as a backstage groupie hoping for a one-night stand. It would be easy to label me that way given I wasn't known by many in the Cliff Wood fan circles. Aside from that, there was our age difference.

I hadn't much considered the years between us as we always had so many things to talk about. In Cliff I saw an attractive, fascinating, and caring man before me, never an age. Sometimes, after we spent time together, I'd feel drunk on the depth of the subjects we'd get into and the sheer bliss of his presence.

Then I met Ramsey. I'd already known she and I were close in age, but seeing her in person made me even more aware of the age difference between Cliff and me. I could be his daughter, too. I wondered if he'd thought about that.

Tossing a pile of tops, bottoms, and jackets onto my bed, I held up each one mentally dressing myself in combinations of the pieces. White jeans and a black iridescent blouse with sheer butterfly sleeves made the final cut. I'd wear a camisole under it and add a choker featuring a decorative coin.

After I tried it all on together and looked in the mirror, I was happy to see it was the right mix of dressy casual. When it was time to go, some large hoop earrings and neutral lipstick would make me look a step more stylish. All that time I'd spent at the magazine and around Sydney had finally given me some sartorial aptitude.

I moved about the rest of the afternoon slowly, taking a shower, then looking online at a couple of cellphone-made videos of Ramsey while I ate a leftover fruit salad. I wanted to be familiar with her music. After only watching a few parts of the videos I'd found, it was easy to see her onstage presence mirrored her father's. She was commanding with a measure of modesty. That aside, she had an ethereal quality, as if she were channeling another part of herself, an old soul she only brought out when she sang.

Leaving my apartment in my not-meant-to-be-too-sexy-but-still-stylish ensemble, I journeyed along Downing Street toward the venue. I'd been there once years ago to hear a local singer but hadn't had reason to go since.

The performance was a big thing for Ramsey and for Cliff's dedicated fans, too. They liked seeing him do things outside of his regular concerts, and some had made special trips from out-of-town to be there.

I felt bad I wasn't more enthusiastic about it. I was looking forward to seeing Cliff side by side with Ramsey on the duets they had planned, but with trying to secure tickets before telling Sydney about my spending time with Cliff, and then so much happening in between, the show had become more of a symbolic reminder of our friendship's collapse.

I wouldn't tell him about that, wouldn't ever get into the logistics of what happened and how he had been the center of it, though based on the little I'd shared, he already had some inkling. He had been polite enough not to ask questions.

What I was more excited about was telling him about my talk with Nina and how she had finally helped me create a plan for my writing aspirations. I had a little bubble of joy swirling in me for taking a significant step toward that end. Cliff had been the encouragement behind it. Our conversations over pie and on no-plans afternoons had both renewed and amplified my desire to get on track with my own writing.

He wouldn't want to take any credit, but I knew he'd be more than happy for me. I'd save the news for later. Tonight was all about Ramsey.

———

May had already spilled into June, leaving a trail of springtime blooms throughout the city.

I rambled slowly along Bleecker Street enjoying the bohemian vibe and scenery on my way to the venue. Being in the sun's warmth always made me feel good along with the flowering plants, especially the cotton candy view of the Japanese cherry tree with its double flowers.

I reminded myself to take more daytime walks. Sydney and I had been on so many concert trips over the last months. Now I would have more time.

The Bitter End, a rock club that had been around since the earlier 1960s, was wedged in between two pubs. Lost in thought along the way, I'd forgotten my instructions from Thomas Yale. He'd said to come to the stage entrance but standing under the blue awning at the front of the place, I didn't see a way to locate the backside of the building.

I looked through the tall glass-paned door to see what was happening. It was too dark to see inside. After a text to him sharing my ignorance, he arrived in seconds.

"Sorry." An embarrassed smile formed on my lips. "You'd thinking living near here I'd have a better idea about things."

Thomas held the door open further, waving me in, and ushered me toward the backstage area. "I'm not sure where Cliff is. There was some trouble with the sound system, but they got it fixed, fortunately. He gets frustrated when the sound isn't right."

It was hard for me to picture Cliff frustrated. He was always so easy-going, but I'd never been around him as he prepared for a performance. I'd never been part of anything backstage-wise. Now I felt a little excited about being there.

We headed down a slim corridor and around a corner into a small room where Alternative Kyle stood by a table holding a selection of food trays. When he looked at me, his expression said *what are you doing here?* I thought the same of him until Thomas casually motioned at him. "You probably know my brother, Jackson."

Jackson? "I've seen him around." Wow, that explained a lot.

Jackson's narrow eyes briefly caught mine again and then he returned his attention to an array of sandwiches, eating one where he stood.

"I think I hear his voice." Thomas looked back as if waiting for another signal of Cliff's presence and then poked his head around the edge of a door jamb. "They did a run-through and were going to take a break. The stage is through there. You can go look for him." He offered a hand toward the doorway. "Hang out wherever you want. Doors open at seven. It's going to be a packed crowd. Be careful. Cables are everywhere."

I found myself back in the same hallway, now noticing it was adorned with posters from previous bands' performances. Icy Blues, Zoot, MPD Ltd,

The Jordy Boys, Rock House, Wickedy Wak. Their once well-thought-out designs now appeared antiquated and amateurish. Being displayed beneath yellow lights hadn't promoted preservation either as the vivid colors had faded with time. I wondered how things had turned out for the members of those groups.

"There you are." Cliff had his hand cupped to his forehead under the lights as he stood at the edge of the waist-high stage.

I didn't realize I'd made it to the main seating area which was shrouded in an aroma of late nights and alcohol. The room was smaller than I remembered. Off to one side was the bar. Narrow, rectangular tables were situated throughout the room leaving little space to walk between them. Now I understood why the tickets had been so hard to come by.

"There you are!" Ramsey said the same as her dad, appearing from the shadows behind him. She had such a playful presence and always looked cute. Low-slung jeans with a red tank top was her current ensemble. "We've been waiting for you!" And then, "Dad, I'm getting some extra picks to put over here." She patted an amplifier. "They asked about how many bottled waters. I said two each for us, but I don't usually drink that much."

She trotted out of sight, and Cliff followed me with his eyes as I headed toward him. He looked so good. His natural expression could make you feel cozy.

He took my hand helping me navigate the step-up to join him and then drew me into a welcome embrace. "I was getting worried."

"You were?"

He smirked adorably. "I knew you'd come. Is your friend here?"

"Not yet." I didn't want to say she had turned me down after he'd found a way for us to attend the sold-out show. Later I'd casually write it off in an innocuous way. I didn't want him to feel anything but good for the performance, and still, he didn't need to be acquainted with my Sydney troubles.

He pointed to an audio board camouflaged by a curtain. "I think you should watch from stage left. That way you'll be away from the mix guy."

"Then that's where I'll be." I smiled easily as I looked up at him. I wanted so much to kiss him again but knew I had to contain the feeling. I pulled away, folding my arms and wandering around the stage, pretending to examine its layout. "Are you playing the keyboard tonight?"

"That's for Ramsey. She has a bandmate who'll be joining her for a song or two. She's worked so hard."

We went to the area Thomas had brought me when I'd first arrived. Cliff gestured toward the table where I'd learned Alternative Kyle's actual name. "So, there's food here. And you can eat if you want. And when I'm not singing, I'll come stand with you. Ramsey is going to sign some CDs afterward. Then maybe we can all go for drinks."

"Sounds perfect."

As the time neared for the doors to open for the performance, I moved out of the way. At the bar, I ordered a glass of wine and took a seat. I figured it would be good for Ramsey and Cliff to have some space before showtime. Even with the amount of experience Cliff had performing, he looked a little nervous, but it was probably more about Ramsey and wanting it to be a successful night for her.

I needed a little space myself. Things felt so strange without Sydney. The way she experienced the concerts contributed to my enjoyment of them. The nuances important to her added a unique layer of fun including how she critiqued everything from Cliff's wardrobe choice to his mood. And then, of course, there was the mandatory post-concert evaluation—or dissection as I thought of it. But now, she would be having all those conversations with Natasha instead. Looking across the dim room, I wondered where they'd be sitting. It would be hard not to say hi to her when she arrived.

I could have brought someone else as my plus-one guest, but I couldn't think of anyone except Aunt Trudy. A bar scene with loud music wasn't the kind of thing she enjoyed. She was probably curled up right now with Larry or a new beau watching a movie. All the regulars would already be coming, Paige, Evvi, Doreen, etcetera. Oh, and Alternative Kyle, or rather Jackson, who was already there.

I still couldn't believe no one in the fan camp had ever figured out why he always had an inside line on Cliff's whereabouts. Thomas Yale's brother, so funny.

"Hey, whatcha doing out here?" Ramsey's voice behind my high-back chair caught me off guard.

I swiveled to look at her adorable face. "I'm getting ready to see your concert. I figured you would want to get your head in the right place or whatever it is musicians do."

Ramsey winced and kind of shook her head at the same time. "Like some *Zen* time?"

"Yeah, I guess." I took a swallow of my wine. It felt dry and too sour and didn't taste that good. I should have gotten something different.

"We're as ready as we're going to be. I mean for me, anyway. I've been obsessing for weeks. Now, I have to trust myself. But for my dad," she waved a dismissive hand, "This is nothing. Small potatoes."

"I'm sure it gets easier the more you do it. That makes sense."

She picked up my glass and finished the wine. Such a frenetic nature. "Come hang out with us. We have more of this back there. At no charge." She set the glass on the bar.

I slid off the chair. "How long have you been performing?"

"It depends on what you count. I've been playing guitar since I was twelve, but not so much performing. I had bad stage fright at first. I still get it sometimes."

"Not tonight though. You'll do great."

"Thank you. If I do something weird, please just clap." We both laughed.

We moved down the hallway. This time, I noticed it could use a good mopping. I had hoped Ramsey's answer to my question would reveal her age, thinking that if she were more than a bit younger than I, my recent amorous thoughts toward her father would feel better on one count.

She skittered along, stopping to look at some of the posters and leaning in close to examine certain ones. "What about you? How long have you been writing?"

I shrugged. "I guess the answer is the same as yours, depends on what counts. I was always writing stories from the time I was little and keeping journals in middle school and high school. I'm thirty-five now, and I've been at the fashion magazine for three years." *Not that I write for them. Not yet.*

"The thirties feel like you're suddenly running out of time, don't they? Like you need to get stuff figured out or your life is going to be a mess. I used to imagine mine like a huge bucket of whipped cream splattered on the floor!" She so reminded me of her dad. And Sydney, same spunk.

When we reached the room where we could hear Cliff's voice, Ramsey stopped short of the doorway. "Don't say that to my dad though—you know, the bit about running out of time. He lectures me on it when I say anything like that, so you'll also get an earful on how young you are. *Wait till you're my age* and all that."

That was not what I needed to hear from her.

Chapter 26

"HOW DO I LOOK?"

In an alcove outside two small dressing rooms, Ramsey did a twirl in her willowy vanilla-colored dress as beautiful brocade sleeves swayed at her elbows. She was a ballet in real life, having a natural and girlish way about her.

Her attire looked like the kind of thing you'd wear barefooted while picking daisies, and she wore it well but with a twist, of course—a rock star twist. She had combined it with a pair of worn combat boots giving her a goth-hippie vibe. Around her neck was a cameo choker, probably vintage.

A group of her friends had arrived to show their support. One of them was a tall, surfer-haired guy who I thought might be her boyfriend. They all agreed she looked perfect, 'wild yet feminine' one of them had described her. Another had brought her a bouquet of daisies.

Most of the space in Cliff's dressing room was taken up by a loveseat and a lighted dressing table. An array of band posters provided decorations by groups better known than the ones displayed in the hallway. Sahara Snow and the Squirts were two that stood out. Generous Cliff had given the bigger room to Ramsey since it was her special night, though it didn't offer much more room than his.

On a folding chair nearby, Thomas sat, holding a canned drink and looking over the set list. He acted like he didn't want me to see it, and since I didn't have anyone to dazzle with the information, I didn't try for a preview.

I missed the opportunity of watching Cliff do his hair, the one thing I had been hoping to witness in the backstage environment. It was now the picture of tousled perfection. The grey sections of his hair with the black looked as if they had been expertly arranged. Maybe it was best to keep some things a mystique.

I felt lightheaded and attributed it to the wine I'd consumed, though I knew it wasn't enough to affect me. The sensation was primarily coming from feeling out of place in being behind the scenes for such a big show as far as what it meant for Ramsey and also for Cliff's fans who had fought to their death for seats to it. *Or had lost a friendship in the process.*

I was glad when my phone dinged and saw it was Paige. What great timing.

"My friend is here. I'm just going to see her," I said to Cliff.

"Sydney?" He sat on the edge of the loveseat with a guitar, fingering the strings.

I hated to lie, but it came out, effortlessly. "Mmm hmm."

I also hated Sydney wouldn't get the joy of Cliff recalling her name. He wasn't known for that with fans. Sydney had said it was a gripe with some of them who had met him at multiple events through the years.

"You might need this." Thomas reached for a laminated pass with the words ALL ACCESS printed in orange letters across it, and underneath, *A Night with Ramsey Blossom and Cliff Wood*. Thomas handed it to Cliff who slid the black cord over my head.

"Need to keep this with you to get back here. We've got one for her friend, right?" He looked over at Thomas Yale.

I decided before he answered would be a good time to exit and avoid any further lying about Sydney's presence.

After filing back through the hallway of washed-out posters, I found Paige with Evvi by the bar. Earlier when I sat there, I'd had the space to myself, but now it was hopping with customers. Alternative Kyle—ahem, Jackson—sat engrossed by his phone on a chair nearby.

"Hey you!" Paige hugged me in a firm embrace as she held her drink to the side keeping it from spilling. "You look great." She studied the pass Cliff had given me. "Wow, check this out." She showed it to Evvi. "When did you get here?"

"Right after the sound check." As the words came out, I realized my reply could come off as if I were boasting, but I knew Paige wouldn't see it that way.

She took a swallow of her drink. "Oh, gosh, it's so exciting! Did you get to meet Ramsey?"

I nodded. "She's sweet. Definitely looks like him, has the same jawline. I think she'll do great. She's nervous though."

Paige switched her drink to her other hand. It was a clear mixture, maybe a vodka and tonic, with a lime wedge floating in it. Evvi said hello, not with any exuberance but cordial enough. I had never talked to her much since Sydney had presented her as an enemy of sorts, but I had no reason not to be friendly with her. In fact, it felt good she spoke to me.

"Do you have good seats?" I asked only for the sake of conversation. It didn't really matter to me. When Sydney posed that question, it was because she wanted to know if others had better seats than she did. Or it might mean she wanted to keep an eye on them. It was one of her concert quirks.

"We're at that third table to the left." Paige pointed between Evvi and me. Then her expression turned forlorn. "I feel bad for Sydney."

"Is she here yet?" I scanned the room. It had filled in even more since I'd begun talking to them. House music now boomed throughout.

"Here?" Paige had a quizzical expression. "She never found a ticket."

"But she said she was coming with Natasha." I said this as though her name were one they'd recognize.

"Who's Natasha?" Paige set her drink down.

I looked at her and Evvi as if they were obviously confused. "Her best friend from Boston."

They both went quiet while I evaluated the nearby tables, certain Sydney would come into view despite what Paige had asserted. But there was no one to be found with dark, asymmetrical short hair with caramel highlights. I envisioned Sydney in her apartment with Lyric in her lap, maybe scrolling through photos of Cliff on her phone, trying to distract herself from the thought of not being there.

I now understood the reality of things. "Wow. She's so disgusted with me, she'd rather miss this than make amends? She's sitting at home, and I'm here. It makes me feel terrible."

Paige and Evvi exchanged glances.

I felt awkward. "Look, I hope you both have a good time. I better go."

I decided I would avoid Cliff until I could set aside my fresh disappointment. I wondered if I could talk Sydney into coming—if she'd even take my call. She would have missed a big portion of the show by the time she arrived, but she'd get to go backstage with me and see Cliff. Knowing Sydney, that would make it worth coming on its own.

When I started to walk away, Paige caught my shoulder. "Claudine, Sydney is next door. Or she was anyway."

"What? Why?"

Evvi set her empty drink glass down and explained. "She was hoping she could find someone with a last-minute ticket, and then she would already be nearby to get it and come here."

Paige checked her phone. "If she got one, I'd have a text from her by now."

"She *has* a ticket, or at least one of these anyway." I tapped the all-access pass around my neck for emphasis. My disappointment shifted into frustration at Sydney's stubbornness. "I'll see you later."

Hurrying back toward the dressing rooms, I ran right into Cliff. I felt hot and realized I was having a semi-anxiety attack over Sydney's behavior, and more than that, what I should do about it.

Cliff lightly held onto my shoulders. "What's going on?"

"Nothing. Can I get that other pass now?" My breath was short, and my request sounded greedy, but it wasn't the time to worry with politeness.

"Hey, take it easy. It's right here." He reached into his back pocket.

CHAPTER 26

The bar where I found Sydney was not the one next door but across the street. It was the third one I'd tried and looked like it had provided its share of late-night fun. That was how many places along Bleecker were, their appearances full of character as a result of time and history.

When I was on strike two of my search, I thought about sending a text to ask of her whereabouts, but I worried she'd leave if she knew I were looking for her.

Once in the right place, she was easy to spot. Denim shirt, black jeans, one arm covered in bangle bracelets. But the true giveaway was how she played with her hair while she viewed the television screen above the bar. I wondered how long she'd been sitting there.

I took the stool next to her, folding my arms on the bartop. In seconds, she looked over, probably to provide a simple hello to a stranger. When my face registered with her, she recoiled.

"What are you doing here?"

"Don't leave. I know you're upset about every-thing. And I—"

"No, I mean what are you doing *here*? The con-cert is about to start, in like, five minutes."

"Five?" I hadn't checked the time when I'd left. "Then we have to do this quickly. Please listen. I know you're upset with me. But I want you with me for this show. I miss you, and it won't be the same if you aren't there. You can still be mad at me if you want, but please come."

When she remained quiet, I added, "The only reason I ended up—" I paused. I wasn't sure what was the right label for what was going on with Cliff and me, but I couldn't worry about it right then. "...as friends with Cliff is because I was trying to get us into this concert, this one that's happening in less than five minutes. And then it all escalated from there. I kept waiting for the right moment to tell you. I thought the whole thing with him would be a welcome surprise. It wasn't meant in deceit; it was supposed to be for you. Your friendship was always the most important to me."

Everything I'd said was true except maybe the last sentence because things with Cliff had become just as important now—but not *more* important than Sydney.

I waited, ready for her to lambast me for hiding my communication with Cliff and secretly spending time with him, to have her say about it all. But instead, she burst into laughter. She laughed so much she couldn't stop, covering her mouth, her nose wrinkled, eyes closed.

At first, I thought she was making fun of my explanation. Either that or it was a nervous response that was about to morph into a sob, the way someone says they're fine before breaking down in tears.

She composed herself and finally looked at me, grabbing one of my shoulders for support as if the laughter had set her off kilter. "Oh my God. You're too cute. I mean, I love that you said all that, but I've missed you, too. I was so mad and so jealous and then I didn't know how to get back to us, and— Claudine! We need to get over to the venue!"

She laughed again, and I laughed too, an anxious laugh also filled with bitten-back tears having felt so stressed what with leaving Cliff abruptly to locate her and then having no luck at first, and then in the middle of it all trying to prepare the speech I'd present to her. What I had said wasn't what I'd thought out, but it was fast and direct and worked. That was all that mattered.

She set some cash by her empty drink. "What kind of seats do we have?"

"These." I held up the all-access pass for her to better see which had flipped over in my trek to find her. "And here's yours." I draped the cord over her head the same as Cliff had done for me.

She looked at the pass for not even a second. "Are you serious? Let's get out of here!"

She grabbed my wrist the way she used to, the way I loved and missed. I didn't care it was the one with the old injury that was easily aggravated.

After she hustled us outside, we dodged a lone taxi as we jaywalked to the venue. Sydney gave a middle finger to the driver who slammed on his horn as we crossed in front of him. He deserved it as he was hardly moving.

When we were inside The Bitter End after getting waved through by security, we stopped in the space between the entrance and the bar. The room was now packed, drinks flowing, house music up a notch. Sydney leaned close to one side of my head.

"Claudine, thank you for not giving up on us. On me. This night means so much. We can never let jealousy come between us."

I didn't say anything. I had said all I had needed to. I held her hand even more tightly as we zigzagged our way through the crowd until we were in the hallway by the dressing rooms.

Sydney stopped abruptly. "Are we going backstage?" I mean, is *he* there?"

"Of course he is."

"Maybe we shouldn't bother him."

I flashed my pass for her to see. "It will be fine. It's what this is for."

It was cute how nervous she was despite all the times she'd met Cliff at meet and greets and other places in her escapades. But I knew this was different, being his invited guests.

We kept moving, and when we got closer, Ramsey and Cliff were rounding the corner through the entrance to the stage area. I whispered, "Break a leg, you guys!"

Cliff looked back with one of his devastating smiles. He was dressier than usual wearing a black blazer emblazoned with velvet designs over a white collared shirt. I thought Sydney would pass out. I understood her reaction. He could be so breathtaking, but by then, I'd had the benefit of spending time with him which helped not to be so jarred by his physical splendor.

Thomas Yale arrived near the doorway through which Ramsey and Cliff had just exited. It was showtime, no room for games. "You need to get out there and get in your places."

Sydney looked up at me. "Our places?"

I had also missed how it felt to have her vibrant eyes meeting mine.

"Go. Now." Thomas motioned with his head.

We passed Thomas and made it to the side of the stage as we stepped around and over cables and gig bags. It was hard to see, and the area smelled of metal and time and an array of artistry from performances past.

Cliff and Ramsey's silhouettes floated in the shadows as they waited to be announced by the venue's manager. I felt nervous for Ramsey and was sorry I hadn't given her a personal well-wish.

But it felt so good to have Sydney with me again.

Chapter 27

THREE GUITARS, A KEYBOARD, AND TWO MI-
crophones with monitors awaited Ramsey and
Cliff as they took the stage to perform one song before Cliff left, giving his daughter the spotlight.

"Don't worry. He'll be back." Ramsey laughed
with a hint of nerves as she switched her guitar with
another on a stand nearby. "I appreciate you sharing your support with me. I already know you're
a fun group. There has to be some reason why my
dad never stops performing, right?"

Everyone laughed, and a few cheered or whis-
tled. Ramsey brushed her fingers across the strings
as she settled onto her stool. "I'm starting with a
song called 'Featherweight.'" She looked across the
room. "'Cause it's one of the easier ones."

She had a humorous and self-deprecating way,
and I could see the audience was already drinking
her in, loving her little quips and her down-to-
earth attitude. Each time she smiled, a look

reminiscent of Cliff graced her face which made it all even better.

He joined Sydney and me in the wings. The very sight and proximity of him caused Sydney to squeeze my hand and sublimate her excitement.

Meanwhile, Cliff's own nerves had become apparent. He tried folding his arms and focusing on Ramsey's performance, holding the expression of a supportive father, but his serious face betrayed the fact he was concerned about her pulling it off. He shut his eyes and nodded his head in time with her tempo. I witnessed him gradually relax into her sound knowing she was nailing it, and he uncrossed his arms.

He was not in rock star mode today which I thought helped soften Sydney's nerves, what with being suddenly thrown into his presence and having to act like she wasn't someone who had been innocently stalking him for years. Despite her anxiety, I knew it was a night she'd hold onto forever, as would I, for different reasons.

The stage was small, enough to fit a four- or five-piece band if no one planned on moving around. From where we watched out of frame, a section of the audience could see us. It felt awkward but fun, the idea that many envied our position including Paige and Evvi who both gave discreet little waves and smiles.

"Where did he go?" Sydney was the first to realize Cliff had left the area.

It was the fourth song in Ramsey's set, and now she delivered a slow, sultry number, only playing the guitar intermittently. During the applause, I looked around and discovered Cliff had covertly taken a spot behind the bar, presumably a place that provided a loose guardianship so he wouldn't be approached by fans.

I motioned with a tilt of my head. "He's right there."

Sydney stood on her toes. "Oh yeah, yep, right there. Hope he didn't leave because of me."

"Why would he do that?"

She threw her hands up palms outward. "Maybe I'm giving off over-the-top-fan vibes."

"You're not. He's just giving Ramsey space to do her thing."

Speculation on Cliff's behavior had always been Sydney's role, and it was plain she was continuing with it, despite the cataclysmic change in our friendship now with me knowing Cliff so well.

I liked this new balance between us, both making our own contributions to the evening. I doubted Sydney was thinking about things quite the way I was though. Cliff's presence had always made her feel good whether the location be a concert, hotel, or a crowded bar in the Village where his daughter shared the billing. I now felt the same about his nearness, the comfort of it, but I preferred it be on the couch in his living room drifting off to sleep to the dialogue of an old movie or gliding along on the back of his cruiser.

For Sydney, having this unrestricted access to his behind-the-scenes environment was bound to be the new pinnacle of all her experiences with him. As for me, I wanted something more. But did he? I still needed to figure that out.

The show progressed as Ramsey continued to hold the room's full attention with her range of vocal talent, strumming her way through the set list, and having an easy repartee in between songs. She had a rhythm and symmetry all her own. The nerves she had mentioned and exhibited at the start went undetected and had likely dissipated.

I kept one eye on Cliff in his new location throughout the performance but hadn't noticed he'd returned until he was behind us and lightly touched the back of my head.

A few minutes later, Ramsey motioned in our direction. "Let's welcome my dad back to the stage. We've worked up a few things for you to close the evening. It's been so wonderful. It really has!"

Applause radiated from the crowd as Cliff brushed past Sydney who tightened her hand in mine once more. A guitar tech waited for Cliff to get seated and then handed him a Gibson acoustic. When the clapping and whistling died down, he and Ramsey began a three-song set.

"Let's go watch the rest from the back." I led Sydney toward the corridor going to the main seating area.

"Good idea, the sound is probably better." Her voice trailed behind me in a whisper. "But we'll come back afterward, right?"

I nodded and kept going until we were behind the rows of tables and in Cliff's line of sight.

It felt different seeing Ramsey and Cliff together from the house view. The wider, more open scene made it easy to observe their individual sensibilities and playing techniques. I wondered if Ramsey had gotten the foundation of her skill from Cliff's genes. Her comfort with the guitar looked as though it were instinctive.

"This next one is called 'Lazy.' It's one of my dad's, an oldie, probably inspired by me never wanting to get out of bed as a kid!" She laughed and then said, "Not really!" Then she tugged at a string with her guitar pick.

"It's only an oldie for some," Cliff cut in.

Ramsey leaned over her guitar completely tickled as the crowd joined her in the amusement. Clearly, the comments had not been rehearsed and the more she laughed, the more the audience adored her.

"Okay, yes, it's an oldie for *some*." She winked at the crowd.

Sydney had the biggest smile on her face as she cupped a hand lightly across her lips, enthralled by the banter between her favorite musician and his daughter.

"Can I tell them what it's really about?" Ramsey swiveled to Cliff for an answer as he fiddled with his guitar.

"It's your show."

I thought he sounded a little perturbed, but apparently Ramsey didn't think so. She doubled over her guitar again even more tickled than the first time. "Okay, sorry. I'm having so much fun. I think I'm stalling." She re-positioned herself on the stool and gripped her guitar, composing herself. "It's a song about love, how it's the most amazing thing in the world and yet we take it for granted. Right?"

Cliff simply nodded.

"And—it's about my mother." Ramsey skated her pick softly across the strings. "A lot of you probably already knew that."

"*I* didn't know that." Sydney nudged me with her shoulder and then bounced on her feet in excitement before readying her phone to make a video.

By the time the show was at its end, we had migrated to the bar and used our all-access passes to cut through the packed area and get the bartender's attention. Maybe it wasn't what all-access meant, but it worked. A few minutes later, we were clinking two martinis in celebration of being together again back where things had started for us—because of Cliff.

He left the stage, and Ramsey was now closing things out with a song of her own. "You've all been so great. Thank you for coming tonight! Please buy my CD and meet me after!" Her voice bounded through the sound system, enthusiastic and grateful, more boisterous than she'd been when speaking otherwise.

"We definitely need to get her CD and show her some support." Sydney looked around. "Is there a merch table around here somewhere?"

"I'm not sure."

"There has to be one. I'll figure it out." She finished her drink. "We should get in line early for the signing."

I didn't reply. I wanted to congratulate Ramsey separately on her performance backstage after I'd disappeared without explanation earlier. I wasn't worried about getting her CD at the moment. I wanted to see what was happening with Cliff.

I left Sydney to go find him. He had said we'd go for drinks after the show, and I knew Paige and company would be hopeful and even expecting me to share insider details on those plans. I needed to see how he felt about me giving out such information.

I was secretly hoping he wouldn't be up for a night with fans around other than Sydney and me. Ever since I'd had that first dinner with him at the bar in Jamestown, I had wanted to give her some direct time to talk with him as she'd always wanted. This night probably didn't lend itself to that kind of intimate gathering since Ramsey would undoubtedly be coming along with her host of friends, an even larger group of whom now congregated in the room beyond the archaic poster passageway.

A plump, middle-aged security guard with frizzy grey hair stood at the room's entrance. After glancing at the pass around my neck, she motioned for us to keep going.

I immediately started scoping the space for Cliff. Instead, my eyes found Ramsey, dressed again in her jeans and tank top and talking with the surfer-haired guy and someone else seated, someone I couldn't see.

I decided I'd give my congratulations to her on the success of the show and find Cliff after. Maybe I'd even grab Sydney first. There was no need for us to wait at the signing table when we could see Ramsey in private.

"Oh hey!" Ramsey turned and flung her arms around me in one of her teddy-bear-style hugs. "I'm so glad you're here. I want you to meet my mom."

The woman who had been seated stood and smiled warmly. She had a Faye Dunaway quality about her, an airy beauty, like a fine painting. I recognized her within seconds.

"Mom, this is Dad's friend, Claudine; Claudine, my mom."

The elegant, mature blonde extended one hand to me. Her nails were beautifully manicured and painted a blush pink. "Hello, I'm Genevieve." Perfume drifted from her and made me think of a plumeria tree with its violet chandelier-like blossoms.

I felt like I was meeting royalty from the fashion world. Genevieve Phillipa had been a top cover model back in the day and now was a stylist to A-list film stars. I should have known Cliff would have dated someone like her.

"It's nice to meet you. I know who you are. I work at a fashion magazine." I let go of her hand as I looked at Ramsey. "Genevieve Phillipa is your mother?" I sounded more astonished than impressed though I'd meant it to be the latter.

"It's Genevieve Bradshaw now. I got married."

Out of the corner of my eye I saw Cliff coming our way. His presence made me feel better, but I didn't know why I was feeling so ill at ease in the first place. It wasn't as if I were his girlfriend, so Genevieve's status with him, whatever it was at this point, wasn't a threat.

"Hey Gen." Cliff's deep voice filled the space. He leaned in to peck her cheek. "Glad you made it."

"I wouldn't have missed it. Wasn't our girl fantastic?" She touched the side of Ramsey's face, and Ramsey put her own hand over it.

"Thanks, Mom."

As I stood with the three of them, probably with my mouth agape, so much made sense now. I was nowhere close to the type of woman who would catch Cliff's eye in a romantic way. How had I not realized he was so far out of my league?

He was Cliff Wood. Cliff freaking Wood! I was so mad at myself.

This was the guy whose poster had hung on the back of mine and Amelia's bedroom door while he toured across the country and beyond to screaming fans, most of them females with gorgeous hair and perfect bodies. He dated models. Of course he did! What had I been thinking?

I was mortified, cringing with embarrassment inside my mind. I felt ridiculous as this all sank in and was so glad I hadn't shared my inner thoughts about him with anyone, especially Cliff himself.

When Ramsey had introduced the duet about her mother to the audience, it didn't even occur to me she might be there. But it made sense. It was her daughter's big night, and her old flame would be front and center, too. I felt so dumb.

"I need to go find my friend. She was getting one of your CDs." I hoped I didn't sound abrupt or panicked. I spoke as brightly as I could muster to Ramsey and then shifted to Genevieve. "It was great meeting you."

I couldn't even look at Cliff as I turned to weave my way out of the room.

Sydney was in a small group by the stage, probably having made her usual rounds with the regular fans, taking selfies, and no doubt hoping they were appropriately jealous of the backstage pass hanging from her neck.

When she saw me, she waved and flashed the two CDs of Ramsey's she had in her other hand. I motioned for her to join me and waited for her by the bar.

"Is Ramsey coming out here?" Sydney handed me one of the CDs and then wiped her bangs out of her eyes.

"I'm not sure. I mean, yes, but there are a lot of people back there, and they're all talking. Cliff doesn't seem in the greatest mood."

"Really? I'd think he would be walking on air after that performance. They were so good together. Didn't you think so?"

I nodded. I hated seeing Sydney's trusting eyes looking up at me. This was supposed to be the night I made good on things with her by giving her some special time with Cliff.

Instead, here I was lying to her and trying to find a way out of it. Cliff wasn't in a bad mood at all. He was glowing just like she'd suggested.

I shrugged. "Ramsey's mother is here. I think they'll want to have more of a family dinner."

"Genevieve! Wow!" Sydney delightedly bounced on her feet again, ignoring the plausible wrench I'd thrown into the mix to divert us. "I wondered if she'd come. This night just keeps getting better!"

Maybe for her.

The discomfort I felt from backstage moments ago wasn't abating. Rather, it was impeding my ability to come up with a more solid reason to jump ship. I knew there wasn't anything that would make Sydney want to abandon the rest of the night and the opportunity to be around Cliff. He, too, would be hurt if I didn't stay. It had been such a special night in so many ways, but he didn't know about the mortification coursing through my head. He couldn't have understood it.

I would have to participate in the after-show happenings, whatever they were. I owed Sydney that. And my feelings for Cliff weren't his fault. I'd brought that upon myself when I kissed him.

Just then there was applause, and out walked Ramsey with the stout female security guard.

Sydney opened her CD case and pulled out the insert. "I guess we should get in line and get ours signed, right?"

"Yeah. I guess so."

It was going to be a long night.

Chapter 28

I DON'T KNOW WHY IT HAD NEVER OCCURRED to me to think about who Ramsey's mother was much less that she would be at the concert. Naturally she would want to be there for her daughter on such an important night and maybe even spend a little time with the still handsome rock star who had once been an intimate part of her life. How close were they these days?

Cliff's romantic past had never been a topic he and I had covered, and the subject had only grazed mine and Sydney's conversations. I'd never given it any thought on my own. I wasn't into digging around in his past the way she and most fans were. To me he was just Cliff, a guy who liked to ride his motorcycle and eat pie and would kindly listen to my secret sorrows. The rock star side of him was secondary for me now. We were friends. He'd said so himself.

It started raining right after we arrived at the restaurant a block away that Thomas Yale suggested.

The menu offered an array of casual food, pizza, burgers, salads and the like. He'd secured a room in the back which had turned out to be unnecessary as Ramsey had gone off with her friends, presumably with Genevieve, too.

Sydney and I both sat across from Cliff with Thomas next to him. The rest in no order, Evvi, Paige, Doreen, Lorie, Jerry, Jackson-cum-Kyle, plus Bruce who had appeared out of nowhere right before we left the venue. He brought his girlfriend with him, a woman who looked like she'd been pulled right off the older groupie circuit, with wild dark hair, tight jeans, and red lipstick.

With Ramsey and company having gone their own way, I had asked Cliff if he was okay with such a fan entourage coming with us. My discomfort at the end of the evening had changed my feeling from not wanting a big group to a *more the merrier* line of thinking. I thought it would be better having additional people around to make conversation and distract me from the unease I felt from meeting Genevieve and all the thoughts launched afterward.

It would also help keep Sydney in check. Once she got a few drinks in her, I knew she could go gangbusters into things she had always wanted to tell Cliff. But she surprised me by only sharing one story about how she had carried one of his albums around in the eighth grade telling everyone Cliff was her boyfriend. He looked genuinely amused hearing about it. She told me she had wanted to ask about the new songs he'd mentioned on the talk show but was hoping she'd have other opportunities. I hoped so, too.

After Sydney, Doreen jumped in to say she'd made her closest friends at his concerts, to which Lorie added that she had also, including Jerry, her boyfriend. The rest of the time, general chit chat took place among everyone, and when the waiter said pie was not in the dessert selection, Cliff predictably announced he was ready to call it a night. This meant everyone else did as well.

Sydney asked me to suggest getting a group photo before we left. We huddled in as close as we could to Cliff who leaned with his hands on the back of his chair with a smile in his eyes.

When the others had gone ahead of us to leave, Sydney prodded me to ask him for one more of only the two of us with him. He was good-natured about it and complied. I thought he seemed tired from the day and not just disappointed about the lack of pie.

Heading out, the owner of the restaurant offered to take us through the kitchen and let us leave out the backdoor to alleviate fans who might waylay Cliff's departure, but Thomas said it wouldn't be necessary. Most of the other patrons were NYU students with no idea of Cliff's celebrity.

Thomas pulled the door open at the front en-trance, and we spilled onto Broadway in the muggy air. It had started to drizzle again.

"This has been so much fun." Sydney shook Cliff's hand as if she'd never met him.

He chuckled. "I'm glad you had a good time."

I could tell she didn't want to leave. She loitered next to him probably hoping we'd all walk further together, but I wanted to get home and try to rein in my myriad of thoughts.

I gave Cliff a quick side hug. "Thanks for ev-erything. Ramsey was amazing. She really shined tonight."

"You girls be safe." Thomas tipped his head to Sydney and me.

I thought I should say more but didn't know what. It felt like a clumsy farewell as Sydney and I trailed off. When we were a street over, Sydney stepped off the curb flagging a cab. It came to an abrupt stop next to us. She opened the door and tumbled into the backseat and then blew me a kiss, waving as the cab drove away to take her uptown. I watched the car's wet taillights until they were a blur like a poignant scene in a movie.

My shoes smacked the soaked concrete as I con-tinued toward my apartment. I felt envious of both Sydney and Cliff being chauffeured home in their respective cars, probably happily reminiscing in their minds about the successful evening. And dry.

The minor rain shower hadn't lasted long but was enough to dampen my hair and clothes, and my spirit. I didn't like how I had parted with Cliff. The night had all gone so much differently than I had imagined it.

While I felt better being back on track with Sydney, I was now lost about what I was doing with Cliff. When I had regarded him simply as someone with whom I was building a friendship, it had been so much easier.

All of that aside, I couldn't stop thinking about Genevieve. I wondered how much Cliff stayed in touch with her. Probably regularly given they had a daughter between them. Maybe he was headed over to meet them both right now.

Amelia. She would have been able to help me sort all this out. If I could hop on a train and head up 8th Avenue and walk over to her place in Hell's Kitchen like I used to, she might not be able to solve the situation, but talking it out with her would make me feel better. I tried to wish her into being. I had tried so many times.

My apartment wasn't much further. Soon, I could change into something dry and maybe distract myself with a book instead of obsessing about the events of the night.

I had just set down my keys and turned on a lamp when my phone buzzed in my hand with the letters RS bold on my screen. Normally, that was such a welcome sight. Now I stared at it blankly.

Why did you leave? Cliff wrote.

Why indeed, I thought. *Because I have feelings for you. Because I know you're out of my league. And I should have known that! Because I hate this confusion. And more I can't fully articulate.*

I didn't respond. Standing by my couch where Cliff and I had spent such an enjoyable afternoon not long ago, I picked up the Anita Brookner novel lying nearby and toted it with me to my bedroom.

I sat on my bed and pushed off my shoes letting them drop onto the hardwood floor. Then slowly I removed my earrings and watch and set them on the bedside table. All the simple movements felt like a chore.

My phone vibrated. This time I ignored it and climbed into some drawstring shorts and a loose tee. The soft, worn material felt good against my clammy skin.

Tap. Tap, tap.

The sound didn't register to me as a knock at first.

Most people in the city are wary of anyone at their door, especially at night, but this was the sound of someone trying not to cause alarm, a gentle knock, thoughtful and hesitant.

I shuffled back through living area and stood apprehensively evaluating the door's lock. I had been so lost in contemplation I hadn't fully engaged it earlier. When the rapping came again, I cracked the door and peered through the slit prepared to jam it closed and throw the bolt.

Even drenched, Cliff's hair looked like a mop of perfection. It was slicked back with one lock dangling to the side of his forehead. Evidently the rain had started again, harder. I pulled him inside.

He still hadn't changed out of the jacket he'd worn during the show. It was beaded with water, and droplets dripped from his brow. He looked overdressed as I stood in my bedtime attire.

I retrieved a towel from a basket of laundry waiting to be folded and offered it to him. "Shouldn't you be on your way back to Jamestown?"

He pressed the white cloth against his face and ran it over his rain-soaked hair. "Ramsey's not leaving until tomorrow. I'm meeting her for breakfast beforehand."

I took the towel from him and set it aside. "So you're staying in Manhattan tonight?"

"No, at the Bowery Hotel."

He truly was a creature of habit as Sydney had always said. That was the same hotel where I'd seen him those months ago the first time I saw a pop-up show. Now he was in my living room, again. It was strange to think how much had happened over the previous months.

He moved further inside. I went behind him to ease off his jacket and then disappeared to the bathroom where I hung it to dry.

When I returned, he'd taken a spot on the couch.

"Why did you leave? You okay?" His voice was a mix of worry and hurt.

I planted myself next to him on the plump crimson cushions. The leftover mist of rain on him shifted into a scent of cool water.

I knew what I was about to say would change everything, but there was no need to prolong the distress I felt.

"I met Genevieve. I get it now." I looked straight ahead and not at him. If I did, I wouldn't be able to continue.

"You get it now? Get what?"

For a girl who said she loved putting words together, I was dreading the sentences I now tried to assemble. They wouldn't even form themselves inside my head at first.

After taking a deep breath, I clasped my hands in my lap and began my impromptu monologue. "I am ordinary. I know I don't stand out. I am not the girl you'd invite backstage or to your hotel." I stopped and finally looked at him as the next words crawled out of me. "I'm not Cliff Wood girlfriend material. So, I know—I know I'm not someone you'd want to be with. I get now why you didn't respond when I kissed you."

Cliff's eyes registered an uncomfortable inner turmoil. He stood and paced over to my small kitchen, found a glass, and filled it with water. After a few swallows he returned next to me. The edge of his knee rested against mine, warm and comfortable. "You're right."

I suppressed the emotion rising in me but knew I wouldn't be able to keep it at bay for long. If we hadn't been in my apartment, I'd have fled the scene. But I had opened the door on the subject as the case were. I'd have to accept walking through it and hear whatever he was about to say, however awful it might make me feel.

"I used to be that guy. That *rock star.*" He went quiet a moment seemingly having the same trouble I was in choosing the right set of words. "Back in the day, Bruce or whoever was working for me at the time, would study the audience for a girl to bring backstage when the concert was over. And, yes, it was usually the archetype of a certain kind of girl who would get this invitation. For sex. For fun. But not for anything I intended to remember." He paused again. "Not for anything that carried any meaning for me, Claudine. It was all a small part of the whole thing, of this business, being on the road, being young, in a place where my ego loved that freedom. That control." His words were so eloquent again as he spoke.

Despite that, I didn't know how they could apply to me and my situation. Tears coasted down my face leaving their feeble residue. "I wish I could've met you earlier. Then maybe—"

"You wouldn't have liked me, Claudine." He took my hand and softly laced his fingers with mine, then brought up the other hand to wipe tears from my cheek. "I wouldn't have offered you much. Not much more than a couple of hours in a temporary trailer behind a venue. Or if it happened to be a more sophisticated market, a night in my hotel room. Maybe breakfast you'd be eating while I tried to get out the door."

Hearing this only made me cry more. I looked at our hands clasped. I loved the way his skin felt.

Cliff kept going. "Do you see what I am saying? You see how that wasn't the kind of man you'd have wanted to have around? And you wouldn't have wanted to be one of those girls. You *aren't* one of them. What we have is so different. You *are* beautiful. Not ordinary by any means. You're the best of what most guys want, attractive and intelligent. If it helps any, the old me was drawn to you first by your looks when we talked at the bar in Jamestown."

I sat for a moment thinking about what he'd said. I loved his honesty and how he'd tried to help me understand the big picture. Still, it didn't make me feel much better.

"Then, why can't we have more? You don't have anyone in your life like that, do you?" My heart thudded as I asked it.

He brushed his fingers alongside of my head and then placed his hand on his thigh. "It's not that. It's because I'm not that guy anymore. That's what I'm trying to tell you. I care about you in a way that's much bigger, different."

When I did comment, he kept going. "I hope as we've gotten to know each other, you've sensed that. I want you to have what's out there for you, Claudine, whatever that is. You haven't even begun to explore it yet. Especially with your writing. I don't want to be in the way."

His deep, muscular voice was a blanket of consolation even if I didn't like what he was saying, but my tears weren't subsiding. I was amazed by his emotional strength. All through the conversation he sounded so down-to-earth and certain while I wanted to cry endlessly.

I let go of his hand and smeared away the moisture crowding my face and my thoughts. "You're not in my way. I know what it's like when something is in my way. With you—things feel so good. It's like you're the cure for everything inside of me. Everything that keeps me from moving forward. I can't remember ever feeling like that. About anyone."

He put his arm around me, and we leaned into the couch as our bodies fell against one another. "I know. If I were fifteen years younger, even just ten, things might be different. Our lives would be more synced. But that's not the case."

I didn't like hearing that. It didn't make sense if we cared about each other. Maybe later I could think back and understand it. Right now, I only felt a deep longing for him, for all he had done and represented for me.

I curled into him, draping my arm across his torso as he pulled me closer.

We sat there like a couple who had been together for years and no longer needed to speak a word because we simply knew. We understood. We felt each other's thoughts. Enjoyed one another's nearness.

What he'd said about himself wasn't news to me. I knew he had some bad boy moves along the way. Sydney and I had talked about how those experiences gave some of his songs an edge and became hits. So maybe that was fate for him.

He was right. I wouldn't have wanted to be with him back then. That was another Cliff.

But the fact he saw me as someone he *could* have been with had our timing been different didn't help. Especially after all his kind words about wanting me to succeed. Didn't he know it would be so much better if he were part of that, too?

It felt like everything I'd gained in the last six months was slipping away from me.

I lay my head to the side of his shoulder as my eyes connected to his in a sorrowful gaze. "I don't want this to be all there is for us. I wish I were ten or fifteen years *older.*"

Cliff laughed, a compassionate laugh, amused by what I'd said and how I was determined to make it all fit. "You deserve so much," he whispered.

We sat with our eyes fixed on each other's as if doing so would take away the sting of reality. So much was being said in the trance between us. I wanted to stay in his arms like that for days. Longer.

Then he slowly ran his finger along the bridge of my nose to my lips, tracing each one. His hand moved to the back of my neck, and he pulled me toward him. Without hesitation, I followed his lead, leaning into him and letting my hands trail up his arms until I was holding onto him the way I'd often imagined. His lips, plush and sensual, landed on mine, and I was careful at first, slowing into the action, afraid he might change his mind.

Then with a force like a sweeping gust of wind, his mouth closed more fully around mine, powerful and warm, as his fingers began a choreography along my skin. I felt his hand move along my hip to my thigh, and I joined him with similar exploration. The rhythm continued with each step we took until we were unified in the darkness, arriving at the same beat.

Acknowledgements

It takes a lot of work to write a book. You think you're going to do it alone—just sit there typing in the middle of the night at the kitchen table, or in the bathtub, or even sitting in your car in a parking lot. But then it gets going and you realize how much more needs to happen for the story to come together. It's not a solitary undertaking by far.

Thus, I must give my deepest gratitude to the following people:

To Jennifer Bradshaw for being my biggest cheerleader, always available for late night readings, willing to receive odd text messages, understanding my vision, and knowing exactly what I needed as a sounding board. I feel in many ways this is our book. To Sharla Hibberd, for bringing my design needs to life (again) and for walking around Greenwich Village with me on a cold December day. To Katie Sheppard for taking on the role of my assistant and always replying to my updates with genuine excitement. To Terri Semper for phone calls involving maps and subway lines and driving me around New York to close some final loops. To my sister, Jeanna Cunningham, for listening to my writing deliberations and for serendipitously providing the title for this book. To Katie Dahm at Palmetto Publishing for your patience and guidance. To anyone who has ever said an encouraging word to me about my writing, I so appreciate your interest and support.

And to Rick Springfield, the rock star *I've* seen too many times to count and who encourages everyone to never give up.

My endless gratitude goes to the following friends for your generous contributions and for believing in me. I couldn't have done this without your support.

Doreen Harkema	Paige White
Josh Walther	Stacey Seminara
Tara Shaver	Jennifer Goodwin
Lisa Wojnarowicz	Laurie Turley
Linda Newsom	Melissa Sonnier
Tonya Jackson	Jeanna Cunningham
Sharla Hibberd	Lorie Freitas
Pat Guziak	The Sheppard Family
Tricia Mackey	Debbie Kittrell
Kay Gara	Suzie Jagger-Richards
Terri Rehder	Terri Coe
Laura Irwin	Line Hammerstad
Heather Cunningham	Susan Fajen
Maureen McFadden	Jennifer Bradshaw
Cynthia Sexton	Bill Parker
Jan Castillo	Linda Petrella

Melissa Sims
Tracy Henry
Lisa Woody
Chandra Kendall
Ellen Nicholson
Diane Walker
Janice Martin
Lisa Howell
Kery Yanda
Scott Schumacher
Mikki Rosema
Jaclyn Jackson
Kristal Walsh
Jamie Fontaine
Elissa Abrams-Redman
Frances Mullins
Kim Lanzillotti
Jill Bigelow
Lisa Chavers
Dan Burns
Carla Owens
Andrew McFarland
Melissa Leone

Jennifer Curlin
Lisa Wondolowski
Sharon Turnbull
Kimberli Case
Jennifer Heyer
Charlotte Anderson
Ann Ross
Pam Chapman
Ronna Blomgren
Mary Fleming
Kathy Ellis
Wanda Smith
Helaine Fox
Pam Holbrook
Donna McDowell
Melissa Schwegman
Jill Archer
Evelyn Brehmer
Kristi Sweeney
Roxanna Pinner
Anne Hendrix
Angela Eddy
Margaret Dixon

About the Author

Claire Springfield has a B.A. in public relations and has worked in television as both a promotions manager and a studio director. She has logged more than 4,000 hours at concerts, 3,860 of which were spent seeing Rick Springfield perform. When not at a venue, she can be found in a thrift store. She lives with her cats and a large assortment of vegan ice cream in a suburb of Tampa, Florida.